The Fine Art of Murder

A *Murder, She Wrote* Mystery

The Fine Art of Murder

A *Murder, She Wrote* Mystery

A NOVEL BY
JESSICA FLETCHER & DONALD BAIN

Based on the Universal Television series created by
Peter S. Fischer, Richard Levinson & William Link

AN OBSIDIAN MYSTERY

OBSIDIAN

Published by New American Library, a division of Penguin Group (USA) Inc., 375 Hudson Street, New York, New York 10014, USA • Penguin Group (Canada), 90 Eglinton Avenue East, Suite 700, Toronto, Ontario M4P 2Y3, Canada (a division of Pearson Penguin Canada Inc.) • Penguin Books Ltd., 80 Strand, London WC2R 0RL, England • Penguin Ireland, 25 St. Stephen's Green, Dublin 2, Ireland (a division of Penguin Books Ltd.) • Penguin Group (Australia), 250 Camberwell Road, Camberwell, Victoria 3124, Australia (a division of Pearson Australia Group Pty. Ltd.) • Penguin Books India Pvt. Ltd., 11 Community Centre, Panchsheel Park, New Delhi - 110 017, India • Penguin Group (NZ), 67 Apollo Drive, Rosedale, Auckland 0632, New Zealand (a division of Pearson New Zealand Ltd.) • Penguin Books (South Africa) (Pty.) Ltd., 24 Sturdee Avenue, Rosebank, Johannesburg 2196, South Africa

Penguin Books Ltd., Registered Offices:
80 Strand, London WC2R 0RL, England

First published by Obsidian, an imprint of New American Library,
a division of Penguin Group (USA) Inc.

First Printing, October 2011

10   9   8   7   6   5   4   3   2   1

LIBRARY OF CONGRESS CATALOGING-IN-PUBLICATION DATA:
Bain, Donald, 1935–
The fine art of murder: a Murder, she wrote mystery: a novel/by Jessica Fletcher & Donald Bain.
p. cm.—(An Obsidian mystery)
ISBN 978-0-451-23473-5
1. Fletcher, Jessica (Fictitious character)—Fiction. 2. Women novelists—Travel—Fiction. 3. Art thefts—Italy—Fiction. 4. Murder—Italy—Fiction. 5. Murder—Illinois—Chicago—Fiction. I. Murder, she wrote (Television program) II. Title.
PS3552.A376F56   2011
813'.54—dc22   2011020257

Set in Minion
Designed by Ginger Legato

Printed in the United States of America

With gratitude to orthopedic surgeon Ronald Tietjen,
who gave this writer a better leg to stand on

The Fine Art of Murder

A *Murder, She Wrote* Mystery

Chapter One

"This is the Basilica of Santa Maria di Collemaggio, one of the finest in all of Abruzzo. Here you will see two works by the artist Giovanni di Paolo, a fifteenth-century painter who was fond of scenes of the Resurrection. His work is often grisly—much blood and gore. But the subject matter aside, he was quite good." The speaker was Flavio Simone of Great Art, Humble Places. Simone was younger than I'd expected, although I don't know why I'd assumed a tour guide would be older. He was dressed in a rumpled green corduroy sports jacket, a yellow shirt that also was in need of pressing, a skinny green tie, and wrinkled chino pants. Obviously an iron would have been a welcome and useful gift.

Simone stood in front of the wooden door of the church, a square building with a façade of pink and white stone, complemented by three Romanesque portals, each beneath a rose window. To the right was a short, round turret that was attached to the corner of the building, looking as if someone had taken it from a castle and set it down there but forgotten to get its match to put on the other side.

"This church was founded by an aging hermit named Pietro Angeleri at the end of the thirteenth century to celebrate the miraculous appearance of the Virgin Mary. Angeleri eventually became Pope, despite not wanting to be, and was imprisoned by the succeeding pontiff, Pope Boniface VIII, in a castle at Fumone until he died at the age of eighty-one. His body was returned to his church in L'Aquila, where he was canonized as Saint Celestine and buried in a Renaissance tomb within the church."

Simone stepped away from the door to allow another tour group to enter. The church had been heavily damaged in the 2009 earthquake, he'd explained, and for safety's sake—ours and the building's—only one group was being let in at a time.

It was a beautiful time of year to be in Italy, after the throngs of tourists had returned home and while the weather still cooperated with mild, sunny days and just the hint of a chill at night. I'd decided at the last minute to take this vacation, my choice aided by Cabot Cove's leading travel agent, Susan Shevlin, who came up with a reasonably priced package that wouldn't break my budget but wouldn't skip on amenities either. She'd booked me at the Hotel Splendide Royal, where I'd stayed the last time I'd visited Rome. The former nineteenth-century palace had been renovated into one of the city's most handsome Baroque buildings, and was situated in the center of the city and only a short stroll to the famous Via Veneto and Villa Borghese.

It had been a pleasant, on-time flight to Rome. The full

Northern Italian meal was tasty, accompanied by a selection of wines specially chosen for the airline by the Italian Sommelier Association. I spent part of the flight reading a wonderful novel written and sent to me by a friend, and napped for an hour before our descent into Rome's Leonardo da Vinci Airport (even Italy's airport celebrates the country's rich artistic tradition). As I walked to where I would collect my checked baggage, I stopped in a bookshop and was pleased to see that the Italian edition of my latest novel was prominently displayed, a fulfilling sight for any author.

My fellow travelers and I had been picked up the next morning by a small, sleek, modern bus with huge windows— it appeared that the entire vehicle was made of glass. Simone, who had been waiting outside my hotel, had taken my hand as I climbed the two steps inside, and the driver greeted me heartily. Seated behind him were my five traveling companions. Simone introduced us, and I took a seat next to a wiry gentleman with a head full of gray hair the consistency of a Brillo pad. He wore a gray suit, white shirt, and black tie.

"It is a pleasure to meet you," he said, smiling. "My name is Luca Fanello. Your first time in Rome?"

"No, I've been here before. Do you live here?"

"*Si*. Yes. All my life."

"It's a wonderful city," I said.

"In many ways, although there are problems, like in every large city."

"Are you involved in the arts?" I asked.

He shook his head and smiled. "No, but it is my passion. I recently retired from the police force here in Rome. Twenty years. But I have always had a love of great art. My colleagues sometimes teased me about it. Somehow, they don't think that a police officer should enjoy things like art or music."

"What a narrow-minded view."

"It never bothered me. I always found time to visit the museums and galleries. Now that I am free to and . . ."

I waited for him to finish.

"Now that I have retired and my wife is no longer alive, I have all the time in the world to indulge my passion. I understand that you are a famous American writer."

"Well, I am a writer, murder mysteries mostly—imaginary crime, as opposed to the reality of what you must have experienced as a policeman."

"It was interesting, but much of the time it was boring. Tell me about yourself and your writing. I always thought I would like to write a book about my experiences, but, as with most things, wanting to do something and actually doing it are too often very different things. As they say, the road to hell is paved with good intentions."

"My late husband, Frank, often said that."

We chatted easily for the rest of the trip, which took almost two hours. Our destination was the town of L'Aquila, where the Apennine Mountains meet the Adriatic Sea, in the Abruzzo region of Italy, approximately seventy miles east of Rome. As we approached, we passed through lush valleys, with rushing streams and medieval towns perched on terraced hills. I'd read that the Abruzzo region was prime skiing territory, and the snowcapped mountains surrounding the area gave testimony to that.

"I trust we won't run into any witches or *lupi mannari*," Fanello said casually.

"Meaning?"

"Werewolves," he explained, laughing. "Abruzzo is known for its witches and werewolves."

"I'd better be on the alert."

"No need," he said. "It is all legend. Abruzzo is a lovely part of Italy, filled with wildlife, bears, eagles . . . so many magnificent creatures. My wife and I visited often. The weather is perfect, the best in Italy, always cool and pleasant. But we don't come to see bears or to enjoy the weather, *si*? We're here to see the art."

Simone's description of Giovanni di Paolo's paintings was accurate. They were certainly dramatic, and somewhat upsetting, but I recognized the skill that went into creating them. I tried to picture one of them hanging on my office wall at home and shuddered at the thought.

"There have been many earthquakes here in Abruzzo," Simone announced as we came to our second stop, "that have done great damage to this cathedral. But there are works of art inside worth seeing. From here we will visit other smaller, beautiful churches of L'Aquila in which re-markable works by famed artists are proudly displayed."

"Until someone steals them," Mr. Fanello muttered to me as we entered the cathedral.

Simone had been right: There was an assortment of oil paintings that reflected the artists' talents, but none of the names attached to the works rang a bell for me, nor did I find the paintings especially appealing. Of course, it's unfair for someone who doesn't have visual artistic talent to judge the works of others who are blessed with it.

We didn't stay long. Before we left, I asked our guide about two places on a wall where discolored rectangles indicated that paintings might have once been displayed there.

"Stolen," he replied. "Less than a year ago. Never recovered."

I heard a grunt behind me and turned to see Signore Fanello raise his eyebrows at me.

"How sad," I said.

"It's been happening with greater regularity," Simone said. "As you can see, there is no security here in the cathedral, or in most of the churches throughout Italy. Oh, some attempts are made to secure the works to the walls, but that doesn't deter the thieves."

After a lunch of spicy porchetta sandwiches and, for dessert, almond marzipan sweets, enjoyed in a bustling piazza, our tour continued on to some of the dozens of L'Aquila's smaller churches, where works painted by Italian artists were on display. Our final stop was the Church of San Bernardino, named after another saint who'd come to L'Aquila, Saint Bernardino of Siena. He died in the town, which angered the Sienese, who never got his body back. He was honored in L'Aquila with a magnificent Renaissance church, including an imposing mausoleum sculptured by noted Abruzzese sculptor Silvestro dell'Aquila. Of all the churches we'd visited that day, this was the most impressive. Simone had saved this stop for last because it contained the finest work of art we'd seen on the tour, a large oil painting depicting a lush garden in which a seminude woman pleaded with a huge man holding in his bloodstained, beefy hands what one could only assume was her child.

"Bellini was greatly influenced by Mantegna," Simone informed us as we stood in front of the piece, impressed into silence by its power and form. "His most famous work was *Agony in the Garden*, and as you can see, this painting follows through on the garden theme. Bellini's own influence on artists in Venice was profound, and his many students went on to success of their own."

As he spoke, two friars in hooded cassocks entered the church. They stopped at a stone urn that held holy water and waited while a child holding her mother's hand scooped out a handful of water and splashed it on the floor before raising a chubby hand to her face. "No. No. No," I heard the mother say. She apologized to the men in rapid Italian, picked up the child, and hastened out of the church. The friars stood quietly, then dipped their hands in the water, crossed themselves, and slowly walked down the aisle opposite ours.

"The reason this particular work has not been displayed in museums is a debate over its true origins, whether Bellini himself painted it or whether it was his best students who did the work. The consensus is that it is the work of one of his students. As far as I'm concerned, this shouldn't make all that much difference. Many great artists had students who contributed to finished works that bear the name of the master."

Simone moved us up the aisle toward another painting on the opposite side of the church, where the religious brothers stood admiring a statue of the Madonna. As we passed the urn, I noticed footprints on the floor made by someone walking through the spilled water.

"That's funny," I murmured.

"What's funny?" Signore Fanello asked.

"Those footprints," I said, pointing to the pattern that led down the aisle we were approaching. "They look like sneakers."

"Not so unusual," he said.

I looked up. "Yes, but the only people who walked through the water before us were those two robed friars. I guess I never thought of friars wearing sneakers." I glanced around to see where they were. They had circled to the back of the church and one of them was locking the door. Before I could ask myself why a friar would need to lock the church, his companion whipped off his cassock, flung it to the side, and pointed a gun in our direction. He was a young man in black jeans, a black T-shirt, and running shoes, as was his accomplice. Both held out pistols, jerkily pointing them at each of the six of us and shouting in Italian words that were obviously orders of some kind. Their voices ricocheted off the church's sacred walls as they waved us out of the center aisle and into pews. One woman on the tour began wailing and collapsed back onto the pew. In an apparent attempt to silence the crying woman, one of the gunmen shouted at her, brandishing his pistol in front of her. She managed to stifle her sobs, and instead began rapidly chanting prayers in a low, choked voice. Simone muttered, "Don't do anything to anger them. Let them do what they came here to do."

Moments later it was obvious what they were after. While one of them kept us huddled together at gunpoint, the other tucked his gun in his belt and, using a crowbar he'd hidden under his clerical robe, went to work removing the Bellini painting from the wall over the altar.

"Can't you say something to stop them?" I asked Simone.

He put his index finger to his lips and shook his head. He was right, of course. It wasn't worth losing anyone's life in order to rescue a painting. Still . . .

The young man holding the handgun on us kept muttering in Italian, frequently glancing back to see how his colleague was faring. The painting had obviously been firmly anchored to the wall, and I assumed that what both men were saying in Italian contained at least a modicum of four-letter words. Finally, the Bellini was freed and the crowbar-wielding young man carried the painting over to where we crowded together, afraid to move or to speak. One of the thieves barked something at Simone.

"He says no one will be hurt, and we are to keep our mouths shut to the police."

The thief holding the canvas took a few steps toward the doors through which they'd come. At that moment—and it took everyone by surprise, including me—Mr. Fanello, who stood in front of me, reached down, drew a small revolver from an ankle holster, brought it up, and fired a single shot at the young man who held his weapon in his right hand. The shot struck him in the left shoulder. Simultaneously, he got off a shot that hit Fanello in the forehead, directly between the eyes. Blood spurted into the air as he toppled backward, crashing into me and almost causing me to fall on the woman who was praying loudly in Italian. A plume of the downed former policeman's blood filled the air and I raised my hand to keep it from hitting me. I locked eyes with the wounded art thief, who appeared to be in shock. He hadn't moved; his dark eyes were filled with surprise, anger, and hate. We were only two feet apart, and every detail of his dusky, youthful face registered with me—one eye, his left, was slightly lower than his right and the eyelid drooped a bit; he had a tiny scar, which looked fresh, on his right cheek; his prominent nose was somewhat crooked; soft black curls fell over his narrow forehead.

He raised his gun and pointed it at me. His hand trembled and my eyes followed the movement of the muzzle as it shifted back and forth across my face. I heard him cock the hammer. Then a loud noise made him spin around toward the church door. His cohort with the painting had released the lock, and shouted something at him. The injured gunman took a last glance at me, turned, and stumbled up the aisle, clutching his shoulder and mumbling something that sounded distinctly threatening. I sank down onto the pew, next to the woman, who was wailing again, a dead policeman at my feet.

Chapter Two

Aside from the wailing woman, we remained in stunned silence. I looked down at where Fanello's body was slumped on the narrow space in front of a pew. Simone wedged past us, fell to one knee, and placed his fingertips against Fanello's neck. He slowly shook his head and came to his feet. "He is gone," he said solemnly, and added words in Italian that sounded like a prayer for the dead.

I moved away and sat in a pew across the aisle. I tried to catch my breath and to stop shaking. The woman, who'd now become hysterical, and an older man scrambled to leave.

"No," Simone snapped. "We must stay and call the police." He pulled a cell phone from a case on his belt and punched in three numbers. "No one must leave," he repeated after completing the call. "Do not touch anything. Please, take seats and we will wait."

In minutes we heard cars, sirens blaring, come to a

screeching halt outside the church, and four uniformed Italian police officers ran down the center aisle, followed by two men in civilian clothing who I assumed were detectives. Simone directed them to Fanello's body. After a brief examination, the uniformed officers were ordered to seal off the church and to corral us in a pew far removed from the body. Once that had been accomplished, the detectives questioned Simone, who, replied in Italian to their inquiries and provided a summary of what had occurred. When he was finished, one of the detectives asked the remaining five of us on the tour, *"Loro parlano italiano?"*

The hysterical woman and the older man confirmed that they were Italian and spoke the language. The detective turned to the three of us who did not and said in good English, "I will need to question each of you separately." He nodded at me. "Please come with me."

He led me to the opposite side of the church and sat next to me in a pew. "Your name?"

"Jessica Fletcher."

"Americana?"

"Yes. *Si.*"

"You saw what happened?"

"Unfortunately, yes." I explained the purpose of the tour and recounted how we were admiring the Bellini painting when the two young men posing as friars or monks entered the church. I told him what had transpired leading up to the shooting of Signore Fanello, at which point he interjected—

"The victim, he was a police officer?"

"Yes, he told me that. Retired. I didn't know that he was carrying a weapon. If he hadn't—"

The detective shrugged and continued writing in a small notebook.

"Did you recognize either of these two young men?" he asked.

"No, of course not."

"I thought you might have seen them loitering near the church," he said to clarify his question.

I shook my head. "No, I never saw them before."

"Did you see them clearly after they entered the church?"

"Yes. I mean, I clearly saw one of them right after the shooting, the one who actually did it. Mr. Fanello—he's the victim—wounded that man before he was killed. I believe the wound was to the left shoulder."

"I see," he said. "Where are you staying in Italy?"

"At the Splendide Royal hotel in Rome."

His nodded. "How long do you plan to remain in Italy?"

"I'm supposed to fly out at the end of the week."

"We will have further questions for you tomorrow, Mrs. Fletcher."

"That will be fine," I said.

He asked for my contact information in the States, which I gave him.

The bus trip back to Rome was slow and sad. Little was said as we retraced our route from Abruzzo to the busy streets of Rome. After thanking Flavio Simone and receiving his apologies for the way the tour had turned out, I went directly to my suite, stripped off my clothes, and stood under the shower, washing Fanello's blood off my skin and out of my hair but not out of my mind. Later, wrapped in the hotel robe, I fell fast asleep, visions of what I'd witnessed that day dominating my dreams.

I awoke with a start, the face of the young man with the gun vividly in front of me, burned into my memory. I tried to shake it, but he wouldn't go away. I looked around the room. I had been so delighted when the pleasant young woman at the reception desk had informed me that they had upgraded me to a suite as a courtesy to my travel agent, Susan Shevlin. My rooms were tastefully decorated and furnished in sumptuous Baroque style, with colorful nuances and boiseries; the marble bath (and there was a second half bath) was twice the size of my bathroom at home. But what was most impressive was the terrace with a sweeping view of Rome and the magnificent gardens of the Villa Borghese. The gardens constitute one of the largest parks in Rome, and that had been on my list of things to do while there. I'd been especially interested in the Borghese gallery, where some of Italy's greatest art treasures are exhibited, including magnificent sculptures by such artists as Canova and Bernini, and paintings by masters including Caravaggio, Botticelli, Rubens, and Titian.

Now I went to the terrace and sat numbly, the sweet scent of jasmine in full bloom and the lights and sounds of the street below reminding me that I was in Rome. What had started as a leisurely week's vacation to a fabulous country and city had almost immediately turned into a nightmare. Within twenty-four hours of arriving, I'd been witness not only to the theft of a valuable painting but also to the brutal murder of a man.

I seriously considered packing and flying back to the States as soon as I could, but quickly pursuaded myself that there was nothing to be gained by abandoning the rest of my trip. It wouldn't bring back Mr. Fanello's life, nor would it result in the recovery of the Bellini artwork. I decided then and there to make the best of the days I had left, to try to distract myself by soaking up the splendor of Rome and its wealth of beautiful things, to give myself new images to remember and do my best to put that day's horror show behind me.

That resolve lasted until first thing the following morning when I received a call in my suite from a man who introduced himself as Sergio Maresca, a homicide detective.

"Mrs. Fletcher, I understand that you had the misfortune yesterday of witnessing a murder."

"'Misfortune' is the proper word, Detective."

"My apologies for such a thing happening on your holiday, Mrs. Fletcher. I don't wish to intrude on your time more than necessary, but it is important that I have the opportunity to interview you this morning. Do you have other plans? It won't take more than an hour or two."

"No, I don't have plans. But even if I did, I would rearrange them."

"Splendid. I will send a car to your hotel—say at nine thirty?"

"All right."

"We will be joined by Detective Lippi from our art squad, if that is agreeable to you."

"That will be fine," I replied. "I'll be in the lobby at nine thirty."

Two polite young police officers picked me up and drove me to police headquarters, an imposing modern building that would not have been out of place in Las Vegas. I was escorted to a suite of offices and asked to wait in one of them. Minutes later, Detective Maresca came into the room, followed by Detective Lippi. Both men looked to be in their early forties; each was neatly dressed in a suit and tie and had an engaging smile. They joined me at the table.

"We know you are a celebrity, Mrs. Fletcher. Your books are very popular in our country. We are grateful you have agreed to cooperate with our investigation," Detective Maresca said.

"*Si, grazie mille,*" his colleague added.

"No thanks are necessary," I said. "I'm happy to help in any way I can."

"We understand you had a good look at the young man who killed the former police officer."

"Yes."

"May we ask you to examine some photographs? I believe in the States you call them 'mug shots.' Perhaps you will recognize this fellow."

"I'll be happy to do that, Detective, although could he be from here in Rome? I assumed he was from the Abruzzo area."

"That may be," Maresca answered, "but it's possible he's a member of the gang centered here in Rome. Organized crime hires these young punks to steal art from churches. They pay them for it and then sell the art to unscrupulous collectors. The money goes right back into the drug trade."

"I had no idea of the extent of it," I said. "To think that money from stolen art ends up in illegal drugs is dismaying at best."

They placed the first book in front of me and I went through hundreds of photographs. I didn't recognize any face. I was given a second book, and then a third, but the results were the same. I was unable to identify any of the criminals in the books.

"I wish I could be more help," I said.

"If you would give our sketch artist as detailed a description of the young man as possible, that would be useful."

I spent the next half hour doing what he'd suggested. The artist, a young woman, slid a series of features across a computer screen, each slightly different, until I found one that most closely approximated the gunman's eyes, nose, mouth, the shape of his jaw, and his brow. She added the scar on his right cheek and the soft black locks that had curled over his forehead. She did a remarkable job. "Perfect," I said.

"*Grazie,*" she replied.

"Well," Lippi said, "we appreciate you taking the time this morning."

"If we happen to get lucky and apprehend the punk who did this, we'll be asking you to return to Italy to make a positive ID," Maresca added.

"I hadn't thought of that," I said.

"It will be an inconvenience, Mrs. Fletcher, but I assure you that we will make it as painless as possible. Naturally, all your expenses would be paid."

As they walked me through the building to where a car was waiting to bring me back to the hotel, I said, "I wish I'd never seen that young man's face. I'm afraid it will haunt me for a long time."

"We can't always be in the right place at the right time," said Lippi. "Or avoid being in the wrong place at the wrong time."

"Unfortunately, that's true," I said.

Maresca excused himself and Lippi took me to the waiting police car. "We really appreciate your cooperation, Mrs. Fletcher," he said. "Would you let me treat you to lunch as a way of saying thank you?"

"There's absolutely no need for that," I said, "but I do admit to now having an interest in the world of stolen art. I might even use what I've learned in a future book. Perhaps learning as much as I can will give me a sense of control over a situation in which I felt so terribly helpless. Yes, I'd like to join you for lunch."

He gave me the address of a restaurant and we agreed to meet at one o'clock.

A fleet of taxis was poised outside my hotel when I came downstairs to keep our appointment. I remembered from my previous visit to Italy that the cabdrivers I'd encountered spoke little English, which had surprised me. For some reason, we Americans expect the rest of the world to speak our language, and many citizens of other nations do. I'd spent some time before leaving Cabot Cove browsing an Italian-American phrase book and had nailed down certain useful expressions.

"*Voglio andare al Hosteria Romana, Via del Boccaccio, per piacere,*" I said to the next driver in line in what I hoped was the proper pronunciation.

"*Si, signora,*" he replied, indicating that I was to get in the backseat of his cab.

Driving through Rome was as chaotic as I'd remembered, with seemingly suicidal men and women behind the wheels of their vehicles cutting one another off, horns blaring, emissions toxically clouding the air, and verbal insults being hurled at fellow drivers through open windows. My driver was no exception, and I said a silent prayer of thanks once we pulled up in front of the restaurant.

It was a charming trattoria, with a table up front laden with platters of meats, cheeses, fish, marinated vegetables, and other appetizing items designed to catch your eye and entice your palate before you were even seated. Detective Lippi, whose first name was Filippo, had already secured a table in the back and stood as the elderly waiter pulled out a chair for me.

"This is a special place in Rome," he said when we were both seated. "It was at one time the secret headquarters of the anti-Nazi movement during the Second World War. Only the locals know it exists, so I am counting on your discretion."

"You mean you don't want me to tell anyone at home about it?"

"Only your closest friends, and only if you swear them to secrecy."

It was the first time I had smiled since the nightmare of the previous day.

"Ah, I like to see that smile," he said. "I was beginning to think it wasn't there."

"It's kind of you to look for it," I said.

As a parade of waiters brought us dish after dish of antipasti, followed by pasta, spaghetti carbonara for him and spinach ravioli for me, I grilled Lippi about art theft in Italy.

"How bad a problem is it?" I asked.

Lippi raised his eyebrows. "Huge," he replied. "Your own FBI estimates that the international trade in stolen art is worth more than six billion dollars a year, the third most profitable criminal enterprise after drugs and weapons. Our Carabinieri Internet-accessible database lists more than a million stolen works of all kinds—paintings, sculpture, rare books, and antiquities of every description."

"I had no idea it was that prevalent," I said.

"Caravaggio, Degas, Cézanne, van Gogh, Monet, Picasso—paintings by all the masters have been stolen in recent years," he said. "Caravaggio's *Nativity* was stolen from a church in Palermo in 1969 and is still missing. Unfortunately, despite our best efforts only a small number of stolen works have been recovered, and when they are, they invariably lead to organized crime—the Mafia here in Italy—and to international drug rings."

"These thieves must be very skilled," I offered. "I assume that museums and art galleries have sophisticated security systems that have to be overcome."

"They do," Lippi said. "The problem is that here in Italy, as you have so unfortunately discovered, many great artworks are in the hands of small churches and other less secure venues." He smiled. "The Carabinieri art squad is the largest in the world—more than three hundred officers assigned to it—but they can only do so much. They've been trying to encourage smaller repositories of art, particularly churches, to improve their security, but—"

"Do they believe that their churches are holy grounds that no one would dare defile?" I asked.

"Precisely," Lippi replied. "The fact is that theft from churches is six times what it is from museums, and seven times that of galleries."

The subject changed as we worked our way through the various culinary courses, but we returned to theft in the art world during dessert, a sinfully delicious and fattening pistachio crème brûlée.

"This has been quite an education," I said.

"You think you've learned enough to use in one of your books?" Lippi asked.

"I do, but I may need to consult you again when I have a question," I replied.

"If I can be of any assistance, you have only to ask," he said.

"You've already been enormously helpful," I said, "pointing my thoughts in a different direction."

We exchanged business cards at the end of our lunch and promised to stay in touch.

I wasn't contacted again by the police during the remainder of my stay in Rome, for which I was grateful. On the one hand, I was anxious to see the young man who had murdered Mr. Fanello brought to justice and would have happily provided identification if it came to that. But I had a suspicion after speaking with the two detectives that finding and arresting him would be nearly impossible, which meant it was highly doubtful that I would be called upon to help them make a case.

I spent the rest of my week in Rome haunting galleries large and small and taking in as many major museums as I could fit in. It was a bittersweet couple of days, and I breathed a sigh of relief when I climbed on the Alitalia jet to return home. That young man's face kept popping up at odd hours, sometimes replacing a portrait on a museum wall, other times coming out of the blue. I hoped that being back in my own home in Cabot Cove would serve to erase his face forever.

Chapter Three

Time has a way of masking unpleasant memories. Never completely, of course. My experience in that small church in L'Aquila had replayed itself now and then since my return to Cabot Cove from Italy, although each episode became less traumatic. I suppose it's the brain's way of filtering out horrific moments in our lives, allowing us to forge ahead without being crippled by past events.

I hadn't heard anything from Detective Lippi, which said to me that they'd been unsuccessful in apprehending the young men who'd stormed the church, stolen the Bellini painting, and murdered Luca Fanello, and whose faces I had described to the police artist. I had mixed feelings about that. On the one hand, I wanted to see those two young men brought to justice. But there was another side of me that hoped I wouldn't be called back to testify at their trial.

I had, of course, recounted my experience to a number of Cabot Cove friends, whose primary reaction was relief that the shooter hadn't pulled the trigger when he turned his weapon on me. I certainly shared in that feeling. Staring down the barrel of a loaded weapon has a way of putting one's life in perspective, and I was well aware how fortunate I was to have left that church alive.

I'd spent the two months since my return working on my next crime novel and had made significant progress. The word had gotten around town that I was in the midst of a new book, and my friends honored my need for some solitude. They're wonderful that way, and I'm blessed to have them in my life. There were, of course, dinners and some involvement on my part in selected civic projects, but in the main, my computer and I were left alone, and the pages began to pile up.

But that idyllic period was marred by something I read in the newspaper. It was an Associated Press article with the headline CHICAGO CIVIC LEADER MURDERED. It took a few seconds for the name in the lead, Jonathon Simsbury, and the accompanying photo to register.

Jonathon Simsbury!

I read further. Yes, it was the same Jonathon Simsbury I knew, the husband of my friend Marlise Morrison Simsbury. The article said that he'd been shot to death in the study of his home on Chicago's fabled Gold Coast. It was sad enough to read that he'd died, but that he'd been the victim of murder was especially jarring. It was the next paragraph that shocked me, though. The writer reported that Simsbury's wife and son had been at home at the time of the shooting and were being questioned closely by Chicago police.

*　　*　　*

Jonathon Simsbury had married Marlise Morrison, a woman whom I'd met many years ago when we both lived and worked in New York City. Marlise, vivacious and strikingly beautiful, had been an up-and-coming New York television news reporter when she met Simsbury, the handsome and dashing son of a wealthy Chicago family whose money had come from a thriving import-export business. He'd taken over the firm upon his father's death.

The fact that they lived in two different cities half a continent apart notwithstanding, Jonathon's courtship of Marlise was of the whirlwind variety, featuring dinners in the fanciest restaurants, lavish gifts, and weekend getaways on his private plane. He'd swept my friend off her feet, and they announced their wedding plans within two months of having been introduced. It would be Jonathon's second marriage; he'd had a son from his previous marriage, whose name, as I recalled, was Wayne. Marlise had confided in me the week before the wedding that her only apprehension about marrying Jonathon was the son.

"I don't know what kind of a stepmother I'll be," she'd told me one evening when we'd gotten together for a quiet dinner, just the two of us without the entourage that seemed always to follow Jonathon. "I've never been a parent."

"I'm sure you'll be a wonderful stepmom," I assured her. "The important thing is to respect his relationship with his natural mother and not try to be too many things to him too soon. I'm sure it will work out just fine. Have you been able to spend time with your stepson?"

"No. He's away at some fancy boarding school. I wasn't even sure whether he'd be at the wedding, but Jonathon assures me that he will."

"Well," I added as we left the restaurant, "my only advice is to be patient when it comes to the boy. He may have mixed emotions about his father marrying again, but I'm sure he'll fall in love with you just as his father did."

"Do you really think so?"

"I do. Let things develop naturally, Marlise. I'm sure everything will work out just fine."

The wedding was held at a posh Chicago hotel. I had been invited, but my schedule got in the way. Marlise sent me a page from the *Chicago Tribune*'s society section that featured an array of photographs from the ceremony and reception I'd missed. She was radiant in an off-white designer suit, and the groom was every bit the captain of industry. I looked for his son, Wayne, but there weren't any youngsters in the photos.

Marlise and I kept in touch, but as is so often the case, our contacts became less and less frequent as the years passed, eventually reduced to the requisite Christmas card. I did occasionally learn something of their lives through various news reports about Jonathon and his philanthropic projects. He was a dependable supporter of the arts in Chicago and sat on numerous boards, including the Joffrey Ballet of Chicago, the Art Institute of Chicago Museum, the Chicago Symphony Orchestra, and the city's Lyric Opera company, and as a couple they appeared in newspaper photos of those organizations' social events. Jonathon was an ardent collector of fine art, with holdings rumored to be

worth more than eighty-six million dollars. I'd always wondered whether Marlise would attempt to resume her TV
news career in Chicago, but she never did as far as I knew.
And, of course, I was naturally curious about the sort of
relationship she'd developed with Jonathon's son, Wayne. I'd
asked about it in earlier letters, but she ignored the question.
I never knew if it was a tender topic or simply one she wasn't
interested in discussing.

I reread the article, my mind flooded with memories of
when Marlise and I were friends in Manhattan, the good
times we enjoyed together, and the arrival of Jonathon in
her young life. I stared at his photo. He'd aged, of course, but
there were still the rugged good looks and an attitude that
exuded confidence and power. As far as I knew, they'd lived
a charmed life, although my evaluation was based solely
upon their smiling faces in the society pages and the little I'd
read about them in later years. Could it even be possible that
Marlise had killed her husband? It seemed outlandish at
best, although I reminded myself that what actually goes on
between two people in a marriage doesn't necessarily match
up with an outsider's public perception of the relationship.

I considered finding Marlise's number, picking up the
phone, and calling her, but I stifled the urge. We hadn't spoken in years, and this was hardly the time for me to intrude
upon her. A letter would be more appropriate, and I set
about writing one. The words wouldn't come. What could I
possibly say at such an unfortunate, wrenching time in her
life?

I put aside the letter, made myself a cup of tea, and sat at the kitchen table immersed in memories. I was deep into my reverie when the doorbell sounded. *Who could that be?* I wondered as I left the kitchen and went to the foyer.

I opened the door, looked into the face of my visitor—and gasped, *"Good heavens!"*

Chapter Four

I suppose that my overblown reaction at seeing my visitor was as upsetting to him as his presence was to me, at least for that brief moment. All I saw was the silhouette of a young man with familiar features. My initial reaction was that I was face-to-face with the young Italian art thief who'd murdered Mr. Fanello. He was the same age and height, had a dusky complexion, a prominent nose, and a full head of black hair that curled over his forehead. When I realized that this was not the same person, I quickly pulled myself together to greet my visitor.

"Mrs. Fletcher?" he asked.

"Yes?"

"I didn't mean to startle you."

"That's quite all right," I said. "It's just that—"

"I know I shouldn't have just shown up like this, but I came here at the last minute and haven't been thinking clearly."

"You are . . . ?"

"Oh, I'm sorry. I should have introduced myself right away. My name is Wayne. Wayne Simsbury."

Hearing his name brought about the same visceral reaction I'd experienced when I'd first opened the door. I stumbled before finally getting out, "Marlise's son?"

"Stepson," he corrected.

"Yes, of course," I said. "You'll have to excuse me, Wayne, if I seem somewhat befuddled. The timing of your arrival is—well, it's really remarkable. I was just reading about your father and—"

He nodded as though he knew precisely what I was thinking, that maybe I shouldn't have mentioned his father's murder. "That's okay," he said softly. "I guess you were pretty shocked to read about what happened. I didn't know whether you knew, and I wasn't sure how I would tell you."

There was an awkward silence as we tried to decide what to say next. Standing at the open door, with me inside and him outside, didn't seem right, so I invited him in.

"Sure it's okay?" he asked. "I know I'm probably interrupting something, maybe one of the books you're writing. Marlise told me that you're a pretty famous murder mystery writer."

"That's what I do for a living, Wayne. Come in, come in."

He stepped into the foyer and I closed the door. He followed me to the kitchen, where he didn't hesitate to take a chair at the table.

"Would you like a cold drink?" I asked. "Or tea?"

"A Coke or something would be great," he said. His eyes went to a lemon pound cake on the table and I encouraged him to have a piece. He didn't hesitate and energetically consumed a slice.

"Would you like some lunch, Wayne? I have some crab cakes and a salad left over from dinner last night."

"If it wouldn't be too much bother," he replied. "I guess I forgot to eat today."

I pulled the leftovers out of the refrigerator and put the crab cakes into my toaster oven. "Did you just arrive in Cabot Cove today?"

"About an hour ago," he said. "I flew into Bangor last night and took a bus here first thing this morning."

I had a dozen questions to ask but decided to wait until after lunch. The way he attacked the meal gave credence to his having forgotten to eat.

"Delicious," he said when he was finished.

"I'm glad you liked it," I said. I took the chair across from him. "I'm sure you understand that your unexpected arrival here raises some questions, and I hope my asking them won't be perceived as prying."

He sat back and shook his head. "I suppose the big question is why I'm even here," he said.

"That's a good place to start."

He drew a deep breath as he gathered his thoughts. "Marlise always talks about you, Mrs. Fletcher—how you were good friends in New York years ago. She says you're the most levelheaded person she's ever known."

"That's quite a compliment," I said. "Your stepmother and I were good friends when we were both living and working in New York. I have many fond memories of her, including the time when she met your father. I was so happy for her when they decided to marry. You were just a small boy then."

He snickered. "Yeah, I was just a spoiled little brat. I'm sure I didn't make it easy for her to come into our home and our lives."

I gave what I hoped was a reassuring smile. "It's never easy for a child to accept a father's new wife," I said. "I know that Marlise was anxious about becoming your stepmother. She wanted so much to do the right thing and to establish a loving, positive relationship with you."

"I guess I was too young and spoiled to appreciate that," he said. "I had some growing up to do before I could accept her. She turned out to be a terrific stepmom, and I know she made my father happy, which was the most important thing."

"How old are you, Wayne?"

"Twenty-three."

"Are you in college?"

"I was—the University of Chicago. I didn't have a great academic record in high school, but Dad was on the board of directors at the university and got me in. I dropped out after my second year, but I'm thinking about going back."

I was well aware that I was avoiding the obvious set of questions—about his father's murder. I suppose I was hoping that he would get into that without my having to prod.

"I guess I'm typical of kids my age," he said, "trying to figure out what to do with my life. Dad always kept pushing me to focus on something, some career, some profession, but I haven't been very good at that. I got involved with this girl. She's a singer with a rock band. I play bass guitar, not great but good enough to work with her group. We went on the road for a few months, but that went bust—lots of drugs and booze and not getting paid. My father was furious that I dropped out of college to do that. I've been a real disappointment to him." He'd been looking directly at me. Now his eyes became moist, and he lowered them as he added, "Looks like he won't be disappointed anymore."

It occurred to me that he'd arrived on my doorstep without luggage. He'd obviously traveled with only the clothes on his back—black jeans, a pale blue T-shirt, beat-up white sneakers, and a lightweight tan jacket.

"Wayne," I said, "I think it's time you told me why you've come here."

He raised his eyes and looked at me again. "Like I said, my stepmother always said that you were the most level-headed person she knew, and I really need to talk to somebody like that."

"I'm listening."

He got up from his chair, went to the kitchen window, and stared out of it, his shoulders hunched as he pressed his hands into the countertop. I waited patiently. He eventually turned, leaned against the counter, and said, "I had to get away from there."

"From Chicago?"

"Yes. It was like a nightmare. There was my father in a pool of blood in his study, a bullet hole in his chest. It was awful. The police were all over the place, and the damn media was everywhere, up and down the street, TV trucks and reporters hanging around, hoping to get some juicy tidbit about what happened. Once it was on the news, the phone never stopped ringing, over and over, ring, ring, ring. It drove me crazy."

"I can certainly understand that," I said, "but did you just pick up and leave? What about your stepmother? She must've been frantic, too. In the article I read it said that police were questioning her about your father's murder. I can't imagine that they suspect her, but wouldn't you have been helpful to her by staying?"

"I wasn't thinking about her, Mrs. Fletcher. That may seem selfish, but all I wanted to do was get away, escape, go where I could clear my head and think things through."

"What about the police? Did you tell them that you were leaving?"

He shook his head. "I didn't tell anybody. Nobody knows where I am."

"Well," I said, "I can understand the need for clarity, Wayne, but what you've done is wrong. Coming here isn't going to solve any problems. My suggestion is that you pick up the phone, call your stepmother, and arrange to return to Chicago."

"I can't do that, at least not right away. I was hoping I could camp here for a few days. I promise I won't be any trouble."

"I can't help but feel, Wayne, that there's something you aren't telling me. I understand how traumatic your father's murder must have been and that you wanted to get away. But surely leaving unannounced as you did and traveling here to Cabot Cove is not the answer. Again, I urge you to call your stepmother and tell her that you're returning home. If you'd like, I'll make that call."

"No, please don't do that, Mrs. Fletcher. Maybe I made a

mistake coming here to your house. I'll leave and go some-place else."

He got up from the table and started out of the kitchen. I grabbed his arm and stopped him. "I don't want you get-ting on another bus, Wayne, and running to God knows where. Come, sit down again. Let's talk. I don't know whether I am levelheaded, but I do consider myself a good listener. Maybe together we can figure out the right course of action for you."

He pondered whether to stay or leave. Then he managed a small smile and returned to the table.

I poured him another Coke and asked, "What about Marlise, Wayne? Finding her husband shot to death must've been horrific. How is she handling it?"

He looked up at the ceiling, deep in thought, his elbows on the arms of the chair, his hands clasped tightly above his chest. Finally, he leaned forward and said, "She became hys-terical, of course. Mrs. Fletcher, do you mind if I lie down for a little while? I haven't slept in days."

"No, I—"

"I know I'm imposing on you, showing up here like this, hungry and—well, I'm really beat. I didn't sleep at all last night. I just hung around the bus depot until this morning. I can't keep my eyes open."

"All right," I said. "Why don't you stretch out on the couch? I have things to take care of in my office."

We went to the living room, where he removed his sneakers before curling up on the couch.

"I'll wake you in an hour," I said.

"Thank you," he said, closing his eyes and emitting a contented sigh.

I watched him doze off almost immediately, and then I left the room and went to my home office. He had looked so peaceful, even angelic, lying there. At the same time, I was apprehensive. Although I had no reason to doubt that he was Marlise's stepson, he was still a total stranger who, having enjoyed lunch in my kitchen, was now fast asleep on my couch. But I was happy that he'd needed a nap. I wanted time alone to sort things out. His unexpected arrival had happened so suddenly that I hadn't had a chance to process what it meant.

I sat in front of the computer, clicked on Google, typed in "Jonathon Simsbury murder," and watched the search results appear on the screen. While the Associated Press piece had contained some information, the local papers gave a fuller account. Simsbury's murder was big news in Chicago. He'd been an imposing figure in the city's art scene, having donated millions of dollars to various artistic endeavors. A variety of photographs accompanied the articles, including a recent one of Marlise and Wayne. If I'd had any doubt that the young man resting on my couch was indeed Wayne Simsbury, the article's photo of him put my mind to rest. Despite Marlise's having aged, her youthful beauty still shone through. She seemed radiant in the photo, happy and at peace with the world as she stood with her arm around Wayne's shoulders.

According to the longest article, which appeared on the front page of the *Tribune*, the lead detective in the case acknowledged that the victim's widow was considered a person of interest, but so were several others, and no formal charges had been filed. The detective viewed it as an open case with the investigation ongoing, and he pledged that the murder would be solved and the killer brought to justice.

I looked for mentions of Wayne, who was cited only in passing. It had struck me that his stated reason for having left Chicago might not have represented the entire truth. If Marlise was considered a person of interest, it was likely that he was, too. I hated to think that he might have been his father's killer, but that possibility lingered.

I printed out a number of the articles, made a file folder for them, and returned to the living room, where Wayne still slept soundly. I thought about waking him but decided not to. Instead, I went back into my office and called our sheriff, Mort Metzger. I'm not a paranoid person, but I wanted someone to know that I had a visitor.

"Hello, Mrs. F.," he said. "Surprised to hear from you. Thought you were hibernating these days, working on your book."

"I have been hibernating, Mort, but I've taken a break. I've had a surprise visit from the stepson of an old friend. He's in from Chicago, and I'm enjoying spending time with him. His name is Wayne Simsbury."

"Always nice to touch base with old friends," he said. "He staying long?"

"I'm not sure. I doubt it. Just wanted to say hello."

There was a pause on his end, probably because he found my call to be unusual.

"Well, good to hear from you, Mrs. F. When you come

up for air, Maureen and I would love to have you for dinner. Bring your friend along, too."

"Thanks, Mort. I may take you up on that."

I was about to see whether Wayne had awakened when the phone rang.

"Jessica?"

"Yes."

"Jessica, dear Jessica. It's Marlise. Marlise Simsbury."

"Oh, my goodness! Marlise?"

"I know. It's been ages since we talked."

"I read about—"

"That's why I'm calling, Jessica. I'm trying to find Wayne, Jonathon's son."

"I—"

"I know it's a shot in the dark, but I'm frantic. He's disappeared, vanished, not a word to anyone. I'm calling everyone I know in case he's tried to contact them. You have so many connections to the police. I thought perhaps you could help me get the word out. He's not being accused of anything, of course, but his leaving at this point in the investigation is very inconvenient. His father's murder was a terrible shock for him. I'm afraid he might do something stupid, or even harm himself."

What had been a two-month period of relative calm and productivity had suddenly deteriorated into a series of unwelcome shocks.

First, I read about Jonathon Simsbury's murder and that his wife, my old friend Marlise Morrison Simsbury, was home at the time of his death.

Then, her stepson, Wayne, whom I'd never met, shows up unannounced at my door.

And now Marlise calls out of the blue.

"Marlise," I said, "Wayne is here."

"He *is*?"

"Yes. He arrived earlier today."

"Let me speak with him."

"He's sleeping at the moment, Marlise. He was exhausted when he arrived. And hungry, too."

"I don't care, Jessica. I must speak with him. He's got to come back to Chicago immediately. We've had a terrible tragedy here and—"

"I know, Marlise. I'll—"

A man came on the line. "Mrs. Fletcher?"

"Yes."

"My name is Willard Corman. I'm an attorney representing Mrs. Simsbury. I'm with her now. She just told me that her stepson, Wayne, is with you."

"That's right. I've already spoken with him about the importance of his returning home, but he threatened to run away. So you see—"

"You're aware of the tragedy that's happened here. Mr. Simsbury has been murdered."

"Yes, I read about it," I said. "A terrible tragedy."

"Mrs. Simsbury is under great pressure from the authorities, and Wayne's statement to the police is urgently needed."

"I'm sure it is, Mr. Corman. And I understand she's upset that anyone suspects she could have been involved."

"I'm convinced that she wasn't," he said, "and it's my responsibility as her attorney to prove that to the authorities. That's why it's vitally important that I reach Wayne and see that he returns to Chicago. He can provide an alibi for her."

"Oh?"

"She was in the house when the killing occurred, but she wasn't feeling well and had gone to bed early, much earlier than when the crime occurred. Wayne's testimony to that is crucial."

I went through a quick series of mental calculations.

Obviously Wayne had to return to Chicago as soon as possible to corroborate Marlise's claim. My initial instinct was to rouse the young man and put him on the phone with the attorney. But I hesitated. On the basis of what Wayne had said to me, there was every possibility that instead of cooperating, he would bolt. He'd left Chicago in a troubled mental state, and I doubted that this lawyer would be successful in ordering him to return. If Wayne balked at going back to Chicago, I wondered, could the attorney arrange for some arm of law enforcement to force his return? I had a feeling that if it came to that, Wayne would be out the door and on his way to another temporary sanctuary.

I made a decision.

"Mr. Corman," I said, "give me some time with Wayne. I don't know whether I'll have an influence on him, but I'll try to persuade him to come home on the next plane to Chicago. I'll let you know later today whether I'm successful."

"Thanks for your cooperation, Mrs. Fletcher."

"You're welcome. Could I speak to Marlise again?"

I heard him tell Marlise what I'd suggested before she took the phone. "Jessica, dear, please do everything you can to get him to do what's right." She forced a small laugh. "I'm counting on you. I know how persuasive you can be."

"I'll do my best. One way or the other, you'll know what he's decided to do before the day is up. Marlise, I'm so sorry about what's happened."

"Thanks, Jessica. Ironic, isn't it, how it's taken this tragedy to put us back in touch again?"

I agreed and we ended the call after exchanging phone and cellular numbers for her and for her attorney.

I went to the living room, where I found Wayne awake and sitting on the couch, his head in his hands.

"Wayne, we have to talk," I said.

"Boy, I really conked out," he said.

"Why don't you go in the bathroom and splash some cold water on your face?"

"Huh?"

"It's important that we have a talk, Wayne," I said in a tone that indicated I was serious. "Go on now. Wash up."

When he returned, he sat on the couch next to me.

"I received a call from your stepmom," I said, "and the attorney who's representing her, Mr. Corman. He told me that Marlise went to bed early the night of the murder and that you can corroborate that for the authorities, but you ran away."

He stiffened. "You told them I was here?"

"Yes. I promised to call them later today about your plans, whether you'll agree to return to Chicago as soon as possible. Marlise needs your testimony. She needs you,

Wayne. Surely you can see that. Regardless of your relationship with her, at least you owe it to her to tell the police the truth."

He started to say something, but I continued.

"I can understand your wanting to get away from what was obviously a wrenching situation. I'm not judging you for doing that. But you're an adult, and you have adult responsibilities. You and Marlise have both suffered a terrible loss, and you can help console each other. She's not only lost her husband under dreadful circumstances, but now the police are pursuing her as a suspect. You must go home, Wayne, and do it immediately."

He leaned his head back against the couch and closed his eyes.

"Wayne," I said, "you have to listen to me."

His eyes opened, and he slowly shook his head. "You want me to go back for her sake, Mrs. Fletcher?"

"Yes, and for your sake, too. You need each other at this time. You want to do the right thing, don't you?"

"What is the right thing?" he asked.

"Supporting each other during this ordeal."

"I don't know."

I stood and walked out, pausing in the doorway to address him. "You're an adult, and I can't tell you what to do. I only hope you'll behave as your father would expect you to. It's your choice, Wayne," I said. "I'll leave you alone to think about it. I'll be in my office in the event you want to discuss it further."

I hadn't been back in my office for more than five minutes when there was a knock at the door.

42

"Come in," I said.

Wayne entered and stood across the desk from me. "You're right," he said. "I have to go back to Chicago."

I smiled at him and nodded. "You've made the right decision. I'll make some calls and see what travel plans we can arrange for you."

"Will you come with me?" he asked.

I'm sure my expression mirrored my surprise. "Me? Come with you? That's out of the question."

"Then I won't go," he said, a suggestion of a pout on his lips.

"You had no problem coming here to Cabot Cove by yourself, Wayne, and I'm sure you can find your way back to Chicago. There's absolutely no reason for me to accompany you."

"I mean it," he said. "If you won't come with me, I'll take off from here and go someplace else. I thought you were Marlise's friend."

"I am, but—"

"She really needs a friend, Mrs. Fletcher, and so do I. At least do it for her."

I was a jumble of conflicting thoughts at that moment. The notion of just picking up and flying to Chicago with him was troublesome, to say the least. I'd been making good progress on my latest book and didn't want to interrupt the momentum.

On the other hand, delivering Wayne back to Chicago and helping Marlise fed my natural instinct to rally to a friend in need. I began to rationalize. Taking a day, or perhaps two, away from my work certainly wouldn't pose much of a burden. Accompanying him to Chicago would ensure that he didn't change his mind and run away again, and it would put me back in direct touch with Marlise, someone for whom I had nothing but warm memories and fond feelings. My heart went out to her, losing her husband in such a brutal way and carrying the heavy yoke of suspicion of having been his killer.

"You will go back to Chicago if I come with you?" I said.

"Yes."

"I want to believe you, Wayne, but—"

"No, no, Mrs. Fletcher. I promise."

"I'll have to make a number of last-minute arrangements, but I'm willing to do that," I said, my mind calculating the myriad details I'd need to handle before we left. "I won't be able to stay in Chicago very long, but I do want to see Marlise again. Maybe having an old friend there even for a day or two will help boost her spirits. You go get a soft drink from the refrigerator while I check travel options for us. I must call the attorney and tell him we'll be there. It's unlikely that we can make reservations for tonight, but I'll do my best. If not, you can stay here overnight and we'll go to Chicago tomorrow."

"That's great, Mrs. Fletcher. I'm sure Marlise will be happy to see you again."

"What's really important is that she'll have you to help prove her innocence. Go on, now—get something to drink. I'll join you as soon as I make my calls."

I felt good about having made the decision. As psychiatrists are fond of saying, "Any action is better than no action."

I called the number Marlise had given me for her, but Corman answered. "Mr. Corman, this is Jessica Fletcher. We spoke earlier."

"Yes. Is he coming?"

"Yes. I've convinced him to come back to Chicago. He's asked that I come with him, and I've agreed."

"When will you be here?"

"Not before tomorrow. He's a very confused and frightened young man, Mr. Corman. I think it best that I make his trip as easy as possible."

"Mrs. Simsbury will be greatly relieved," he said. "So am I. May I disclose your plans to her?"

"Of course. And please tell her that I'm looking forward to seeing her again and that she not only has Wayne's support to count on, she has mine, too."

He gave me his office address and said that once he knew our travel arrangements he would send a car to pick us up at the airport.

My next call was to Jed Richardson. Jed had been a commercial airline pilot, but eventually he tired of big-airline bureaucracy and left to establish his own charter air service in Cabot Cove, providing flights to nearby cities and giving flying lessons. I had become one of his students a few years back and was now the proud owner of a private pilot's license, which always amuses my friends, since I don't possess a driver's license.

"Hello, Jessica," Jed said. "Planning another trip so soon?"

"As a matter of fact I am, a very last-minute one. A young man who's visiting me and I need to go to Chicago tomorrow. I've checked schedules out of Bangor, but there doesn't seem to be any service from there."

"Boston?"

"All booked. That was my first option, but I'm also checking Hartford."

"Either way's fine with me. I've got a free day tomorrow. Happy to ferry you and your friend wherever you want to go."

After I booked two seats on a late-morning flight from Hartford to Chicago, I called Seth Hazlitt.

"How's the book coming?" he asked.

"Fine. I'm about to take a break for a day or two. I'm going to Chicago tomorrow."

"A book signing?"

"No, I'm going to see an old friend, Marlise Morrison Simsbury."

"Don't recall you mentioning her, Jessica."

"We go back a long way, to when I was living in New York. She was a TV reporter then and—"

"Simsbury? Seems I just read about a wealthy fellow in Chicago named Simsbury."

"You did?"

"Ayuh. There was a piece in this morning's paper. Fellow was murdered, as I recall. He wouldn't happen to be any relation to your old friend?"

"Well, as a matter of fact, Marlise was married to him. Her stepson, Wayne, dropped in to see me unexpectedly today and I'm accompanying him back home."

There was a long, meaningful silence on Seth's end before he said, "Why do I have the feeling, Jessica, that this little jaunt of yours to Chicago isn't as innocent as you make it sound?"

"I suppose there is more to it, Seth, but nothing I can't handle. My friend, Marlise, needs her stepson's support and I'm just making sure that he returns home to provide it."

"Seems to me, Jessica, that it was only a few months ago that you took a pleasant little trip to Italy and ended up not only witnessing a murder but almost getting killed yourself."

"That was just a matter of me being in the wrong place at the wrong time. Going to Chicago with my friend's stepson is—well, it's just something that I feel I must do. Not to worry, Seth. I'll be back in a day or two. I just wanted you to know that I'd be away in case you tried to reach me."

"As you wish, Jessica, but my advice is to deliver your friend's stepson, turn directly around, go back to the airport, and take the first available flight back home."

"Which is exactly what I intend to do. Talk to you in a few days."

I weighed whether to take Wayne out to dinner that evening, but decided to stay home. Chances were that we would run into friends, who would naturally have questions, and I wasn't eager to put myself or Wayne in the position of having to answer them. Instead, I ordered Chinese food from a new restaurant outside town that had delivery service, and we had a pleasant dinner together. When I raised the topic of his family, Wayne resisted talking about his father and stepmother, but opened up when I asked about his band and the music they played. Clearly, it was a passion of his, although not an interest he'd been able to share with his father.

Before retiring for the night to my guest room, he put on

an old bathrobe of mine and used my washing machine and dryer. I admit to being somewhat on edge as I tried to fall asleep knowing that he was in the next room, but I reminded myself that such fears were unfounded and eventually fell into a deep, albeit fitful, sleep.

The next morning I was up early and had to make several attempts to wake Wayne. He finally arrived in the kitchen wearing his freshly laundered clothing, eagerly consumed the breakfast I put out for him, and was ready to leave the moment the taxi arrived. The driver took us to Jed Richardson's hangar at the airport, and fifteen minutes later we were airborne and on our way to Hartford, Connecticut, where we would connect for our flight to Chicago. I love flying in a small plane—you feel the experience of flight so much more powerfully than you do in a jetliner. Wayne didn't seem impressed that we were flying on a private aircraft, although I suppose years of having flown on his father's private plane left him blasé to such experiences. He insisted on paying for his share of the flight, including half of Jed's fee, using a platinum American Express card. This was a young man with access to anything he wanted, no matter the cost, and I wondered to what extent his exposure to easy money and luxury had spoiled him. He was far more self-assured than he'd initially led me to believe when it came to spending. Yet he also seemed to be brooding much of the time, his brow and mouth set as though he were pondering heavy thoughts. I attributed his somber demeanor to the death of his father and the violent circumstances in which it came about. What son wouldn't mourn the loss of a parent, even if the relationship hadn't always been ideal? Yet I wondered how much his pensive pose was a true expression of his thoughts and how much it was a screen to avoid having to deal with simple issues of humanity. A scowl discourages others from approaching you. But I noticed that when he wanted something, Wayne was capable of using a different strategy. When he did smile on occasion, his face lit up, and I was convinced that those around him wished he would do it more often.

Wayne said little during the trip and dozed for much of the flight to Chicago. But when we deplaned, he suddenly became animated and looked around the vast terminal as though searching for something that might pose a threat.

"We have to find the driver that Mr. Corman is sending for us," I said.

He said nothing.

"Are you all right?" I asked.

"I dread this," was his response.

I spotted a man wearing a black suit, white shirt, and black tie and holding a sign with my name on it. Minutes later, Wayne and I were in the backseat of a large black SUV and on our way to the attorney's office.

Chapter Five

Willard Corman's law offices were in a high-rise building on Michigan Avenue. Wayne and I got out of the SUV and I did a three-sixty turn to take in the city. I've always found Chicago to be beautiful, cosmopolitan yet down-to-earth, its architecture inspiring, its people unfailingly friendly. It's particularly lovely at night, when its lighting rivals that of Paris. On this day, with the sky a cobalt blue with tiny white, puffy clouds coming and going behind the skyscrapers, I felt very much alive and happy to be there despite the seriousness of my visit.

The final call I'd made before going to bed the night before was to book a room in a hotel that's always been a particular favorite of mine when visiting Chicago, the fabled Ambassador East, now part of the Omni chain. It's conveniently located in a neighborhood of multimillion-dollar homes, just a short walk from Lake Michigan and Lakeshore Drive, and in the other direction is Chicago's "Miracle Mile" of upscale stores and restaurants. If nothing else, I would have a little one-day vacation before returning to Cabot Cove and the work that awaited my attention.

The driver had been instructed to wait for us; he was at our disposal for the rest of the day and evening. I asked him to deliver my small wheeled suitcase to the hotel while we met with Corman, and he readily agreed, assuring me that he would be back in plenty of time to pick us up. Obviously, Wayne would stay at his family's home.

We stepped out of the elevator, told the receptionist we were there to meet with Mr. Corman, and took seats in the reception area. Wayne was visibly nervous. He fidgeted with his hands, and his legs were in constant motion, doing a seated tap dance on the carpet. It wasn't long before Corman arrived to gather us. He was younger than I'd expected—I'd say no older than forty or forty-five—with just enough gray at his temples to add gravitas, and a ready smile. We shook hands and he led us into a conference room with floor-to-ceiling shelves containing the firm's law library.

"Thank you for coming, Mrs. Fletcher. Please, have a seat," he said, holding out a chair for me at the long conference table and indicating that Wayne was to sit next to me.

"Will Marlise be here?" I asked.

"No. I thought it best that I get a formal statement from Wayne without her present. She's at home waiting for you to arrive after we finish up. She's delighted that you've come back, Wayne, and was absolutely ecstatic when I told her that you would be here, too, Mrs. Fletcher."

"I'm eager to see her," I said. "It's been a long time."

A young woman entered the room carrying a court stenographer's apparatus. "This is Ms. Robertson, one of our paralegals," Corman said. "She'll be recording Wayne's statement. You and she can act as witnesses, Mrs. Fletcher, if you don't mind."

"Not at all. Happy to do anything I can to help."

"All right," Corman said, "let's get started." He nodded at the paralegal. "First of all, Wayne, I want to compliment you on behaving in an adult and responsible manner. You are a key witness in your father's unfortunate killing, as are all the people who were in the house at the time. We will take your statement today, but the police will also want to question you again. It's imperative that you be clear and consistent in your communications with both of us, that you think through exactly what you heard and what you saw carefully, so that the police can pursue the case with all the facts on their side. Are you ready?"

Wayne nodded but said nothing.

The attorney swore the younger man in, asking whether what he was about to say would be the whole truth and nothing but the truth. Wayne hesitated, then affirmed that he would be truthful and lowered his hand. Ms. Robertson had already begun speaking into a stenomask that covered her mouth, repeating what was said into her recording machine.

"Your stepmother has already given us her statement," Corman said. "Please tell us in your own words what occurred that night."

All eyes went to Wayne, whose nervousness hadn't abated. He looked back and forth among the three of us. We sat quietly, waiting for him to begin providing the details that the attorney was seeking. Finally he said, "I was home that night because the date I had fell through. She called me late in the afternoon to tell me she wasn't feeling well, which was a bummer. I really liked this girl. We have a lot in common, including our taste in music. Anyway, I ended up at home with nothing to do, so I hung out with Marlise. I kind of enjoy spending time with her. She can be really cool. She used to be a TV news reporter, and she's always yelling at the TV, criticizing the reporters, for their lame questions." He laughed. "Anyway, she's a trip.

"What I mean is that she really keeps up on the news," he continued. "I couldn't care less what's going on in the world, all the wars and killing, all the political BS. They're all crooks and liars, the politicians. You can't believe anything they say."

I cast a quick glance at Corman, who kept his frustration in check. I was sure that he wasn't interested in Wayne's view of the world and politics, or in a recounting of his love life. I waited for Corman to redirect Wayne's focus, but he allowed the young man to continue without a prompt.

"She's always watching the news shows on TV, all the talking heads, stuff like that. She really keeps up with what's going on. Anyway, it was late afternoon. I watched a couple of shows with her. I had nothing else to do. My date for the night had canceled on me, so I didn't mind sitting around. My father was away at some meeting—he was always at some meeting—so Marlise suggested we have dinner together. She'd been complaining about an upset stomach and told the cook she just wanted soup and salad. Oh, yeah, and some bread, too. I was in the mood for fried chicken, and Consuela—that's our cook—made it for me. We had a nice time together at dinner, some good conversation. Marlise was never without something to say, always had an opinion about things. Anyway, after dinner she said she still wasn't feeling right and was going to her room. She and my father had three bedrooms, one for her, one for him, and one for when they wanted to get together. I thought it was weird, but I kept my mouth shut about it. She said she was going to read and get to bed early."

Corman interrupted. "About what time was that?" he asked.

Wayne shrugged. "Seven. Seven thirty, maybe. I wasn't sure what to do for the rest of the night. I thought about hooking up with some buddies, maybe hitting a few clubs, but they don't open till late. I decided to hang in my room, play some video games and watch TV. I went into the kitchen, and Consuela—she's really a terrific baker—gave me a slice of coconut custard pie that she'd just made. I was eating it when Dad got home. He came into the kitchen and told Consuela that he'd already had dinner and would be working late in his office."

"His office is in this house?" Corman asked.

"Yeah. Just down the hall."

"Okay. Go on."

"Anyway, we talked for a couple of minutes. He got on my case about what I was going to do with the rest of my life, which I didn't feel like hearing. I know he meant well and wanted me to make something of myself, get a college degree and go into business with him. That didn't interest me. I didn't make a big deal out of it. I just finished the pie and went to my room.

"I stayed there until maybe nine thirty, ten o'clock. I'm

not sure. I remember dozing off and being bored when I woke up. I decided to come downstairs for another piece of that pie." He rubbed his chin and a small smile played on his lips. "It was really good pie. Consuela had left the rest of it on a platter with a clear cover over it. I cut a piece, sat at the table, and started to eat. Then I heard Marlise's voice coming from Dad's office. I couldn't make out what she was saying, but she sure sounded angry. Then I heard my father, and he sounded mad, too."

There was an instant tension in the room, a heavy silence as Corman leaned forward in his chair, his face creased. Obviously he hadn't been aware that Marlise had left her bedroom and confronted her husband.

"I'm not sure I understand, Wayne," the attorney said. "Marlise told me that once she'd retired for the night she stayed in her room until she heard a loud noise and came downstairs."

Wayne took in those of us at the table, then avoided our eyes as he said, "I left the kitchen and went down the hall to his office. The door was half open and I saw my dad and Marlise standing face-to-face. They were arguing. I figured it wasn't right to be eavesdropping on them like that, and I started to walk away."

"And?" Corman said.

Wayne drew a deep, audible breath, looked at me, and said, "Before I turned, I saw Marlise pull a gun from the robe she was wearing."

We all tensed.

"And she pointed it at my father and pulled the trigger."

Chapter Six

Corman slumped in his chair and rubbed his eyes as
though to massage away what he'd just heard. The
paralegal looked to him for guidance but received
a blank stare in return. As for me, I wasn't sure if it was appropriate to say anything, so I waited.

Finally Corman spoke. "I know that my hearing is good,
Wayne," he said, "so I don't doubt that I heard right. You say
that you saw—actually *saw*—Marlise kill your father?"

For a moment I thought that Wayne might correct what
he'd said, rescind it, modify it. He didn't. He simply nodded.

"That's why I left Chicago," he said. "I didn't want to have
to tell the police what I saw, didn't want to be the one to hurt
Marlise. I wish I wasn't the one to see it. I'd give anything if
it didn't happen. I will never forget that night as long as I
live, the sound of the gun going off, my father groaning,
then seeing him fall to the floor."

"Did you run in and try to save him?" I asked, still un-

sure whether it was my place to be asking questions,
plunging ahead anyway. Corman didn't object.

"I was so scared, Mrs. Fletcher. I didn't know what to
I was sort of paralyzed, I guess. I didn't know whether M
lise might turn the gun on me, so I ran back to my room a
locked the door."

I'm sure that Corman was pondering the same questi
that was going through my mind:

Was Wayne telling the truth?

He'd admitted to me that he hadn't made Marlise's ent
into the family easy. Yet here he'd indicated he enjoy
spending time with her. Had their relationship never real
improved? If so, was he claiming to have seen her murd
his father as a way to get revenge? Why hadn't he told n
this before we set out for Chicago? He'd allowed me to b
lieve that he would be *helping* Marlise by returning hom
Was this some sort of sordid grandstand play on his par
some perverted attempt at becoming important?

I also couldn't help but speculate that he might be lyin
to cover up his own involvement in his father's death.

These were unsettling thoughts, but they did represer
realistic possibilities.

"I suppose what I said really shocked you, huh?" he saic

"A classic understatement," Corman replied. He followe
up with, "Let's backtrack a little, Wayne. What happene
after you saw your stepmother shoot your father? You obvi
ously didn't confront her. She's operating under the impres
sion that you would verify that she'd gone to bed early anc
hadn't awakened until after the shooting."

"I stayed in my room until almost midnight," Wayne said.

"You never went into your father's office to see whether you could help, to see whether he was still alive?" I asked.

"I should have, I know, but I was too scared."

"Did you call the police?" I asked.

"No. Marlise did. The police arrived and all hell broke loose. When I came downstairs she was talking to the cops. I heard her tell them that she had gone to Dad's office to suggest that he come to bed. That's when she said she found him dead on the floor."

"She didn't mention hearing a loud noise and coming downstairs to investigate?" Corman asked.

"No."

"Did the police question you?" I asked.

He shook his head no. "I mean, they did ask me some questions, but I never told them what I'd seen. Marlise said that she had gone to bed early because she wasn't feeling well, and I backed her up."

"But that was true," Corman said.

"Mostly," Wayne said. "I mean, she wasn't feeling well and she *did* go to bed early. But she got up and—"

"Now you're changing your story."

"Now—now I'm telling the truth."

"Did you ever find a moment alone with Marlise when you could tell her what the truth was, that you had witnessed her killing your father?" the attorney asked.

"No, I never did. I guess I was afraid of how she'd react."

"And so you just picked up and left," I said.

Wayne turned to me. "I guess you don't think much of me, Mrs. Fletcher."

"It's not my place to judge you, Wayne," I responded.

Corman said, "That's your statement, Wayne?"

The young man nodded.

"Nothing else to add?"

A shake of the head.

"Well," said the attorney, "I suppose we might as well gear up to tell Marlise about this." He instructed Ms. Robertson to have the statement printed for Wayne's signature.

"You can do that so quickly?" I asked.

"We work with a voice recognition program," he said. "She feeds what she's dictated into the computer. It comes up on the screen. She cleans it up and prints it. Takes only minutes."

Corman left Wayne and me in the conference room, saying he'd be back shortly with the statement.

"I can't go see Marlise," Wayne said.

"What other choice do you have?" I said.

"She'll go nuts."

"It doesn't matter how she reacts." I leaned closer to him. "Wayne, are you certain that the statement you've made here today is the absolute truth?"

His face hardened. "Are you saying that I'm lying?"

"I'm not saying anything of the kind, but this is not the story you told me in Cabot Cove. I just want to be sure that—"

Corman's return interrupted us. He slid the printed pages in front of Wayne and handed him a pen. "Read it over," he said. "If it's an accurate transcript of what you've told us, sign where indicated."

Wayne didn't bother reading, just scribbled his signature and dropped the pen on the desk. Corman suggested that I sign on one of two lines reserved for witnesses. Ms. Robertson had signed in the other space.

"I'll call Marlise," Corman said, "and tell her we're on our way. I'll wait until we're there to break the news about what's occurred here today. I don't want her to be alone when she hears it. It's good that you're here, Mrs. Fletcher. She'll need a good friend."

Had I been honest, I would have admitted that had my suitcase not already been delivered to the hotel, I would have considered hailing a taxi and heading right back to O'Hare Airport. The thought of being a buffer against what was sure to be an anguished reaction from Marlise wasn't a palatable contemplation. There she was, alone at the home in which her husband had been brutally murdered, expecting the arrival of her stepson, who supposedly would validate her claim of what she had done the night of the killing. Instead, he was delivering what could be a death warrant.

Corman's expression reflected abject pain as he said, "Under the rules of disclosure, I'm obligated to inform the DA's office of Wayne's allegation. That's bad enough. It's possible that based upon what he's stated here the DA will bring formal charges against her. I'm not happy having to break the news to Marlise. She was so relieved that Wayne was returning and would vouch for her innocence. She'll be devastated."

Corman's feeling mirrored mine. Of course, he didn't have a choice. As an officer of the court he was legally obligated to turn Wayne's statement over to the prosecutors. For a fleeting moment I wondered whether it would have been better for Wayne to have stayed away, to have disappeared for good, but I knew that wouldn't have solved anything. I also suffered a moment of guilt at having persuaded him to return to Chicago. But such thoughts were unrealistic at best. Wayne had a duty to report what he'd seen, no matter who was hurt in the process, and I'd done the right thing in encouraging him to come home and face the music.

Corman called Marlise from the conference room and simply told her that we'd be there in half an hour. Although I couldn't hear her side of the conversation, it was obvious that she asked the attorney questions that he deftly avoided answering. At one point he said, "We can get into that when we get there, Marlise. What? Yes, Wayne and Mrs. Fletcher will be with me. See you soon."

The driver was waiting when we came down from Corman's office.

"Your suitcase is at the hotel, ma'am," he said.

"Good. Thank you."

Although it took only twenty minutes to reach Marlise's house, it seemed like a multi-hour drive. No one said anything, each of us deep in our own tormented thoughts. It wasn't until we'd pulled into a circular drive that Wayne said, "I should go stay with friends."

The harsh, skeptical look that Corman gave Wayne said to me that he questioned the young man's truthfulness, and although I had nothing tangible upon which to base a judgment, I questioned it, too.

Chapter Seven

Before we were able to get out of the SUV, Marlise came through the front door and bounded down the steps. Although many years had passed since I'd last seen her, she had the same youthful, winning smile and spark in her eyes that I remembered. Her platinum hair was pulled back into a ponytail that bounced when she moved. She wore tailored tan slacks, a white silk blouse, and sandals. As she approached, the driver lowered the windows on the passenger side.

"Jessica?" she said as she leaned in the open window.

"Marlise," I said, taking her hands in mine. "I'm so sorry about Jonathon."

Her smile disappeared and her eyes became moist. "Oh, dear, dear Jessica. It's the most awful thing—but we can talk about that later. I'm just so happy that you're here."

She looked past me at Wayne. "Welcome home, darling," she said. "I've been so worried about you. I'm relieved that you sought out Jessica. I've always told your father you had a good head on your shoulders. You couldn't have picked a better person to confide in."

"Hello, Marlise," Corman said.

"Willard, thank you for bringing these two precious people to me. Come, come inside. I know we have a lot to discuss."

We exited the vehicle. Marlise linked her arm in mine and led us into a spacious foyer with a white marble floor and large, impressive pieces of art on the walls. At the end of the foyer was a set of stairs leading up to a landing and the second floor. To the right of the stairs was a corridor that gave access to the rear of the house. Calling it a house wasn't quite accurate, though. I noticed as we drove in that it was huge; "mansion" would be a more apt word for it. The spaciousness of the inside rooms added to the perception of being in a very special place, as did the pieces of art that dominated every inch of wall space.

"This is lovely, Marlise," I commented as we passed through two rooms before reaching a parlor or den of sorts. The floor was covered with expensive Oriental carpets. The furniture was oversized and inviting. A huge flat-screen television set was set against one wall. Bookshelves took up another wall. In addition, dozens of oils and watercolors were hung around the room as well as etchings, drawings by Picasso that I recognized, and a large work that resembled in style the Bellini painting that had been stolen at gunpoint from the church in L'Aquila.

"This has always been my favorite room in the house," Marlise said. "Please, sit down and make yourselves comfortable. I'll be back in a minute."

She returned with a woman she introduced as Consuela, their cook. "Coffee, tea, a drink?" Marlise asked. Wayne asked for a Coke. I opted for tea. Corman said he would appreciate a drink, scotch or bourbon, neat, which didn't surprise me. He looked as though he was about to face a firing squad.

I'd noticed that Marlise hadn't initiated any physical contact with her stepson until now. He stood in a corner of the room looking out a window, obviously wishing he were somewhere else. She crossed the room, put her hands on his arms, and said, "I am so relieved that you are home, darling. I was worried sick. I had no idea where you'd gone, and so I gave Willard—Mr. Corman—every name I could think of. Thank God I thought of Jessica. I admit that there was also some selfishness involved. If anything had happened to you and you wouldn't be able to tell the authorities about what happened that night I'm afraid I'd be—well, let's just say I'd be in a difficult situation." She looked at Corman: "Thank you for tracking him down, Willard."

She sat in a red leather wing chair. "It's been horrible here since Jonathon was killed. The police took the crime scene tape only down an hour ago. I've kept the door to Jonathon's office closed. The company that cleans up after such dreadful events can't come until tomorrow. I suppose Jonathon's isn't the only murder to be cleaned up in Chicago."

Corman cleared his throat before saying, "There's something we have to discuss, Marlise."

"Oh, yes, I'm sure there is. How do we go about this? Does Wayne have to give some sort of formal statement?"

"He already has," Corman said.

She looked at Wayne and smiled. "Thank goodness you were here that dreadful night, Wayne."

Wayne looked at me as though I might be able to provide him with an out. When it was obvious I couldn't, he said to Marlise, "Look, Marlise, there's something you should know."

She waited for him to continue.

"I know," he said, his eyes lowered.

"You know *what*, darling?"

"I know that you—" He turned his back to her.

Marlise looked at Corman. "What's going on?" she asked.

"Wayne has given a statement at my office, Marlise," the attorney said. "In it he claims to have witnessed you shooting Jonathon."

Marlise's face went blank, as though she'd suddenly been drained of all emotion, all feeling. I could almost hear her mind racing, trying to fathom what had just been said and the meaning behind it. After a few moments of sitting ramrod straight, she looked to Wayne, who now stood in a corner of the parlor, his hands splayed against a bookcase.

"Wayne," she said.

He slowly turned and faced her.

"Is what Mr. Corman just said true?"

He nodded.

"My God!" she exclaimed. "Why would you say such a horrible thing? You know that it isn't true."

"It *is* true," he said, his voice gaining strength. "I saw it, Marlise. I was there when you killed my father."

Marlise had remained calm, even stoic during this initial exchange. Now she seemed to collapse within herself. Her body sagged as the meaning of what she'd just been told finally sank in. She extended her hands to us in a gesture of pleading.

"I know this comes as a blow, Marlise," Corman said, "and I was as surprised as you are."

"Jessica," she said, "did you hear what Wayne has said about me?"

"Yes, I heard," I said. "I was there when he gave his statement." I got up, knelt in front of her, and took her hands. "I'm sure this can be worked through," I said. "I think that—"

She wrenched free of my hands, got to her feet, and approached Wayne, her fists clenched. "How could you tell such lies?" she demanded. "Are you out of your mind? Kill your father? I *loved* your father. Tell them that you're lying, Wayne. Tell them that—"

"I told them the truth," he yelled, and stormed out of the room. Marlise took a few steps after him, but Corman intercepted her. "Let him go, Marlise," he said. "He's confused. Let's sit down and go over the events of that night—from your perspective."

She sat on a love seat and I joined her.

"Surely there's got to be an explanation for Wayne's behavior," I said.

"Oh, yes," she replied bitterly. "There's a good explanation for his vile lies. He's resented me ever since I married his precious father. He was a spoiled brat then and he still is. He's hated me all these years and is trying to get rid of me so he can collect all the money."

"I'm not sure I understand," I said.

"That miserable, pathetic excuse for a man." She got up and crossed to the door. "Excuse me. I'm sorry that you've come all this way, Jessica, to be privy to this sordid mess."

Corman and I looked at each other as she left the room, slamming the door behind her.

"I can't believe this has happened," I said. "I thought that convincing Wayne to come here would be beneficial to Marlise."

"He had me fooled, too," said Corman. "Not that I spoke with him. He'd flown the coop before I became involved."

"You're the family's attorney?"

"No. I'm a criminal defense attorney. I was retained by Jonathon Simsbury's lawyer, Joe Jankowski. The minute he got wind that Marlise was being looked at by the police as a suspect, he called me. I met with Marlise immediately, and she told me that Wayne could verify her actions the night of the murder."

"I wonder . . ."

"You wonder what, Mrs. Fletcher?"

"I wonder why Marlise would have put so much stock in what Wayne might say. After all, his being in the house that night didn't mean that he had an eye on her at every moment, knew what she did at every step. He said he'd spent time in his room and fell asleep there. Obviously Marlise was free to move about as she wished without being observed."

"As was he, for that matter. I didn't know the details of what he'd done and where he'd been that night until his statement today," Corman said. "There are others who were in the house that night, like household staff. There are staff quarters, I'm told. We've met Consuela, the cook. I've also met the live-in housekeeper, a Mrs. Tetley. And there's Jonathon Simsbury's mother."

"She lives here?"

"Yes. Marlise told me that the mother is well into her eighties, and a bit cranky."

"She's entitled at that age."

"I suppose you're right. The tone in which Marlise describes her tells me that she isn't especially fond of her."

"What's going on in here?" said a gravelly voice as the door swung open.

Sitting in the entry was an old woman in a wheelchair. Her steel gray hair was piled atop her head. She wore a red-and-black plaid caftan many sizes too big for her, and bulky gold chains adorned her neck. Her wrinkled face was heavily made up; she looked like a character from a play or motion picture.

She wheeled into the room, stopped in the middle, and stared at me. "Who are you?" she asked in a surprisingly strong voice.

"I'm Jessica Fletcher. You must be Mrs. Simsbury."

"How would you know that?"

"A guess."

She pivoted to face Corman. "You the attorney she retained?"

"I am. Willard Corman, ma'am. Nice to meet you," he said, going to her and extending his hand, which she ignored.

Her attention returned to me. "Fletcher," she said. "The mystery writer. She told me about you."

"I brought your grandson home," I said.

She scowled. "He told me that. Poor baby, having to watch his father gunned down in cold blood. Not that it would bother *her*."

I noticed that Mrs. Simsbury didn't use Marlise's name. It was "she" or "her," which confirmed that she was not a fan of her daughter-in-law.

I gathered that she knew about the claim that Wayne had made about witnessing the murder, and I wondered when she'd learned that bit of information. I was debating whether to ask when Corman said, "Since you're here, Mrs. Simsbury, this might be a good time for you to answer some questions."

She sneered at him. "Questions? About what?"

"Your son's murder."

"What do you expect me to say about that? Wayne told me what he saw. Doesn't surprise me. She's a cold one if I ever knew one. No sense in you wasting time trying to defend her. As far as I'm concerned, they should lock her up and toss away the key." She wagged a bony finger at him. "Oh, I know, you're one of those slick lawyers who'll use tricks to get her off. I've got no use for lawyers. Can't believe a word they say."

During their exchange, I pondered why Mrs. Simsbury wasn't exhibiting any fear of Marlise. Her grandson had told her that he'd seen Marlise shoot Jonathon. It seemed to me that if I were in that situation, I'd be concerned about being in the house with a cold-blooded murderess. But the old woman seemed more interested in berating lawyers than worrying about sharing close quarters with Marlise— assuming, of course, that she believed Wayne's story.

"You were here the night your son died?" Corman asked.

"Of course I was. I don't get out very often."

"And did you hear anything?"

"Hear him get shot? No. I was watching TV, had it on loud like always."

"Wayne said that he heard Marlise and Jonathon argue before the shooting. You never heard that?"

"You hard of hearing?" she shot back. "I told you I had the TV on loud. *She's* always complaining about it."

"I have a question, if you don't mind," I said.

"Everybody's got questions. The police had lots of them. Might as well hear yours."

"What was the tenor of the relationship between Wayne and Marlise?"

She looked at me as though I'd asked for a definition of quantum physics.

"Did they get along?"

"She couldn't stand him, treated him like some foreigner, not her husband's son. That's how they got along. Made nice in public, in front of Jonathon, but I knew the truth."

"I only asked because Wayne told me how much he liked Marlise."

She ignored my comment and addressed Corman. "Well," she said, "what are you going to do?"

He cocked his head.

"Get her locked up. You think I want me and Wayne to be sleeping in the same house with a killer?"

"She hasn't been proven guilty of anything," Corman replied.

"You heard what Wayne said, didn't you?"

"Yes, I did, Mrs. Simsbury, but you don't lock people up based upon an unsubstantiated accusation. Would you be more comfortable staying someplace else tonight?"

"Leave this house?" she fairly snarled. "This is my house. I own it. She's the one who should leave, spend the night in a jail cell." With that she spun her chair around and left. "I'd better barricade my door."

Corman exhaled and raised his eyebrows.

"What *will* you do?" I asked.

"Deliver a copy of Wayne's statement to the DA's office. They'll want to—"

Marlise reappeared. She'd changed clothes and pulled a small rolling suitcase behind her.

"Jessica, dear, I am so sorry that you had to walk into this mess. Please forgive me."

"There's nothing to forgive, Marlise. I feel terrible for you. Are you leaving?"

"I couldn't possibly stay the night in this house filled with hate, that nasty old woman and now Wayne turning against me."

"I need to know how to contact you," Corman said. "The district attorney and the police will want to question you based on Wayne's statement."

"The Four Seasons on East Delaware," she said. "Jonathon kept a suite there that he used for business visitors." She turned to me. "Jessica, dear, this awful situation has made me lose my manners. You're welcome to stay with me, of course. There's plenty of room."

"Thank you, Marlise, but I've already booked a hotel."

"Well, I hope I can count on you to stick around a little

while. I can see I'm going to need all the support I can get, with everyone I thought I had on my side turning against me. Willard, surely there's a way to make the district attorney see that Wayne is lying."

"I'll do everything I can. Mrs. Fletcher and I were just leaving. Can we drop you at the hotel?"

"That isn't necessary. Carl, our driver, is taking me. He should be out front by now. Again, Jessica, I can only apologize for the scene you've been forced to witness."

"Don't give it a second thought, Marlise. I just want to see you exonerated."

Which was true, assuming that her stepson was lying.

But if he wasn't . . .

Chapter Eight

No one else came to the room after Marlise left, so Corman and I let ourselves out. His driver was waiting and we climbed into the backseat. "The Ambassador East," Corman instructed.

"Quite a day," I commented.

"I've been thrown curves before by witnesses, but this takes the cake. A stepson charging his stepmother with the murder of his father. He didn't give you any inkling that he intended to make the charge?"

"No, he didn't. He spoke highly of Marlise, quite a different perspective than the one given by Mrs. Simsbury."

"And it's not what he told the police when they questioned him the night of the murder." He paused before saying, "I'm not saying this because she's my client, but I don't believe him."

"Based on?"

He shrugged. "Just an instinct. You question enough

witnesses and you develop a sense of who's telling the truth and who's lying."

"Pretty serious lie," I offered. "I assume that his statement will be enough for them to charge her with the murder."

"Not necessarily. He'll have to recant his initial statement to the police. I can make a case that his testimony is tainted. He's already lied to the authorities once, and there's the strained relationship between them. His allegation is the only evidence against her. And frankly I wouldn't put it past him to have done the deed himself."

"What about the weapon?" I asked.

"It wasn't found at the scene. And Jonathon's pistol is missing. There's no way to know if his own gun was used, but it was registered. Ballistics should be able to show if the bullet that killed him was the same caliber as his own gun, but without the weapon in hand, there's no proof. The police did a pretty thorough search of the house and surrounding property but came up empty. Whoever did it got rid of the weapon."

"Or took it when they left," I said. "If it was Wayne, he would have had plenty of opportunity to dispose of the gun between here and Cabot Cove."

"Are you still planning to head back there tomorrow? Maine, isn't it?"

"That's right. I should catch a plane tomorrow, but I feel terrible that I haven't had a chance to sit down with Marlise. I'd like that opportunity."

"Well, sounds like she might like that opportunity, too," Corman said as we pulled up in front of the Ambassador East.

"Can't blame her, Mr. Corman."

"Please, it's Willard."

"All right, Willard—and it's Jessica."

"Can I buy you dinner?" he asked. "It's the least I can do to thank you for bringing Wayne back."

I laughed and said, "I'm surprised you'd even offer, considering the way it turned out."

"Not your fault."

"Thank you, but I think I'll settle in my room, order room service, and decide what to do about heading home."

"Whatever you do, call me before you leave. It was nice to meet you. Have a good night."

The clerk at the reception desk welcomed me warmly, and a bellman escorted me to my room, a lovely minisuite on a high floor. The Ambassador East is a historic hotel in the heart of the Gold Coast, not far from Marlise and Jonathon's mansion. As charming as it is today, it's the hotel's history that fascinates me. Its Pump Room restaurant and the hotel itself had been home to Hollywood's elite for many years. Sinatra reigned there when in town, and Bogart proposed to Bacall in the restaurant's favored "Booth Number One." I've never considered myself celebrity-bitten, but sensing the ghosts of show business greats who'd made the Ambassador East their home when in Chicago gave it a special ambience for me.

My bag had been brought up and placed on a luggage rack. A vase of colorful flowers and a bottle of champagne were on a coffee table in front of a couch. I hung up my jacket, put my toiletries in the marble bathroom, sat in a flowered tufted chair by a window, and took a moment to digest everything that had occurred over the past two days.

I must admit that I was impressed at how Marlise seemed to be holding herself together, considering that her husband had been murdered only days earlier. Maybe "surprised" would be a more accurate description of how I felt. She had always had a certain controlled way about her, which served her well when she was appearing on television in New York City. Still, the stereotypical grieving widow image was lacking from her current deportment, and the more I thought about it, the more it nagged at me, although Jonathon's son and mother were no more expressive than his wife. I had to remind myself that everyone deals with emotion differently. Prosecutors are too quick to point the finger of guilt at someone who doesn't grieve for a victim in a way that the prosecutor thinks is appropriate. Some people fall apart and stay that way for weeks, even months or years. Others are more philosophical about death and accept it as part of the human condition. As an old friend was fond of saying, dying is the price you pay for living. But because Marlise was now being accused of murdering her husband—the accusation coming from her stepson, no less—her composure was a little off-putting. She had come unraveled upon hearing Wayne's accusation, but that seemed to be fueled more by anger than by grief.

I was deep into those thoughts when the phone rang.

"Jessica, dear, I'm so sorry I ran out on you that way. Will you forgive me?"

"Of course, Marlise. You didn't need to call to apologize, but I'm pleased to hear from you. I was telling your attorney, Mr. Corman, how disappointed I was that you and I haven't had a chance to sit down and have a good talk."

"I was thinking the same thing. I'm afraid I was terribly rude, but the shock of hearing Wayne accuse me of killing Jonathon was too much to bear. I just had to get away, out of that toxic atmosphere, out of that house."

"I understand completely, Marlise. I want you to know that when I persuaded Wayne to come back to Chicago, I was encouraging him to return to help you. He never gave me any indication that his intentions were the opposite. Obviously, you were under the same misapprehension."

"I can't believe he said that, absolutely cannot believe that this young man to whom I've been so good, so loving, could turn on me like that. Jessica, would you be up for dinner tonight, just the two of us? I know some nice quiet restaurants where we can catch up on things. I'd feel terrible if you made the trip out here and returned home without us having some time together. Please. I need someone to talk to, an old friend, someone who isn't directly involved in this tragedy."

I was torn. The emotional roller coaster of the past two days had taken its toll on me, and I was very much looking forward to a quiet night alone in my suite. But this was the reason I'd come. I couldn't turn my back on this friend who was in such trouble.

"I'd like that very much, Marlise."

"Jessica, you are a dear. I'll meet you at Les Nomades on East Ontario Street, just off Michigan Avenue. Do you know it? It's my favorite French restaurant in Chicago, quiet, reserved, a perfect place for us to get together. Can you be there in an hour?"

"An hour it is."

The taxi dropped me in front of a charming brownstone. Marlise was waiting for me in the entryway. We hugged. She looked beautiful in a buff pantsuit that hugged her stunning figure. I'd hastily put myself together in preparation for the dinner, but she looked as though she had just come from a salon.

An attractive blond woman told us that our table was ready.

"Jessica, say hello to Beth Liccioni. She owns this charming restaurant."

She greeted me warmly, but her smile faded when she said to Marlise, "Are you all right, Marlise? I was so sorry to hear."

"I'm holding up, Beth. Thank you for asking."

Marlise had requested a secluded table when she called for a reservation, and we were seated on the second floor, far from other diners. "Perfect," Marlise proclaimed to the owner. "I knew I could count on you."

"Jonathon and I used to come here on special occasions," Marlise told me.

"Maybe another restaurant would be—"

"No, no, Jess. I like being here in familiar surroundings. I need a drink. You?"

"A glass of wine would be fine."

She ordered a glass of Cabernet for me and a double scotch on the rocks for herself. She held up her glass and said sardonically, "Here's to family values, Jess."

We touched the rims of our glasses.

"Thanks for being here for me," she said. "It's just beginning to sink in how much trouble I'm in."

"I spoke with your attorney on the ride to my hotel. He doesn't think that Wayne's allegation will carry that much weight with the prosecutors, certainly not without corroborating evidence."

She slowly shook her head. "I can't believe this is happening, being accused of murdering my husband. It's like a bad dream."

"Your attorney seems like a capable fellow."

"Joe Jankowski says he's the best in the city, although I'm never sure whether to trust Joe."

"Jonathon's attorney," I said, remembering what Corman had told me.

"Right. Joe is an old-school Chicago lawyer, heavy political connections, not an honest bone in his body. He had Jonathon twisted around his little finger. A lot of people didn't know that about Jonathon, how naïve he could be."

"I thought he was a successful businessman."

She guffawed. "Jonathon's *father* was the successful businessman, Jessica. From the day Jonathon inherited the import-export firm from the old man, it started on a slow but steady downhill slide. It happened over a period of time, and it took me all those years to realize what was going on. Jonathon never included me in any business discussions. A big mistake on his part. He kept everything under wraps. When I'd ask about something I'd heard or read, he'd say that I shouldn't concern myself about business and sort of pat me on the head. Not that I complained. There was always plenty of money for me to indulge myself. When I think about it, I realize that keeping me in spending money was Jonathon's way of shutting me up. Of course, he always confided in his mother. Jonathon was—I hate to say it—he was certainly a mother's boy. And the old biddy held that over me from the first day we met." Her grimace testified to her displeasure at that thought.

"How bad had things gotten with his business?" I asked.

"I'm not really sure. As I said, Jonathon kept me in the dark about his business dealings. I do know that he surrounded himself with questionable people who took him for a ride."

Our waiter appeared, and we ordered dinner—arctic char for me, roasted duck breast for Marlise. I passed on a second glass of wine, but she ordered a second double scotch. She seldom drank alcohol when we knew each other in New York, and I hoped that her wealthy lifestyle in Chicago hadn't turned her into a problem drinker. She would need a clear head to navigate the troubles she faced.

"You were saying that Jonathon was involved with questionable people," I said after our salads had been delivered. "In what way?"

"Hustlers," she said. "Joe Jankowski is one of them. Edgar Peters is another. He became Jonathon's partner a few years back."

"Why did Jonathon need a partner?" I asked. "If his father left him the business, I would assume that he didn't need one."

"He didn't in the beginning, but as the company continued hemorrhaging money, Jonathon brought in Peters as a partner. Edgar was good at raising money through investors and generated enough to keep things afloat for a while. At least that's my understanding from picking up on bits and pieces of conversation. Jonathon never let his money problems get in the way of his philanthropy. He loved being a patron of the arts. He was never happy with running a company that imported and exported gadgets, household items, junk. Being involved in the arts allowed him to be viewed as being more—more cultured, I suppose."

We fell silent for a few minutes, and then Marlise said absently, "Settling the estate will be a circus."

I suppose my puzzled expression mirrored what I was thinking—that I hadn't expected the subject of estates or money would be raised.

Marlise smiled. "I don't mean to bore you with all this, Jess."

"Bore me? Not at all. I don't doubt that Jonathon's estate is a complicated one."

"The art collection alone will be messy."

"I wanted to mention art," I said. "Your home is filled with priceless art. Jonathon's reputation as an art collector was well-known."

The effects of her second drink were now evident in her speech. She leaned across the table and said with what could almost be described as a giggle, "Let you in on a little secret, Jess?"

I opened my eyes wide to invite her to continue.

"All that so-called 'priceless' art you see hanging on the walls at home? Most are fakes."

"Really?"

She nodded. "Jonathon spilled the beans right after we

were married and I moved here. I guess it's really not a surprise to people who know about that sort of thing. Jonathon says other collectors do it, too."

"I don't understand."

"The art is too valuable to just hang on a wall in the house, so Jonathon had copies made of every piece he bought by some art forger in Los Angeles. The originals are stored in a small, climate-controlled warehouse Jonathon had built just for that. He took me there once." She laughed. "I thought it was silly, paying all that money for a piece of art and then having to pay more to some forger to make a copy. I teased Jonathon about it, but he never found it funny."

"I wasn't aware that collectors routinely did that."

"That's what Jonathon told me. Oh, here's our meal. I'm famished."

We said little during dinner, and I was relieved when she waved off the waiter's offer of another drink.

"The food is so good here," she commented after we'd finished eating.

"Yes, it was excellent," I agreed. "Marlise, what do you intend to do during this period?"

"Do? Do about what?"

"Where will you stay? At a hotel until things are settled?"

"I don't know. I certainly don't want to go back to the house with Wayne there, not to mention Jonathon's mother. Don't get me started on her."

"I can't blame you for that. Still—"

"I'll figure that out tomorrow. Dessert?"

"I'd better not."

She motioned for the bill and insisted upon paying for both of us. We said good-bye to the restaurant's owner—"If there's anything I can do, Marlise, please just ask," she said— and hailed a taxi, which dropped me first, at the Ambassador East.

"I'm planning to return home to Maine tomorrow," I said before getting out of the cab.

"Sure you can't stay, at least for a few days? I certainly could use a friend I can trust about now."

"Let me think about it. We'll touch base in the morning."

I hadn't been in my room for more than fifteen minutes when the phone rang.

"Jessica, dear, it's Marlise. I just got off the phone with Willard Corman. He delivered a copy of Wayne's lie to the prosecutors. I can't believe he didn't give me time to absorb all this. He said he had to do that. Anyway, two detectives are coming to the house at nine in the morning to question me again."

"That was inevitable," I said.

"I tried to get Willard to have them come to the hotel, but they insisted that the interview be held at the house. I hate to ask it of you, but would you be there with me?"

"Oh, Marlise, I really don't think that—"

"Please, Jessica. I know it's an imposition and that you intended to go home, but it would mean so much to me. Please."

"All right," I said. "I can put off my flight a few hours. I'll be there before nine."

"I knew I could count on you," she said. "That's what old friends are for, isn't it? Here we are, not having seen each other in years, and it's like we were never apart. Thank you, thank you, thank you, Jessica, dear. I'll see you in the morning."

Yes, I thought, *that's what old friends are for, only it's rare that one of them has been accused of killing a spouse in cold blood.*

Chapter Nine

When I arrived at the Simsbury home the following morning, the housekeeper, Mrs. Tetley, answered the door. She was a solidly built woman with a round Irish face and a no-nonsense expression.

"Yes?" she said.

"I'm Jessica Fletcher. I was to meet Mrs. Simsbury here this morning."

She said nothing as she turned and led me to the same room in which I'd been the previous day. It was only a few minutes past eight. I hoped it wasn't too early, but I wanted to have some time with Marlise prior to the detectives' arrival, and thought I'd catch her as soon as she arrived from her hotel. I assumed that I'd preceded her to the house and was surprised when she walked in a minute later.

"Did you change your mind and stay here last night?" I asked.

"God, no! I just couldn't sleep. I got here hours ago."

We heard the sound of a distant door chime. Marlise looked at her watch. "That should be Corman," she said.

"Mrs. Fletcher," the lawyer said as he entered the room. "I didn't expect to see you."

"I asked Jessica to be with me this morning," Marlise said. "I need all the moral support I can get. God, how I dread this."

"You don't have to answer their questions," Corman said.

"Why wouldn't I answer? I haven't done anything wrong. I told you exactly what I did that night. It's the truth."

"That aside, if they get into areas you're uncomfortable with, just refer the questions to me."

The door chime sounded again. A minute later Mrs. Tetley escorted a large, gruff-looking man into the room. He was easily six feet, four inches tall and slightly stooped. His short black hair was fringed with gray. A healthy patch of gray and black hair protruded from his ears. His face was gray, too, an unhealthy look enhanced by a premature five o'clock shadow. His suit matched his other grayness.

"Hello, Joe," Corman said, getting up from his chair and shaking the new visitor's hand. The man accepted a peck on the cheek from Marlise, then looked at me and scowled.

"Meet Jessica Fletcher," said Corman. "She's an old and dear friend of Marlise's. They go back to their days together in New York."

The newcomer grunted his name, Joe Jankowski.

"I wasn't expecting you, Joe," Marlise said.

"We need to talk," Jankowski said.

"The detectives are coming at nine and—"

"There's been a turn of events, Joe," Corman said.

The big attorney settled in a chair and said, "What's that mean?"

Corman told him of Wayne's allegation that he'd seen Marlise shoot Jonathon.

"That's nuts," Jankowski said. "When did this happen?"

"Yesterday," Corman replied. "We thought he'd come back to Chicago to back Marlise up. Instead, the kid made this accusation."

"Why wasn't I told?" Jankowski asked angrily.

"It was a busy day, Joe," Corman said.

The chime was heard again.

"Must be the detectives," Corman said.

Mrs. Tetley arrived and said to Marlise, "The cleaning people are here."

"It's about time," Marlise muttered. "Show them to Mr. Simsbury's office and tell them to be quiet while they work. I want the rug removed, burned." She turned to me. "Not that there's much left of it after the police cut out several big pieces."

As Mrs. Tetley turned to leave, the chime sounded again.

"I'll go," Corman said. "It's probably the detectives."

He returned with two men, one middle-aged, the other younger. Both wore off-the-rack suits. The senior detective introduced himself as Larry Witmer; his younger colleague was Walter Munsch. There was no need for an introduction to Marlise. They'd been part of the team that had responded to her call the night Jonathon was murdered.

Once they were seated, Corman said, "We appreciate you coming here to interview Mrs. Simsbury. Having to go to headquarters would have been awkward."

"We'll still want Mrs. Simsbury to come to headquarters to make a formal statement," Munsch said.

"Of course," Corman said.

Witmer looked at Jankowski. "Your reason for being here, Joe?" he asked.

"I represent the estate," Jankowski replied. "I was Jonathon Simsbury's legal counsel."

The detective's attention turned to me, his raised eyebrows and cocked head asking the same question he'd asked Jankowski.

"I'm a friend of Marlise Simsbury," I said. "She's asked me to be here this morning."

"That's right," said Marlise. "I want her here."

"All right," Witmer said, turning to Marlise and directing his next statement to her. "As you know, your stepson, Wayne Simsbury, has given a sworn statement to your attorney, Mr. Corman, in which he claims to have witnessed you shooting your husband."

"It's preposterous," Marlise said. "I did no such thing, and I can't imagine what would cause him to lie like that."

Detective Munsch jotted notes on a pad while Witmer continued. "His accusation makes you a person of interest, Mrs. Simsbury."

"But you did some kind of test on me the night my husband was killed, and you told me I was cleared," Marlise said. She turned to Corman. "I'm sorry. In all the confusion, I forgot to mention that to you."

Corman's face turned red. He addressed the detective. "What did you do? A paraffin test?" he said, referring to a procedure to detect gunshot residue. "You had no right to examine my client without my being present."

"We use a chemical test kit in the field now, and yes, we swabbed her, but we asked her permission first," Witmer said, "and she agreed."

"Of course I agreed. I have nothing to hide," Marlise said.

"And?" Corman said.

"It was negative for nitrates," Witmer said.

"Which only proves the kid is lying." Corman clapped his hands on his knees and rose. "I guess that settles that."

Marlise flashed me a grin, relief clearly written on her face.

"Not so fast, Mr. Corman. Please keep your seat," Witmer said, and I saw Marlise tense up again. "A positive result would be confirmatory, but a negative one is not. If the gun was new, never fired before, it might not leak nitrates. Without the weapon, we can't be sure. I'm sorry, Mrs. Simsbury, but that still leaves you as a person of interest."

Marlise dropped her head, and I thought she might cry, but instead she took a deep breath and faced the detective.

Detective Witmer looked at Corman, who nodded.

"What we'd like you to do," Witmer said, "is to give us a play-by-play of your movements the night of the homicide."

"I already have," she said. "I told you when you answered my 911 call that I'd gone to bed early—I wasn't feeling well—and that I came downstairs to ask Jonathon to come to bed. He'd been working late night after night and I wanted him to get some rest."

"How did you know he was home?"

"Well, I thought I'd heard some noise downstairs."

"See? Those are the kinds of details we need," Witmer said. "Our conversation with you that night was necessarily brief. You were distraught. Possibly not thinking clearly. Maybe you can be more precise in a relaxed atmosphere."

As they talked, I took in the senior detective. I judged him to be in his late forties, maybe early fifties. He was a tall, reed-thin man with a pleasant, long face and clear, inquisitive blue eyes. He spoke in well-modulated tones; I didn't detect any trace of a Midwestern accent. Because he was low-key and likable, I assumed that he was an effective interviewer, one who quickly gained the trust of those on the receiving end of his questions. His younger partner's expression was one of youthful enthusiasm, quick to smile and to indicate agreement with whatever Witmer said.

Corman told Marlise, "Go through your movements that night, Marlise, but only if you want to." He turned to the detectives and said, "Since you're now looking at Mrs. Simsbury as 'a person of interest,' citing her Miranda rights might be in order."

Witmer smiled. "I was just about to do that, Counselor, but thanks for reminding me."

He gave the classic Miranda rights speech without referring to notes—"You have the right to remain silent and—"

"I understand," Marlise said.

Marlise and the detective spoke for the next fifteen minutes. He interrupted her only occasionally to clarify something she'd said. The younger officer continued taking copious notes. When they'd finished, Corman said, "I suggest that we end this, unless you intend to charge her with something."

Given what Corman had told me earlier, I doubted the detective would place her under arrest solely on the strength of Wayne's accusation. I was right. Witmer stood and said, "We'll arrange for you to come to headquarters in the next day or two. You're not to leave the city, ma'am."

Marlise asked Corman, "Do they have the right to demand that?"

"I'm sure Mrs. Simsbury has no intention of leaving," Corman told Witmer, then aimed a stern glance at Marlise.

Witmer thanked Marlise for her time and cooperation, and he and Detective Munsch followed Corman out of the room. Marlise excused herself, leaving Jankowski and me alone.

"What do you know about this statement that the kid gave?" Jankowski asked me.

"I'm afraid you'll have to ask Mr. Corman about the particulars. I was there when Wayne gave the statement, but I don't remember all the specifics. He tended to ramble a bit. The bottom line was that he claims to have seen Marlise shoot Jonathon."

"They believe him?" Jankowski growled. "The kid is an inveterate liar."

I certainly hadn't expected such a vehement condemnation of Wayne Simsbury. I was, after all, a complete stranger to Jankowski. As though suddenly realizing that he was talking to someone he didn't know, he asked, "What's your connection with this?"

"I'm a friend of Marlise."

"From here in Chicago?"

"No. I live in Maine. Marlise and I knew each other in New York years ago."

He grunted and lowered a leg that had been crossed. "You live in Maine, but you're here. How come?"

I recounted for him how Wayne had arrived on my doorstep and how I had persuaded him to return to Chicago. "He said he'd only come if I came with him, so I did. I'm glad that I did. Marlise needs as much moral support as she can get."

"What do you think of the kid's claim that he saw her shoot Jonathon?"

"I prefer to not believe it, but I don't know whether it's true or not."

"That's refreshingly candid," he said. "You know a lot about her marriage to Jonathon?"

"Not very much. I was with her when she accepted Jonathon's proposal back in New York. I wasn't able to attend the wedding, and I hadn't seen Marlise until I came here yesterday with Wayne."

"But you have Marlise's ear."

I shrugged. "I wouldn't know about that," I said.

"You retired?" he asked.

"Hardly. I'm still writing."

"Writing what?"

I felt as though I was on the witness stand.

"Murder mysteries."

He exhibited his first smile of the morning. "Is that so? You planning on writing about this murder mystery?"

"Of course not. I'm here as Marlise's friend, that's all."

He got up out of his chair with some difficulty, yawned, and stretched. "Come on," he said, "I'll buy you breakfast."

"Breakfast?"

"You don't have breakfast back in—where did you say you live?"

"Maine. Cabot Cove, Maine. And yes, we do have breakfast, very good ones, I might add."

"Don't get huffy, Mrs.—what was your name?"

"Fletcher. Jessica Fletcher."

"I'll tell them we're leaving," he said as he lumbered out of the room.

He returned with Corman.

"What do the cops say?" Jankowski asked Corman.

"They'll be back to reinterview everyone else who was in the house that night."

We were joined by someone I hadn't seen before, a strikingly beautiful woman in her early to mid-thirties. She had a mane of copper-colored hair, filled out her form-fitting cream-colored suit in all the appropriate places, and had a face that rivaled those of many models I'd seen in cosmetics ads and commercials. She wore a pair of very high heels, and I marveled that she managed to walk in them.

"How are you, kid?" Jankowski said to her.

"Hello, Joe," she said.

"Meet Jessica Fletcher. She writes horror stories," he said.

I extended my hand. "Actually," I said through a smile, "I write murder mysteries."

"I've read some of them," she said. "Marlise has mentioned you. I'm Susan Hurley, Jonathon Simsbury's executive assistant."

"Pleased to meet you."

"We're just heading out for breakfast," Jankowski said. "Join us. You look like you could use a good meal."

She ignored the large attorney and said to Corman, "Marlise is lying down, Willard. She's upset about what happened this morning."

"I need to talk to her later," said Jankowski.

"The detectives will be back at eleven," Corman told her. "They want to interview everyone who was here that night."

"I can't tell them anything," Hurley said. "I left early."

"Still, they want to talk with you," Corman said. "Stay around until they come. Don't make life difficult for them by making them have to chase you. It's a lot more comfortable talking to them here instead of in an interrogation room."

Ms. Hurley said to Jankowski, "Edgar called. He wants to meet with you as soon as possible."

"Call him back and tell him to meet me for breakfast. We'll be at Nookies, the one in Old Town." He turned to me and said, "Best bloody omelets in the city, if you get my drift. You, Willard? Up for a good omelet?"

"No, thanks," Corman replied. "I've got to get back to my office."

Jankowski led the way out of the room, saying over his shoulder to Susan Hurley, "Tell Marlise I need to talk to her when she's up and around. She has my cell number."

"Nice meeting you," I said to her.

She nodded.

Jankowski stopped suddenly, causing me to almost run into him. "Where's Wayne?" he asked Hurley.

"Sleeping."

"Figures," Jankowski growled and continued toward the front door.

I followed. I hadn't eaten before leaving the hotel and was suffering hunger pangs. But more than that, falling in line behind the hulking attorney seemed natural, almost expected. I wouldn't say that he had a "Pied Piper" personality. It was more a matter of it being a lot easier to say yes to him than no.

His black Cadillac was parked down the street at a fire hydrant. As I got in, I noticed that a sticker from the Chicago Police Department was prominently displayed on the windshield. Joe Jankowski obviously knew his way around Chicago, and those who counted in the city knew him.

Nookies was a bustling place with an inviting array of outdoor tables strung along the sidewalk and a line of people waiting for inside space. A man suddenly appeared and pointed to one of the outside tables. "Didn't know if you were coming, Joe," he said. "I had to give away your table inside, but I held this one for you."

Jankowski mumbled a thank-you and we sat. I was pleased that we were outdoors. It was a splendid day in Chicago, sunny and pleasantly warm, with low humidity and a refreshing breeze.

"I'd rather eat inside," he grumbled, squinting at the sun. "You hungry?"

"Yes."

"Crazy name, huh? Nookies. They named it after a breakfast nook. Nook. Nookies. Best omelets in the city."

"So you've said."

He ordered for us, cheese-and-bacon omelets, whole wheat bread, coffees, and orange juice.

"So, you write murder mysteries. Figured out this one yet?"

"'This one'? I haven't even tried."

"Marlise didn't kill her old man. You can take that to the bank."

I didn't get a chance to reply because two men came to the table to greet Jankowski. They engaged in playful, masculine banter and left, soon replaced by someone who'd just gotten out of a taxi. Jankowski spotted him and waved him over to the table, where he took the remaining vacant chair. He was a short, thin man with limp flaxen hair that blew in the breeze, and beneath an aquiline nose he had a pencil mustache that was darker than his hair. He wore a tan suit and a colorful striped button-down shirt open at the collar. He carried a folded newspaper.

"Hi," the newcomer said, extending his hand to me. "Edgar Peters."

"Jessica Fletcher," I said, surprised at how slender his hand was, almost feminine.

"She writes horror stories," said Jankowski.

"Murder mysteries," I corrected, wondering when Jankowski would get it right. "I'm an old friend of Marlise Morrison Simsbury."

"Oh," he said. "Wait a minute. Jessica Fletcher. Sure, I've just been reading about you. Here."

He unfolded the newspaper and laid it in front of me. A headline on the front page popped out at me: SIMSBURY SON POINTS FINGER AT WIFE. It was accompanied by a photograph of Jonathon and Marlise Simsbury that had obviously been taken a number of years ago. They stood on a beach with their arms around each other, their wide smiles as dazzling as the white sand. I started reading the article, but Jankowski pulled the paper in front of him.

"Shoot!" he said.

"You said you were reading about me," I said to Peters.

"The writer mentions in the piece that you'd arrived in Chicago with Wayne Simsbury."

I gave an abbreviated explanation of my trip to Chicago, which was cut short by the delivery of our breakfasts. Peters asked the waiter for coffee and a dry English muffin.

"Have an omelet," Jankowski said as he continued to read, his face set in a menacing scowl. "You could use some flesh on those bones."

Peters ignored Jankowski's culinary suggestion and said, "We need to talk, Joe."

"I'm listening," Jankowski said, tucking the newspaper under his arm.

Peters glanced in my direction.

"If you'd prefer to have a private conversation, I can move to another table."

"No, stay and eat your omelet before it gets cold," Jankowski commanded. To Peters, he said, "Who leaked it?"

"Who knows? Who cares?" was Peters's response. "Look, Joe, what Wayne said aside, there's the matter of the art collection to consider."

"Jonathon was quite a noted art collector, wasn't he?" I said.

Jankowski, who was in the process of raising his final piece of omelet to his mouth, stopped his fork in midair and said, "Jonathon Simsbury appreciated pretty things, Mrs. Fletcher. He liked his fancy sports cars and his yacht and all the pretty pictures he surrounded himself with. That's why he hired Susan. Now *that's* a piece of art." He chuckled and finished eating.

I don't know why I felt compelled to defend Jonathon, but I said, "There's nothing wrong with liking 'pretty things.'"

"Yeah, well, too bad he didn't pay more attention to his business. He was so busy liking pretty things that he let his business go down the tubes."

Peters ignored him and said to me, "Are you an art collector, Mrs. Fletcher?"

"Not at all, although I do enjoy good art." That comment led me to tell the tale of when I'd visited Italy and was witness to art theft and murder.

"Lucky you're alive," Peters said.

"Yes, I am," I agreed. "I'd like to read what this reporter said about me."

Jankowski handed over the newspaper. Whoever gave the story to the paper had given the reporter a lot of detail about Wayne's statement to Willard Corman. Had Corman, or someone from his office, been behind the leak? Or had it come from the district attorney's office or from someone in the Chicago PD? I suppose it didn't matter at that juncture. I was pleased that the mention of me was fleeting, just a line indicating that Wayne had returned to Chicago with "noted mystery writer Jessica Fletcher, a longtime friend of the victim's wife, Marlise Morrison Simsbury."

"How did you end up with Wayne?" Peters asked.

This time I gave a more complete explanation of how Wayne had arrived unannounced at my door and the phone call I'd received from Marlise and her attorney.

"Must have come as a shock when the kid came up with the story that he saw Marlise shoot Jonathon."

"It was certainly a surprise," I said.

"Enjoy your omelet?" Jankowski asked.

I looked down at it. I'd barely started it. "It was fine," I said.

Jankowski reached with his fork and speared an untouched portion of it, popping it into his mouth. "Excuse me," he said as he pushed himself out of his chair and disappeared inside Nookies.

"Tony Curso would love your story about almost being killed in Italy," Peters said to me when we were alone at the table.

"Who's that?" I asked.

"An art historian here in Chicago. I've asked him to evaluate our collection."

It wasn't lost on me that he'd said "our collection." I suppose my quizzical expression prompted him to explain.

"Jonathon and I jointly own the art collection, Mrs. Fletcher. Maybe it's more accurate to say that we are— were—partners in a corporation that owns the art. Anthony Curso is a world-renowned appraiser. A real character. He's also an expert on mixing drinks. And he loves murder mysteries. I know he'd be thrilled to meet you."

"Sounds like a fascinating gentleman."

"Like to meet him?"

"Well, perhaps another time. I wasn't planning on staying in Chicago, but I do want to spend some time with Marlise before I leave."

"Tony and I are having dinner tonight. Please join us."

I thought a moment.

"You have to eat, Mrs. Fletcher," he pressed. "And we provide great dinner table conversation."

I laughed. "All right. I'd like that very much. But if we're to dine together, you have to call me Jessica."

"My pleasure. I'm Edgar."

Jankowski emerged from Nookies holding a cell phone to his ear. "Come on," he said to me as he headed for his car. I hurriedly made arrangements with Edgar Peters to meet that night for dinner, tagged along with Jankowski, held my breath as he sped through city streets, and heaved a sigh of relief when he pulled up in front of the Simsbury home.

Marlise had gotten up from her nap and looked refreshed, with newly applied makeup and a different outfit. Before Jankowski whisked her away for a private conversation, she asked if I was free for lunch.

"As long as it means spending time with you, Marlise."

"Great. Let's go to your hotel. The police are due here to interview everyone in the household except me, thank God. I've already told them twice what I know, which isn't much. Sit tight until Joe and I have our little confab. Carl will drive us unless they've arrested him. Tea or coffee?"

"Tea would be fine."

"Be back soon."

By now the room in which I waited had become familiar. Mrs. Tetley brought me tea (I thought how apt her name was), and I sipped it while more closely examining the art on the walls. What Marlise had said about the works in the house being copies of the originals cast a different light on them. Jonathon had attached a small brass plate to the bottom frame of each painting, giving the artist's name and the title of the work. There was a "Sargent" and a "Pollock," and two small pieces by "Van Eyck" were grouped together. Of course, according to Marlise, the art I perused was actually painted by a skilled forger from Los Angeles.

The detectives arrived at eleven and disappeared into the recesses of the house. I kept wondering where Wayne was. I hadn't seen him since Corman and I delivered him to the house, and I wondered whether he'd rethought his allegation about Marlise. It would be wonderful if he did, of course, but I doubted he would change his story. As long as his charge hung in the air, Marlise was under the harsh scrutiny of the investigating officers and would continue to be. I thought I heard his voice a few times but couldn't be sure.

The hands of an antique clock on the wall were approaching noon when Marlise reappeared, accompanied by Jankowski. She looked less composed than an hour earlier, and I assumed that what he'd said to her hadn't gone down well.

"Ready for lunch?" she asked.

"Yes."

"I'd join you, but I have another lunch to go to," the hulking attorney said, though he hadn't been invited. "Remember what I said, Marlise," were his final words as he left the room.

"Sometimes I could strangle that man," Marlise said

I raised my brows. "Maybe that's not the best way to put it," I said.

She managed a smile. "I suppose you're right," she concurred. "Let's go eat. I'm famished."

Chapter Ten

When Marlise had suggested that we have lunch at my hotel, I'd assumed she meant the Ambassador East's famed Pump Room. But she had something else in mind. "They don't serve lunch in the Pump Room," she said as Carl Grundig, the family's chauffeur, a taciturn middle-aged man with shaggy gray hair that covered the collar of his black suit and white shirt, drove us to the hotel. "I don't feel like being around people," she explained. "We can order up lunch to your room."

I was pleased that my suite had already been serviced by the chambermaids, and glad that I'd tidied up before leaving that morning. Marlise said she wanted only a shrimp cocktail and a double shot of single-malt scotch; I ordered a club sandwich and tea. We fell into an easy conversation while waiting for the food to be delivered, sitting across from each other at a small table next to the window.

"I really like Chicago," I commented.

"I used to," she said, "when Jonathon and I were first married. I hate it now."

I wasn't sure that the tragedy that had befallen her was reason to condemn an entire city, but I also understood how external things could be tainted for her.

"I remember when you and Jonathon first met in New York," I said lightly. "It was like something out of a romantic Hollywood movie."

She'd kicked off her shoes and now tucked her feet beneath her. "Those were happy days, Jessica. I never dreamed that the happiness would fade."

At first I thought that she was referring to how things had changed because of his tragic and sudden death, but then she added, "It started going sour a few years after we married."

I was surprised that she was sharing this with me. I felt as though we were back in New York trading confidences over dinner and glasses of wine. Marlise had never been reticent in voicing her feelings. She'd always been frank, which held her in good stead while she was working as a TV reporter. Being trusted enough to be on the receiving end of another person's innermost thoughts is always flattering. I would never have pried into the state of her marriage with Jonathon, but I was willing to be a sympathetic, nonjudgmental listener.

"I wasn't aware that you were having marital problems," I said.

Marlise guffawed. "Is there any marriage that doesn't have problems?"

"Of course not," I replied. "Those looking in from the outside only see the good."

"Don't get me wrong, Jessica," she said. "There were many wonderful things about being married to Jonathon Simsbury. He was always so alive and eager to try new things. But in many ways, he was like a little boy not satisfied with one piece of fudge. He had to have the whole box."

"I remember so clearly, Marlise, that it was his little-boy quality that you found so appealing."

"You're right, Jessica. His youthful enthusiasm was infectious. But I have to admit that it eventually wore thin. I suppose you could say that Jonathon never grew up."

"That isn't necessarily a bad thing," I offered, "remaining youthful as we age."

"As long as you're a grown-up when you need to be, before your childishness negatively impacts the way you run a business."

I remembered what Joe Jankowski had said about Jonathon enjoying "pretty things," as he put it, at the expense of his role as a businessman. I debated whether asking the questions that I'd formulated would constitute prying but decided it wouldn't. Marlise had brought up the topic without any prodding. Besides, if I went too far she could always change the subject. As long as she was leading the conversation, I was willing to follow.

"You've said that Jonathon's business wasn't doing very well."

"That's putting it mildly, Jessica. Despite advice from knowledgeable people like Joe Jankowski, Jonathon just kept playing Lord Bountiful while the business went to hell.

Oh, don't get me wrong. I was happy to go along for the ride. What girl wouldn't be? It was all very heady—a private plane available at a moment's notice, the expensive vacations in exotic places, the unlimited expense accounts at the best stores, the yacht, the servants, all of it. As far as I knew, the business was doing fine. At least he never indicated to me that it wasn't. But there were hints, subtle ones, and even when they became more obvious, I chose not to recognize them, until the last few years when they were impossible to ignore. I started to pick up pieces here and there that Jonathon was in financial trouble. I didn't want to believe it at first, but then again I've always been somewhat naïve. I'm sure you'll agree with that."

"When you were young, Marlise. We're all naïve when we're young."

This time her laugh was mellow and self-effacing. "Yes, I was young once. Funny how you keep thinking you're young until suddenly one day you're not. The selling of our yacht was the turning point for me, the moment when Jonathon's money woes became real. He loved that yacht. So did I. He named it *Marlise*; I was thrilled to have my name on such a beautiful boat—maybe 'ship' would be more accurate. It was big enough to cross the Atlantic, and we took it to Europe a few times, and down to South America, too. We had a crew that waited on us hand and foot. I felt like Cleopatra or the Queen of Sheba or some glamorous Hollywood star. It was all make-believe, of course, and I shouldn't have expected it to last forever. When Jonathon announced he was selling it, I knew that something was very wrong."

"Did he tell you why he was selling it?" I asked.

"Oh, sure. He said he had a feeling that the economy was headed in the wrong direction and that as a smart business-man he was taking difficult but prudent steps to be ahead of the curve. Yes, that's what he said. He wanted to be ahead of the curve, whatever that meant. But he wasn't fooling me. I knew that selling the yacht meant that his business was in financial trouble. I didn't press him about it, at least not then. But in the past year I'd become more bold in questioning him about our finances. He just kept saying how good things were and that I wasn't to be concerned, always with that big, boyish grin and enthusiastic voice. But I knew better, and Joe Jankowski sat me down one day and told me the grim facts. I am no fan of Joe's, but he does give it to you straight."

Our conversation stopped when a young uniformed man arrived with our lunch, taking great pains to set it up neatly on the table between us. I signed the bill, including a tip, and he left the room.

"I thought you said you were famished," I said, eyeing the four cold shrimp in front of Marlise.

"I am, but it doesn't take much to satisfy my hunger. Besides, I'd better get used to doing with less."

As we ate, the subject shifted to Jonathon's involvement in Chicago's art scene.

"He loved being a patron of the arts," Marlise said, "and kept pledging funds even when it became increasingly obvious that he didn't have the money to back them up. I heard from Joe that Jonathon had been borrowing to keep the company afloat, to meet the payroll and other expenses. As far as I know, he never laid anybody off. In fact, he even did some hiring, including his so-called administrative assistant."

"Ms. Hurley?"

"You've met her, I take it."

"Only briefly. She's very attractive."

"I suppose she can type, too," Marlise commented sarcastically. "Jonathon's boyish enthusiasm wasn't restricted to his toys like the yacht and the plane. He appreciated a pretty face and a shapely bottom, too."

I fell silent. Was she about to tell me that Jonathon was having an affair with Susan Hurley? I hoped not. The police would see jealousy as a powerful motive for murder, and Marlise had enough going against her already.

"Jonathon spent more time at home than he did at the office, especially lately. He had a few other administrative aides, but they were male. He told me he hired Susan because he needed someone with a good head for numbers and an understanding of the accounting process." She closed her eyes and slowly shook her head. When she opened them, she said, "I knew early on that something was going on. I raised my suspicions with him a few times, but he told me I was being paranoid. But I could tell from the way they interacted, the way she looked at him and him at her. Women have a good sense of that, don't we, Jessica?"

"So I've been told. Marlise, when you learned about Wayne's statement, you said he'd been trying to get rid of you for years, something about him being after the money. If I'm off base in asking this, please stop me, but I assume that Jonathon had a will?"

"Of course he did. Joe Jankowski drafted the original and the new one."

"'*New* one'?"

Marlise finished the last of her shrimp and nodded. "I haven't been entirely honest with you, Jessica. It wasn't just my womanly intuition that led me to believe that Jonathon and Susan Hurley were having an affair. I caught them together, twice."

I winced. How hurtful that must have been.

"I know I claim to be naïve, but I was a reporter for too long not to know how to get to the bottom of a story. I confronted Jonathon and threatened to sue him for divorce and take every penny he had left. He was really upset, swore he loved me, and said if I stayed, he would change his will. The original left half of his estate to me and half to Wayne. I told Jonathon I thought I deserved more. I was surprised when he didn't argue. He said that he couldn't cut his own son completely out of the will and that he felt compelled to leave Wayne something. I certainly understood that. Even though Jonathon was always terribly disappointed in Wayne and the direction his life was taking, I knew that he loved him. Jonathon said that he would have Jankowski draw up a new will leaving ninety percent of his estate to me and ten percent to Wayne. It was a lot more than I had expected. He said he hoped the new will would force Wayne to take control of his life and plan for the future. I suppose that Jonathon was making that point with Wayne by cutting back on what he would inherit."

"Was Wayne aware that this was happening?" I asked.

"Oh, yes, as recently as a week before Jonathon was killed. They had quite a shouting match. I overheard much of it. Jonathon's death was tragic in many ways, including the fact that he never got to execute that new will. As Joe just informed me, the new will was ready to be executed and Jonathon was scheduled to sign it the week following his death. I didn't realize that he hadn't already signed it."

I didn't voice what was becoming obvious—Wayne Simsbury had a strong motive for killing his father. However, Marlise read my thoughts.

"I know what you're thinking. That Wayne had a good reason for killing Jonathon. I'm well aware of that."

"And a reason for pointing the finger at you," I added.

"Sure."

"He was in the house the night that Jonathon was killed," I said. "And the way he left Chicago could be considered, as the lawyers call it, consciousness of guilt. Marlise, do you have any idea who might have killed Jonathon?"

"From what you've just said, the finger of guilt, *Wayne's* finger, should be pointed at him."

"Are there others?" I asked.

"Who might have wanted to kill Jonathon?"

"Yes."

"Susan Hurley may not have been happy to learn of Jonathon's recommitment to me. And you know as well as I do that anyone who has a lot of money makes enemies. Are you going to help me defend myself here?"

"I can't promise anything, Marlise, but I'll see what I can do."

She'd finished her drink and looked sleepy. She placed a hand on my arm and squeezed. "You find out who your friends really are when you're faced with something like this. I know so many people here in Chicago through Jonathon, but there isn't anyone I would call a close friend."

She appeared to be on the verge of tears but held them back. What she'd said touched me, but I resisted allowing myself to become maudlin.

"Marlise, about this new will that Jonathon never got to sign. From what you've said, I gather that Jonathon's estate has been considerably diminished. How much is it worth—*really* worth?"

"I can understand why you'd ask that, Jessica. Yes, his business is in terrible financial shape. I know that he'd borrowed to keep it afloat, but that doesn't take into account his investments outside the business. Although Jonathon didn't share much information with me about his personal worth, Jankowski says it's sizable, most of it tied up in his art collection. That lovely creature you met this morning, Ms. Hurley, has access to all of Jonathon's personal accounts."

"Really? That seems unusual."

Her sardonic laugh said volumes.

I thought for a moment before saying, "I had breakfast this morning with Edgar Peters. He claims that he and Jonathon were partners in the collection and that it's owned by a separate corporation."

"How did you end up with Edgar?" she asked.

"He came to meet Mr. Jankowski where we were eating. I'm having dinner tonight with him and an art appraiser named Curso."

She sat up straighter. "You haven't wasted any time getting to know the players in this sordid little drama, have you?"

"That wasn't my intention. But now that I'm involved, I might come across something that will help clear you. I'm willing to give that a go if you want me to."

"Do I? Oh, Jessica. You're the only one on my side, the only one," she said before erupting in tears.

I put a hand on her heaving shoulder and said, "You'll get through this, Marlise, and I'll be with you all the way."

After Marlise left my suite, I sat by the window and pondered what she'd revealed to me during our lunch, what my commitment to her would mean. There was a lot to digest besides the food, and I made some notes to ensure that I would remember the most salient things that she'd said. I'd meant it, of course, when I said I would do the best I could to help her. But I was equally aware that my efforts to help identify Jonathon's killer could easily prove futile. There was also the possibility—I hated to admit—that were I successful in helping solve Jonathon's murder, it could end up that Wayne's accusation that Marlise was the killer had been truthful.

No matter how it turned out, I was now, as the saying goes, in for a penny, in for a pound.

Whether I'd made the right decision remained to be seen.

Chapter Eleven

Edgar Peters had arranged to pick me up at the hotel at six, but I was ready far in advance and used the time to Google the gentleman who would join us, Anthony Curso. The sources of information about him seemed endless—I started with the first and worked my way down through a dozen. A few of the articles about him included a photograph, which helped me feel as though I'd already met him. Assuming the photographs were of recent vintage, Mr. Curso was a man of about sixty with a wide face and chipmunk cheeks. He wore half-glasses in the pictures and displayed a small smile that said he found amusement in many things, including having his photo taken. He hadn't lost much of his black hair, if any, nor had it grayed. He wore it relatively short and plastered to his head, which reminded me somewhat of Agatha Christie's famous fictitious detective Hercule Poirot.

His credentials as an art historian, appraiser, and professor were substantial and distinguished. He was currently a visiting professor of art history at the University of Chicago.

Simultaneously, he was a consultant to leading museums around the world, including the Met in New York City and the National Gallery in Washington, D.C. The more I read, the more eager I was to meet him.

I also used the time to make a phone call back to Cabot Cove.

"Hello, Jessica," Seth Hazlitt said. "Where might you be calling from?"

"I'm still in Chicago. That's why I'm calling. I'll be staying here longer than I'd planned."

"Oh? What brings about *that* change of plans?"

"It's a long story, Seth, and I won't bore you with it now. Let's just say that my old friend Marlise needs me here now, and—"

"Needs you to help her prove she didn't shoot her husband."

"That's part of it."

"Knowing you're there, I've been keeping up with the news about the murder. I suppose there's no sense in my trying to *talk* sense into you about not getting involved."

"I didn't choose to become involved, Seth. It just happened."

He started to hum. "Seems to me I've heard that tune before."

I chuckled. "I guess you have," I said, "but there's no danger here. I'm just giving a friend some much-needed moral support at a difficult time in her life."

"Mebbe so, but just remember, if your friend didn't kill her husband, someone else did. And that someone may not appreciate your meddling."

"I don't consider it 'meddling,'" I said, bristling at the accusation.

Seth laughed. "Got your goat, didn't I? My real concern, Jessica Fletcher, is this: Do you have enough clothing with you? You said you were only going to Chicago for a day. You must be running low by now."

I couldn't help but smile. He knew that I was getting riled and had shifted gears to make light of it.

"Your concern is well placed," I said. "I do need some additional clothing for my stay. It's a good excuse to replenish my wardrobe."

"Shopping for clothes is a mite less dangerous than hanging around with murderers," he said.

"Seth, I—"

"Pleased that you called, Jessica. Always enjoy talking with you. Stay in touch."

The conversation was over.

As much as Seth can nettle me at times, I love him dearly and have seldom experienced real anger at his overprotective ways. And I have to admit that he's been right on more than one occasion.

Was this one of those times? I wondered as I put on last-minute makeup before heading downstairs to meet Edgar Peters. Had I jumped into the fray without giving it sufficient thought, injected myself into Jonathon Simsbury's murder investigation to satisfy my own curiosity and psychic needs rather than out of a true desire to help? Marlise seemed genuinely pleased that I'd decided to stay, which tempered my ambivalence of the moment. As I waited for the elevator, I admitted to myself that my intrusion into the case might prove useless, no help at all. But that unpleasant thought was replaced by anticipation of the evening when I stepped off the elevator and saw Edgar Peters waiting for me.

"Ah, Jessica, right on time," he said, taking my hand and leading me to the street. "I'm sure you were looking forward to dinner at one of our city's best restaurants, but Tony convinced me to come to the Quadrangle Club at the university. Really quite nice, renovated a dozen times over the years. It's been around since the late eighteen hundreds. A little stuffy, but that's to be expected of a private faculty club—professors hunched at a round table tackling the meaning of life and such."

"I'm sure it's lovely," I said as he held open the door of his sporty metallic blue car, which was a little hard to fold myself into.

"The food is good at the club," he said, starting the engine and driving away. "And I know you'll love Tony. He's a true Renaissance man, with a limitless number of interests besides art. He's a walking encyclopedia of the history of alcoholic beverages, and he's just recently decided to become an expert on the history of steamship travel."

"I admire people with varied interests," I said. "Keeps the mind young."

We chatted amiably during the drive to the club, a graceful redbrick building on the corner of Fifty-seventh Street and University Avenue. Peters found a parking spot only a few car lengths from the entrance, came around to help me out of the car—"Sorry for the tight squeeze"—and we entered the building, where Anthony Curso, whom I immediately recognized from my Google foray, stood chatting with a man and a woman. As he excused himself and bounded across the lobby, I was struck by how short he was, no taller than five feet, five inches. He wore a beige linen double-breasted jacket, a navy blue shirt, a floppy red-and-yellow bow tie, and black sneakers.

"How wonderful that you're here!" he said in a voice considerably larger than his stature.

"I'm delighted to be here," I said. "It's a beautiful club."

"Creaky and stodgy, like its members," he said cheerfully. "Come, I've reserved a table in the main dining room."

Our table in the nicely appointed room was set with white starched tablecloth and napkins and heavy silverware. A vase of fresh flowers brightened up the expanse of white. Curso's reputation as an expert on alcoholic beverages was immediately evident when ordering drinks. "Martinis?" he asked as though the answer was preordained.

"Not for me, thank you," I said. "A little too strong for my taste."

Curso made a face as though he'd been mortally stabbed. "Not even a vodka martini?" he said. "It distresses me to see vodka used in a martini, but it's what so many people, mostly younger ones, ask for these days. For me, a martini made with anything but gin and vermouth is sacrilege."

"I think a glass of white wine would be fine," I said.

"You, Ed?" Curso asked.

"Looks like I'd better have a martini."

"Splendid," said Curso, motioning for a waiter. He said to me with enthusiasm, "I've taught the bartenders here how to make a martini to my liking. Always a glass tumbler, never metal. I put the gin in the tumbler and place it in a bed of ice. The same with the glass. I don't like chilling glasses in a cooler. The air in them is invariably stale and picks up odors. I fill the glass with shaved ice and drizzle the smallest amount of vermouth over the ice, which slowly coats the inside of the glass. The ice is discarded and the chilled gin poured into the glass. Add the garnish—I prefer the traditional olive—and voilà! The perfect martini."

I had to laugh at the zeal with which he explained his martini-making technique.

"It's tragic how people have bastardized the world's most perfect drink," he said, his face now set in sorrow. "Chocolate martinis, apple martinis, *vodka*! We've become a barbaric society, Mrs. Fletcher."

"I never equated variations on the martini with the fall of civilization," I said lightly, "but I'll take your word for it."

"Such a proud history," he continued. "You remember, of course, how Hemingway described the martinis his character enjoyed in *Across the River and Into the Trees*. Montgomery Martinis, Hemingway called them, fifteen parts gin and one part vermouth, named after Field Marshal Montgomery, who commanded the British Eighth Army in North Africa during World War Two. Montgomery, it was said, refused to engage his German foe, Erwin Rommel, unless he had a fifteen-to-one advantage in manpower."

"Fascinating," Peters said, not sounding entirely truthful.

"I'm afraid I could go on all evening about mixed drinks and their origins," Curso said. "Forgive my enthusiasm for the subject."

"I always enjoy learning new things. I'd love to hear more," I said, meaning it.

But Peters said, "Tell Mrs. Fletcher about the art collection, Tony."

"Oh, poor Jonathon," Curso said. "I didn't know the man well, you understand—ran into him a few times at gallery openings and museum shows. He was most generous where the arts were concerned. What a dreadful way to die, gunned down like that. You knew him well, Ed. You must have been devastated when you received the news."

"Devastated—and in total shock."

"I understand that you'll be appraising the collection that Jonathon and Edgar owned," I said.

"I've already gotten a good start," Curso replied.

"I never thought I'd see the day when the collection was being appraised because of Jonathon's death," Peters said.

"Untangling a large estate must be difficult," I offered, "especially when it involves millions of dollars' worth of fine art."

Curso raised his eyebrows but said nothing.

"Tell Tony about your Italian adventure with the art world," Peters suggested.

"Oh?" Curso said. "You're a connoisseur of Italian art, Mrs. Fletcher?"

"Hardly," I said. "I was in Italy, on a tour of art outside museums—places like churches, municipal buildings, private homes—when two young men who'd been posing as priests burst into the church we were visiting. They had weapons and trained them on us while they stole a Bellini."

"A man in the tour group, a retired Italian police officer, was killed during the robbery, as I recall," Curso said.

"You know about it," I said.

"Oh, indeed. I keep up with such shenanigans in the art world. I wasn't aware that you were part of the tour group."

"Unfortunately I was," I said. "Wrong place, wrong time."

"Tell me again what happened from your perspective," Curso said.

He listened with great interest as I retold the tale, interrupted only by the delivery of our drinks. When I was finished, Curso lifted his glass and said, "To you, Jessica Fletcher, and your survival instincts."

We touched rims.

"There was some question as to whether Bellini had painted the piece himself or whether it was the work of some of his students," I said.

"That's always a problem with the great masters who also taught," said Curso. "But I'm interested in your mystery novels. I've read a few, although that was a year or two ago."

We spent the rest of dinner discussing murder mysteries and mixed drinks; Curso knew a great deal about both subjects. He was partial to classic British writers like Agatha Christie, Dorothy Sayers, Margery Allingham, Wilkie Collins, and, of course, Arthur Conan Doyle. But he had an appreciation, too, for hard-boiled American writers like James M. Cain, Raymond Chandler, Dashiell Hammett, and John D. MacDonald.

As spirited and interesting as the conversation was— actually, it was more of a monologue by Curso in which he dissected the differences between authors, as well as the British and American approaches to writing crime novels—I was eager to bring the talk back to the subject of art, particularly the collection jointly owned by Edgar Peters and

Jonathon Simsbury. I took advantage of a lull in the monologue to ask Peters about it. "Who are some of the artists in the collection?"

"It's an eclectic collection, Jessica," he replied. "Cézanne, Monet, Pollock, Picasso, all the usual suspects. Jonathon's taste in art was wide-ranging. I questioned some of his purchases, but once he'd set his heart on a piece, he'd move heaven and earth to obtain it."

"Did he have a primary source for pieces he purchased? One gallery, perhaps?" I asked.

"Not at all. His sources were many and varied," said Peters. "He had a network of people throughout Europe who kept their eyes open for works that they knew would interest him."

"To be honest," said Curso, "the collection is a little *too* eclectic for my taste. That waters down its value."

His comment didn't sit well with Peters, who said, "That's a cliché, Tony."

"No, it's not," Curso countered. "Collections with a theme are invariably more valuable than those that have been put together through a more scattered approach."

"You've already come to this conclusion in evaluating the collection?" Peters said in a voice that bordered on a growl.

"No, no, Edgar, of course not. I'm speaking hypothetically. I haven't come to an overall impression yet. I'm still working on appraising the individual pieces."

I said nothing during this exchange, content to take in the meaning behind their words. Obviously Peters wanted the collection to be valued at top dollar, while Curso's responsibility was to honestly and fairly put a price tag on the works. I concluded from Curso's comment that his final evaluation might not be as high as Peters would want it to be. I was also confident that Anthony Curso wasn't the sort of man who could be persuaded to violate his professional standards. He would call it as he saw it.

Curso turned to me. "So tell me, Jessica, what is your analysis of the murder investigation currently under way?"

"I'm not sure I'm in a position to comment on that," I said.

"Of course," said Curso. "But your modesty, while admirable, doesn't necessarily represent reality. I did some prowling on the Internet before enjoying this evening and it's obvious that murder isn't a foreign subject to you."

"Not with my fictitious characters," I replied, "but in real life—"

"That's what I'm referring to," Curso said. "Real-life murder like Jonathon Simsbury's. From what I read, you've been involved with as many real-life murders as with the fanciful ones in your books. You and Mrs. Simsbury are close friends, I believe. Is that how you came to be involved?"

"We hadn't seen each other in years. I came here to—"

"To escort the young Simsbury chap—Wayne, is it?— back to the old homestead to accuse his stepmother of the crime."

"I didn't know at the time that he intended to do that." I explained the circumstances of his arrival at my home in Cabot Cove and how I had assumed that he would help prove Marlise's innocence. "Needless to say, I was as shocked as everyone else when he alleged that he'd seen Marlise shoot her husband."

"And what do you think?" Curso asked.

I glanced at Peters, who seemed uninterested in the conversation.

"I really don't know," I said to Curso. "Naturally, I prefer not to think that my friend, Marlise, did such a dreadful thing. What interests me is the dynamic between Wayne and his stepmother, whether he has some underlying reason for claiming to have witnessed the murder and identifying her as the murderer."

"Wayne Simsbury is a good kid," Peters said. "He wouldn't lie about something like that."

"So you think that Mrs. Simsbury actually *did* the dirty deed," Curso said to Peters.

"I don't know who did what," Peters said. "All I *do* know is that Wayne Simsbury was the apple of his father's eye. The sun rose and set on him. Why would he kill a father who doted on him in every way?"

Peters's analysis of the father-son relationship was not exactly what I'd been led to believe by others, but I didn't challenge him.

"Would you be interested in seeing the collection, Jessica?" Curso asked.

I looked to Peters for a reaction.

"May I give Jessica a personal tour of the collection, Edgar?" Curso asked. "I plan to spend the day there tomorrow."

Peters seemed conflicted but agreed. "I guess there's no harm in it."

"Splendid," said Curso. "Shall we say ten in the morning?"

"That's fine with me," I said.

Peters drove me back to the Ambassador East and walked me into the lobby.

"Thank you for dinner," I said. "You were right. Tony Curso is a fascinating man."

"He is amusing," Peter said, granting Curso a less than enthusiastic endorsement. "Mind some advice, Jessica?"

"I'm always interested in good advice."

"I know that you and Marlise are close and that you don't believe that she killed Jonathon."

"Am I mistaken in that belief?" I asked, wondering where he was going.

"Jonathon's murder is going to get messier as time goes by, and I think that you'd be wise not to become entangled in it."

"I certainly don't intend to become 'entangled,' as you put it," I said.

"That's good to hear," he said. "The point is that Wayne Simsbury is a fine young man who wouldn't lie about something like this. Sure, he's had his troubles. Like most young people, he's fouled up here and there. But Jonathon was a terrific father who had a close bond with his son, and Marlise would never win the stepmother-of-the-year award."

I wondered whether he was aware that Jonathon had been about to execute a new will that cut his son's inheritance down to ten percent, but I didn't ask. It was interesting how Edgar Peters had a very different perspective on the Simsbury household than Marlise did.

Peters flashed a smile. "Just some idle thoughts, Jessica. It was a nice evening. Tony is obviously taken with you."

"He's charming," I said. "Thank you again."

I watched him leave the hotel, and as I rode up in the elevator, I replayed in my head what he'd said about Wayne and his relationship with his father. The young man had told me while at my house that his father was disappointed in him and that his relationship with Marlise was good. Marlise had said Jonathon was in the process of changing his will in her favor and to Wayne's detriment. Would she have said that if it weren't true? I didn't know where the truth lay, and I realized that if I was to make any headway in solving the murder, I'd need to get a better perspective on the relationships within the family. One source with possibly less-biased views would be the household staff. But would Mrs. Tetley, the cook, Consuela, and the driver, Carl, be willing to talk to a stranger about the family they worked for? I made a silent pledge to seek them out.

In the meantime, I looked forward to the next day's tour of the Simsbury-Peters art collection. If nothing else, admiring fine art would be a welcome reprieve from thinking about the less pleasant topic of murder.

Chapter Twelve

Judging from the car Anthony Curso drove, his career as an art historian and professor paid well. The vehicle was, he explained after picking me up in front of the hotel—and eliciting numerous "oohs" and "aahs" from admiring passersby—a gleaming 1964 Austin Healey 3000. "The color is Healey Blue," he said with obvious pride. "It's the best big Healey ever made."

"It's beautiful," I said as I ran my hand over the burl wood dashboard.

"My baby," he said. "Mind the top down?"

"No, not at all," I replied, untying the scarf I'd fortunately worn around my neck and retying it over my hair. I enjoy a ride in a convertible, but not the rat's nest the wind makes of my hairstyle.

The expression on his face was sheer joy as he smoothly shifted gears while navigating city traffic. He wore a red tam, a pale blue safari jacket over a red button-down shirt, and jeans that were a cut above Levi's or Wranglers.

We eventually left the city and drove into an industrial park that appeared to have recently been built. At the rear of the complex was a one-story concrete and steel building. Curso parked in front, hopped out to open my door, and led me to the side of the building. He punched a code into a keypad, and I heard the door unlatch. He pushed it open, flipped on overhead lights, and entered another series of numbers into the alarm system's keypad. Despite the building's double alarm system, I couldn't help but wonder whether the storehouse was secure enough to be the repository of millions of dollars' worth of fine art. I asked.

"I had the same question," Curso said. "When I mentioned it to Ed Peters, he said that Jonathon was content with the building's security, although Ed didn't seem convinced. An amateur thief could break in here in a couple of minutes. Of course, if no one knows what's in the building, that's unlikely to happen. It goes without saying, I am relying on your discretion."

"And it goes without saying that I would never disclose this location," I said.

"At least it's climate controlled," he said, looking around. "Amazing how some collectors don't have a clue about how to preserve and secure their paintings. But that isn't my problem, Jessica. Come see the latest piece I've been appraising."

Curso had established a work area in a corner of the spacious room. A table contained a large microscope, two magnifying glasses, and various small dishes that held liquids. Dozens of books were piled on one corner of the table, along with a thick notebook. The table and its contents were illuminated by a pair of powerful gooseneck lamps. An easel held a painting covered with a crimson piece of cloth. He removed the cloth and directed one of the lamps on the painting. It wasn't very large, maybe two feet tall by less than a foot wide. The subject was a nude female whose bronze body had been elongated by the artist.

"A Modigliani," I said.

"Yes, probably painted in 1908. Typical of his approach to painting nudes."

"His style is easily recognizable," I said.

"Yes, it is, and apparently easy to replicate. Even so, his works are eagerly sought by collectors around the world, and an expert can usually spot a fake. Modigliani was born in Italy but spent his final years in Paris living the bohemian Montmartre life to the fullest. He was sickly; a typhoid epidemic had almost killed him. As it was, he lived only thirty-six years."

"Another great artist who died young."

"Unfortunately for him, but the consequent limited number of his paintings lifts their value."

"What is a painting like this worth?" I asked.

Curso shrugged as he held a magnifying glass to the canvas, focusing on the lower left-hand quadrant. He was totally engrossed in his examination of the painting. After spending a number of minutes at his task, he lowered the glass, made notations in the notebook, and said, "This particular piece isn't listed in the catalogue raisonné."

"What is that?"

"It's a list of all works known to be executed by an artist. This particular piece isn't in it."

"Which means it might not be a Modigliani?"

"It raises that suspicion, Jessica, although the catalogue isn't infallible."

"Marlise Simsbury told me that Jonathon had copies made of works he'd bought, and that those copies are the ones hanging in their home."

"Not unusual," Curso said.

I laughed. "Somehow I find it strange that someone would buy expensive artworks and have them copied. I think that I'd prefer to enjoy the beauty of the originals every day in my own home."

"Which is why people should buy art that pleases them, not as an investment. Of course, think of wealthy women who own expensive jewelry and have copies made to wear in public while the originals gather dust in a safe-deposit box."

I laughed again. "I know a few of those women," I said.

"The artist who copied many of Jonathon Simsbury's originals is in Los Angeles. A very talented chap who decided there was more money in copying the works of the masters than in creating his own art. He has not only made a decent living copying originals for their owners, like Simsbury, but he receives commissions from people who pass off his work as original art by the masters and proudly display his copies on their walls. Very much like those scoundrels who pour inferior whiskey into empty bottles containing the labels of top-shelf liquor to impress their guests."

"People do that?" I said, demonstrating my naïveté.

"More than you realize," said a voice behind me. Edgar Peters, hands tucked in the pockets of his yellow sports jacket, strolled across the warehouse to where we stood.

"So, you came to check out your investment today?" Curso said to him.

"I knew you both would be here, and decided to see what you're up to."

"I wish I could say we were up to no good," Curso said, winking at me, "but Mrs. Fletcher—Jessica—is, sad to say, able to resist my charms. Perhaps you'll have better luck, Ed." He didn't wait for Peters to reply, but turned to me. "You asked what this particular painting is worth," he said, referring to the Modigliani. "If it was listed in the catalogue, and certified by a Modigliani expert, it would go at auction for, say, two million, possibly more."

"But without the catalogue listing, or certification?"

Another shrug from the art expert.

"Are you saying this is a fake?" Peters said, frowning.

"If it isn't a Modigliani, it's an excellent forgery," Curso replied. "There are collectors who buy such bogus works. But of course its value would be much less. A hundred thousand, perhaps."

I was momentarily confused. "I thought all the paintings and sculptures here in the warehouse were originals. Are you saying, Tony, that some of the works here might be forgeries?"

"He better not be," Peters growled.

"Oh, no, Jessica. You were asking what it might bring on the open market and I gave you two hypothetical scenarios. Don't misconstrue what I said."

I leaned against the table and shook my head. "Frankly," I said, "I never gave much thought to forged paintings. I take it that buying art, especially expensive art, is a risky business."

"Extremely risky. Forgeries are sold to unsuspecting buyers every day."

"But not to people who have experts vet the work before the money changes hands," Peters said.

The three of us spent the next hour looking at the paintings in the warehouse, with Curso providing a running commentary about each piece. His knowledge was encyclopedic; I felt as though I was taking a college course in art history. When we were finished, I suggested that he had work to do and that I was getting in his way.

"Not at all," he said, "but I do have to leave for a luncheon appointment."

"I can drop you off, Jessica," Peters put in. "Would you like me to take you to your hotel?"

"Do you mind driving me to the Simsbury house? I want to see Marlise again. I'll call to make sure she's there."

Marlise was at home, and Peters, Curso, and I left the warehouse. As Peters double-checked that the alarm was functioning properly, I thanked Curso for the tour.

"My pleasure." He lowered his voice. "Free for dinner tonight?"

I glanced over at Peters, who was punching numbers into the keypad. I turned back to Curso. "At the moment, yes," I said, "but I'd like to keep it open, if you don't mind."

"I don't mind at all. Here." He handed me his card with his cell phone number listed on it. "Call if you're free, Jessica. There's something I'd like to discuss with you."

"Oh?"

"I think you may find the subject interesting. Don't mention it to Peters, if you don't mind."

"All right."

"Give my best to Mrs. Simsbury," he said in a loud voice and went to his car.

I watched him drive away and wondered what it was that he wanted to discuss. He certainly had captured my attention.

The housekeeper answered the door when Edgar Peters dropped me off at the Simsbury mansion.

"Hello, Mrs. Tetley. I'm Jessica Fletcher," I said, not sure whether she'd remember me. "I'm here to see Mrs. Simsbury."

"Follow me," she said. "I'll tell her that you're here."

She led me to the same room where I'd been before. As she turned to leave, I said, "Mrs. Tetley, would you have a few minutes for me?"

She looked at me quizzically, hands on her broad hips, narrowed eyes exaggerating the lines around them.

"I'm working with some people to find out what happened the night of Mr. Simsbury's murder. Not officially, of course, but—"

"Working to get her off, you mean."

"Pardon?"

"Get her off. Mrs. Simsbury. The wife."

"No, you're wrong about that," I said. "I don't have any preconceived notion about who might have killed Mr. Simsbury. All I want is to find out the truth. I'm sure you want that, too."

Her expression softened.

"Did Mrs. Simsbury and Mr. Simsbury's son, Wayne, get along?"

"If you mean were they lovey-dovey like she makes it sound, the answer is no."

"What about Wayne and his father? I'm led to believe that there might have been bad feelings between them."

Her deeply furrowed brow said that she was pondering how to answer the question.

"Was Mr. Simsbury disappointed in his son?"

She looked toward the door to ensure that no one was about to walk in, and then she said, "You seem like a nice and proper lady, Mrs. Fletcher, and I know that you're a famous writer. I'll be leaving here soon, so I don't mind telling you what I told the police when they sat me down and asked me their questions. As much as I've never been partial, shall we say, toward Mrs. Simsbury, her hubby, Mr. Jonathon Simsbury, was no saint either, him and his fancy clothes and toys and chasin' after Ms. Hurley." She cast another look at the door before adding, "Now there's somebody you should be gettin' to know, if you get my drift. She and him were disgraceful the way they carried on, and I saw plenty of their grabbin' each other and talkin' sexy and the like."

"Was Mrs. Simsbury aware of what was going on between her husband and Ms. Hurley?" I asked, knowing that Marlise was, indeed, aware of the affair.

"Probably so," was the housekeeper's reply, "only it wouldn't have mattered none to her, not as long as the money kept comin'."

Voices in the hallway caused Mrs. Tetley to place her hand over her mouth and to turn and leave the room as Marlise and the cook, Consuela, came in.

"Jessica, I'm sorry. I know I told you I was free, but I'm

huddled with my attorney and will probably be with him for another half hour. Consuela will make you some lunch while you're waiting."

"No need for that," I said.

"Nonsense," Marlise said. "Tell her what you'd like. I'll be back as soon as I can."

"All right," I said as Marlise left the room. "Anything simple will be fine, Consuela."

The attractive Hispanic woman, who I judged to be in her early thirties, stared at me as though she needed something besides my food order.

"Are you all right?" I asked.

She nodded, but the tears that welled up in her large dark eyes said otherwise.

"Please, sit down," I said, indicating a chair.

"No," she said, wiping her eyes with the back of her hand. "I will make you lunch."

"Would you stay for a minute?" I asked. "I'd like to ask you something."

"No, señora," she said. "Excuse me."

Knowing that something was bothering her only prompted further curiosity on my part. Was her upset the natural result of working in a household where a brutal murder had recently taken place? Or was there something she was afraid to share?

I got up from my chair and went to the hallway. I didn't know where the kitchen was but assumed that it would be toward the rear of the house, close to the large dining room and its table set for sixteen. I walked in that direction and passed a room with closed doors behind which I could hear voices, a woman and a man who I assumed were Marlise and Corman. Eventually I reached the kitchen, which was the size of many a kitchen found in restaurants, with a huge stainless-steel refrigerator, a professional-grade eight-burner gas stove, and a large center island above which gleaming copper pots hung. Consuela was busy at the double sink and didn't hear me come in. I coughed. She turned.

"I hope you don't mind me coming here," I said pleasantly. "I know this is your domain and I don't want to intrude on it."

She leaned back against the sink, her hands clasped in front of the blue-and-white checked apron she wore over a white uniform. Her eyes left me and went to a far corner of the kitchen in which a small round café table and two chairs were wedged. Seated there was Wayne Simsbury, whom I hadn't seen since that fateful afternoon in Willard Corman's law office.

"Hello, Wayne," I said.

He stood. He was dressed in purple pajamas and a matching silk robe. "Hi, Mrs. Fletcher," he said.

"Am I interrupting your lunch?" I asked, even though I could see that the plate on the table in front of him was empty.

"Not really. I'm just leaving anyway." He walked past me, stopping only to cast a menacing look at the cook, who hadn't moved from the sink.

"I will bring the lunch to you, Mrs. Fletcher," she said. "It will only be a moment."

"I'm not looking for lunch, Consuela," I said. "You were here in the house the night Mr. Simsbury was killed. I believe you made dinner for Wayne and Mrs. Simsbury."

She looked to the door, causing me to follow her gaze. Wayne lingered there, obviously interested in hearing our conversation. He smiled and walked away. I looked at Consuela, who had turned her back to me and busied herself at a counter next to the refrigerator. Clearly she didn't want to talk. I decided to pursue a conversation with Wayne instead of trying to break through the wall the cook had erected. He was on his way up a set of stairs at the rear of the house. "Wayne," I called. "May I talk with you?"

He stopped, turned, and looked down at me with what I can only describe as a sneer. "No," he said. "I'm busy."

"It will take only a moment. I wanted to know if—"

My question was cut short by his bounding up the stairs two at a time, disappearing into a room off the landing, and slamming the door.

I was taken aback. What a change in his personality! He didn't have any problem coming to my house and enlisting me as both a listening post and a traveling companion, and now he had no compunction about being rude. I tried to rationalize his behavior. Maybe he was feeling a modicum of guilt about using me as he had, but didn't want to admit it.

I'd come to grips with the fact that he hadn't been upfront with me about what he would say upon returning to Chicago. Of course, he didn't know that even if he had told me in Cabot Cove that he'd seen Marlise shoot his father, I would still have encouraged him to go home and share his accusation with the authorities. In fact, I would have been even more willing to accompany him, if only to hold out a lone hand of friendship to Marlise.

He had no reason to avoid me, although I could understand his wanting to stay clear of Marlise. I'd wondered since coming to Chicago how they could continue to occupy the same house after he'd accused her of being a murderess. True, she stayed in a hotel at night. But she spent each day in the Simsbury mansion. They'd evidently found a way to avoid each other in this large home with its many rooms in which to seek and find seclusion.

The parlor in which I'd questioned Mrs. Tetley now contained a tray on which rested a plate with an egg salad sandwich and potato chips, a small bowl of fresh fruit, and iced tea. I'd just taken a bite of the sandwich when Marlise entered, followed by Willard Corman.

"Hello," the attorney said. "How is your stay in Chicago going?"

Marlise answered for me. "Jessica has already befriended everyone in Jonathon's life."

Well, not exactly, I wanted to say.

Corman smiled. "Hopefully you'll come up with a bit of information from them to help Marlise."

"That would be wonderful," I said. "What's the status of the investigation?"

"The DA has nothing except Wayne's claim that he saw Marlise shoot Jonathon. Without some additional evidence, they're reluctant to bring formal charges. But that can change at any time."

"I had a tour this morning of Jonathon's art collection," I said.

Marlise's nostrils flared. "How did that happen?"

"Anthony Curso invited me, with Edgar Peters's permission."

She looked at Corman: "See what I mean?" she said.

Corman grinned. "You're obviously someone whom people naturally take to," he said.

"I like to think I'm easy to approach," I said. "Marlise, do you have a few moments?"

"Sorry," she said, "but I don't. Willard thinks I should move out permanently."

"Oh?"

"He's right. It's macabre, rattling around in the same house where my husband was murdered and where my dear stepson has accused me of having killed him."

I couldn't argue with his logic, or her acceptance of it.

"I'll be at Jonathon's suite at the Four Seasons," she said. "I can't leave the city. I feel like a caged animal in this house. I'll come back when necessary. Mrs. Tetley is packing my things as we speak. We'll have to find another time to talk, Jessica."

"No problem," I said. "Why don't I call you later at the hotel?"

Corman offered me a ride back to my hotel, which I accepted.

"Marlise seems more upset than she's been before now," I offered.

"The longer this drags on, the bigger the impact on her," said the attorney. "Mind if I ask a question?"

"Of course not."

"Did you decide to tour the art collection because of a love for art, or did you have another reason in mind?"

I had to smile. "Why do you ask?" I said. "Did I say or do anything to indicate that I had another reason?"

"Not at all," he said, laughing, "but I do have the feeling that you've decided to try to get to the bottom of Jonathon Simsbury's murder. From what I read about you, it wouldn't be the first time."

"I'll plead the Fifth Amendment on that."

"Fair enough. I'd be delighted if you came up with something that would help clear my client."

"If I do, you'll be the first to know."

"By the way," he said as he pulled up in front of my hotel, "I've been getting calls from the press asking about your involvement in the case."

"I hope you deny that I have any involvement."

"Yes, that's what I tell them. I assume they'll be coming to you directly at some point."

"Hopefully not. Thanks for the lift."

"Stay in touch, Jessica. I'm always available."

I went directly to my room, where the red light on the phone was blinking, indicating that I'd received calls while I was out. There were three.

The first verified Corman's prediction. It was from a reporter for the *Chicago Tribune*. Her name was Diane Albanese and she was requesting an interview regarding the Simsbury murder. I jotted down her phone number and brought up the second call. It was from Cabot Cove's sheriff and my friend, Mort Metzger. I listened to his message twice.

"Hey, Mrs. F. Mort Metzger here. Sorry to bother you on your trip, but thought you'd want to know about a call I got this morning from an Italian detective named Maresca. He was calling from Rome about that robbery and murder you witnessed a few months back. He says he left messages on your answering machine but thought you might be away, so he called me as the town's law enforcement chief. Seems they've arrested the guy who killed that retired policeman you were with on your tour, and they need you to make an ID on him. I didn't know where you were staying in Chicago, so I called the doc and he gave me your number. Nice fella, this Detective Maresca. Spoke pretty good English." Mort had left the number Detective Maresca had given him, and suggested I get back to Maresca as soon as possible.

The third call was from Anthony Curso, who asked again whether I was free for dinner. He ended by saying, *"I really need to speak with you—alone!"*

I took a chance that Detective Maresca would still be in his office and called Rome. The detective picked up immediately.

"Ah, Signora Fletcher. I was hoping to hear from you."

I explained that I had received a call from Sheriff Metzger.

"A good man, your sheriff," he said. "He told you that we have arrested one of the thieves who took the Bellini? He is the one we believe killed the retired officer."

"Yes, he did. Congratulations!"

"But as I told you before you left Italy, Mrs. Fletcher, it would be of great help if you would come and identify this young man from a lineup."

I sighed, sat back in my chair, and toed off my shoes. "Is that really necessary?" I asked.

"Signora Fletcher, I will be honest with you. While we have gathered other evidence that connects this man with the theft and murder, the case is not as you would call a slam dunk, huh? We have only the one, not his accomplice. If we are able to prove to him that our case is one hundred percent solid, we might be able to get him to make a deal and tell us who he worked with and those who financed his activities. To have you positively identify him would do that for us, I am sure."

"I understand that, Detective, but I'm not sure I can get free to return to Italy, at least not right away."

"And I understand *that*, Signora Fletcher. Naturally, I have no way of compelling you to come and make an identification, but knowing of your reputation as a writer who always sees that justice prevails in her books, I was hoping that it would extend to the pursuit of *real* justice in the *real* world. Please consider it, Signora Fletcher."

"I assure you that I will. Let me get back to you in a few days."

"*Grazie*. I look forward to hearing from you."

I'd no sooner hung up than the phone rang.

"Jessica, Tony Curso here."

"I was just about to return your call."

"I'm hoping that you're still free for dinner."

"I am. You said in your message that you wanted to discuss something with me alone."

He chuckled. "I don't wish to appear to be secretive, but I suppose I do enjoy a certain cloak-and-dagger existence. I would be most appreciative if you would allow me to explain over dinner."

"All right," I said.

"Splendid. May I pick you up at six?"

"That will be fine."

My curiosity was piqued, of course. What could he possibly want to discuss that necessitated our being alone? We'd just met. I decided that as a man of the arts, he undoubtedly had his share of quirks, and the topic of the evening would probably prove to be fanciful. I'd thoroughly enjoyed the brief time we'd spent together and looked forward to simply being in his company again.

My thoughts quickly shifted, however, to my conversation with Detective Maresca and his insistence that I come to Italy to identify the young man now in custody. It was not a trip that I wished to take, and I certainly wouldn't have a problem coming up with reasons to decline his request. On the other hand, a sense of duty and responsibility tugged at me. I'd had the misfortune of being face-to-face with the young man who'd shot and killed the former Italian police officer. Even if it was an inconvenience, how could I not see to it that justice was done?

I put that dilemma on the shelf and returned the call to Ms. Albanese, the reporter from the *Tribune*.

"This is Jessica Fletcher," I said when she answered.

"Oh, yes, thank you for getting back to me. I'd really appreciate the chance to talk with you about the Jonathon Simsbury murder."

"I'm afraid that's impossible," I said. "The investigation is ongoing and it would be inappropriate for me to comment."

"Well, Susan Hurley didn't seem to think so, and as his assistant, she was a lot closer to the victim than you. She was willing to talk; why aren't you?"

"I don't wish to be rude, but I don't owe you an explanation for my decisions. I don't want to be involved in your story. That's all I care to say."

"But you've already become involved in the case, Mrs. Fletcher. After all, you accompanied Wayne Simsbury back to Chicago to testify against his stepmother."

"I realize that," I said, "but I wasn't aware that that was his intention. I'm sorry, Ms. Albanese. I know it's your job to ask questions, but you'll have to excuse me for not wanting to answer them."

"I've been told that you don't believe what Wayne Simsbury has said, Mrs. Fletcher. What do you base that on— your friendship with Mrs. Simsbury?"

"I don't know where you've heard that, Ms. Albanese, but I haven't come to any such conclusion. You'll have to excuse me. I'm late for an appointment."

I don't like lying, but sometimes it's acceptable.

I think in this case it was.

Chapter Thirteen

It had become overcast and misty by the time Anthony Curso picked me up at the hotel. Happily, he had raised the top on his vintage sports car. Again he was nattily dressed, this time in a silver gray double-breasted suit and a navy blue tie over a pink shirt. I was conscious that I wore the same outfit that he'd seen me in last. There hadn't been any time for shopping, and my selection of clothing was very limited, as Seth had pointed out. Curso, however, was very gracious.

"You look absolutely beautiful tonight," he said as he walked me to where he'd parked his Healey.

"Thank you, sir."

"I've chosen what I believe will be a restaurant that you'll particularly enjoy," he said after we'd settled in the car. "It's called Everest, forty stories up in the Chicago Stock Exchange building, splendid views of the city, and world-class food."

"Sounds wonderful," I said, caught up in his enthusiasm.

He tended to talk in superlatives; everything was top-notch or world-class or to die for. I know others who do the same, but their superlatives aren't always to be trusted. Curso meant every word of his praise, and I had the feeling that his evaluation of things was probably accurate most, if not all, of the time.

We pulled into an underground parking garage beneath the Stock Exchange reserved exclusively for the restaurant, and rode the elevator to the fortieth floor, where we stepped into a dazzling space. Curso was greeted warmly by the maître d'—he was obviously a regular there—and we were escorted to a prime table facing huge windows that afforded splendid views of the city's glittering light show below.

"What a spectacular view," I commented.

"The best in the city. Are you up for a martini, Jessica? The bartender is a friend of mine and he'll make it to my standards."

"Do you know every bartender in town?" I asked playfully.

"I believe that I do," he replied with an easy laugh.

"Actually," I said, "I know something about martini making from old movies, at least the way Nick and Nora Charles made them in *The Thin Man* series. Nick—William Powell—claimed there was a proper way to shake a martini and it was all in the rhythm. Let me see if I can recall it. He said that when shaking a Manhattan you had to do it in fox-trot time, and a martini had to be shaken in waltz time."

"You're right," Curso said, "but you forget what else he said. To make a proper Bronx cocktail you must shake it in two-step time."

"A Bronx cocktail?"

"Gin with both dry and sweet vermouth, like a 'perfect' Manhattan, only with gin instead of bourbon or rye."

"I suppose there's a Brooklyn cocktail, too," I said.

"Of course. Blended whiskey, some dry vermouth, a dash of maraschino liqueur, as well as a dash of the apéritif Amer Picon."

"Would you be offended if I preferred a glass of wine?"

"Not at all. The wine selection is superb, including by the glass. May I choose for you?"

"By all means."

Our waiter greeted Curso like a long-lost brother. My host ordered wine for me, an extra-dry martini for himself: "Please tell Juan it's for Tony Curso. He'll know what to do."

"So," he said as we waited for our drinks to be served, "here I am with a beautiful woman who also happens to write bestselling murder mysteries."

"And I'm delighted to be here," I said, meaning it. "But I have to admit that you're behaving very mysteriously. What did you need to discuss with me alone?"

He smiled. "Perhaps it was a ruse to entice you to have dinner with me again."

I looked at him askance.

"Do not worry, my lady. I might sink to subterfuge on occasion, but this is not one of them. However, I would prefer to wait until we've sated our appetites," he said, opening my menu for me and doing the same with his own. "There are two dishes Everest is famous for," he said, "a magret of duck with wild pine honey and marinated turnips Alsace style, or classic baked filet of sea bass, also Alsace style."

I perused the menu before deciding to follow his lead. I ordered the sea bass for myself, and he ordered the duck.

"Notice the art?" he asked after he'd ordered. "These bronze sculptures on each table are by the Swiss artist Ivo Soldini, the paintings on the wall by a fine local artist and good friend, Adam Siegel. Too few restaurants pay attention to the art that accompanies their culinary creations, and the art in hotel rooms, even the most upscale hotels, is, well, to be kind, dismal."

And so went the conversation throughout dinner, jumping from fine art to cocktail making, and on to the history of transatlantic steamship travel, then back to cocktails, art, and the lowering of taste in society, a subject that he was particularly passionate about. I nursed my single glass of wine throughout dinner while Curso enjoyed a second and third martini, which didn't seem to affect him. He hadn't overstated how good the food would be, and the restaurant's chef and proprietor, J. Joho, ventured from the kitchen to welcome Curso and "the lovely lady" with him. Dessert was compliments of the chef. I wasn't able to eat another thing, but Curso ordered a rum-infused baba based upon an eighteenth-century recipe that called for pineapple confit and Tahitian vanilla glacé. He asked for a second spoon and insisted that I at least taste this creation, which I had to admit was everything he said it would be.

"Well," Curso said after we'd been served coffee, "about my reason for wanting to be with you this evening. It's often hard for me to get to the point quickly, but I shall do my best. Simply put, Jessica Fletcher, I wish to collaborate with you on a book."

If I had made a list of things he conceivably wanted to discuss with me that night, writing a book wouldn't have been on it.

"I realize that it's presumptuous of me to even assume that you would be interested in collaborating, and the puzzled expression on your pretty face tells me that I'm right."

"Oh, no, it's just that I wasn't expecting collaborating on a book to be the thing you wanted to discuss."

"Let me be more specific, Jessica. Having spent my adult years immersed in the world of art, particularly the less savory aspects of it, I've amassed a considerable amount of information that isn't well-known to the general public. There is a dark, even evil side to the art world that I feel would make for a wonderful murder mystery in the hands of someone like Jessica Fletcher."

"It wouldn't be the first time that the art world has been the basis for a murder mystery," I said. "I've read quite a few of them."

"Oh, I quite agree with you, and I've made it a point of searching out and reading virtually every one ever published. Many of them are nicely written, but even those fail to truly take the reader inside the world of art forgery and theft. I might not have come up with the idea of a collaboration had you not experienced a firsthand example of the greed that permeates much of it. Frankly, I can't imagine that your horrific experience in Italy didn't set your creative wheels spinning."

"If you mean did I come back from Italy thinking about writing a novel based upon my experience, the answer is yes. But it was only a fleeting notion and I haven't given it a second thought. Many experiences and ideas intrigue me, but I don't always follow them up with a book."

His ebullience subsided a bit. He took a sip of his coffee and sat back, a frown on his face.

"Which isn't to say, Tony, that I wouldn't be interested in working with you. It's just that I've never collaborated with anyone before and I'm not sure how it would work."

His face brightened as he leaned forward, elbows on the table, a twinkle in his eyes. "Does that mean that you'll consider it?"

"Perhaps, but I can't promise you anything."

"I believe that a little candor on my part is called for. Besides my work as an appraiser, and my teaching responsibilities, I'm also a consultant with the Italian police, particularly members of its art squad. I'm told that you will probably be traveling to Italy to help identify the young *farabutto* who stole the Bellini and killed the man on your tour. *Farabutto*. 'Villain' in Italian."

I wasn't pondering the meaning of the word he'd used. Instead, I'd put my brain on rewind. Had I mentioned to him during our first dinner together that I'd been asked to return at some future date to make an ID on the suspect? I was sure that I hadn't. Was he assuming, without having been told, that the police would want me to return?

He read my mental process and laughed. "Let me be forthcoming with you, Jessica. After you recounted for me and Edgar Peters your hair-raising experience in L'Aquila, I called a good friend on the art squad in Rome, Filippo Lippi."

"I met with Detective Lippi when I was there," I said, my

voice mirroring my surprise. "We had a delightful lunch together."

"That devil Lippi. He appreciates a pretty woman as well as recognizing a fake Titian or Caravaggio."

"He was the consummate gentleman."

"They have arrested the perpetrator."

"So I've been told. I didn't know that you would know, too."

"Lippi called me this afternoon."

"He did? I was called by another officer, a Detective Maresca."

"Ah, Sergio. He works closely with members of the art squad, including my good friend Filippo."

My head was spinning and it wasn't because of that single glass of wine.

"You will go to Italy to make the identification?"

I gathered my thoughts and said, "Why do I have the feeling that you and the Italian detectives are working together to ensure that I go?"

He shrugged and extended his hands in a gesture of submission. "Guilty as charged," he said. "But think of it as fate, Jessica. We can travel together to sunny Italy and accomplish two things at once. You can do your civic duty and see that a murderer is put away where he belongs, and we will have time to discuss working together on our book."

"Travel together?"

"Of course. The timing is perfect. I am due in Rome within the next few days to confer with the police on other matters, and you have your responsibilities to discharge. And please, do not allow my forwardness to be off-putting.

Like Detective Lippi, I am the consummate gentleman. I assure you that it will be strictly business between us."

I hadn't been thinking along those lines, nor had it occurred to me that he might think I would consider traveling with him to be inappropriate. No doubt about it, Anthony Curso was a charming man, but hardly my type. What appealed to me about his suggestion was having someone as knowledgeable and well connected as he was run interference for me with the police. Was I also interested in writing a book with him, using his vast insight into the underbelly of the art world as a basis for the story? At that moment the answer was no, but I hadn't ruled it out completely.

"Well?" he asked.

"I think it's a very good idea," I replied, hoping that it would turn out to be exactly that.

Chapter Fourteen

I don't consider myself an impetuous person. I like to take time to weigh the pros and cons of decisions I'm called upon to make and to factor those decisions into the overall scheme of my life. Reaching an agreement to join Anthony Curso in Rome after only a discussion at dinner might strike some people as being rash. I didn't view it that way. If it was a matter of deciding to make a last-minute trip to Rome without a mission of my own, their assessment would be justified. But I'd decided late that afternoon to make the trip at the behest of the police; having a noted art appraiser (and, now I knew, a consultant to the Italian police on matters of art fraud and theft) at my side gave me a sense of comfort and well-being that traveling alone might not provide.

Impetuous or not, my decision put a lot of pressure on me. I would have to leave Chicago, swing through Cabot Cove to repack, and go to Boston to catch a flight to Rome. Curso had wanted us to fly together, but I ruled that out. He was leaving in two days, which was too tight a schedule for me. Instead, we would fly separately, meeting up three days hence at the hotel he'd chosen, the d'Inghilterra, one of Rome's finest, according to Curso. He was at his superlative best when describing the hotel: "All the great writers have stayed and drunk there—Henry James, Twain, Hemingway. The d'Inghilterra bar is the best in all of Rome, one of only twelve authorized Bond Bars in all of Italy."

My puzzled expression prompted him to explain.

"Bond Bars offer a choice of James Bond's twenty favorite drinks, including the 007 martini Vesper, created for the lovely Vesper Lynd in *Casino Royale*: gin, vodka, and just the right amount of Kina Lillet. Or the stone martini, which uses real stones soaked in vermouth for twelve hours prior to pouring gin over them. I consult with the bartender there whenever I am in Rome."

Not only did he seem to know every bartender in Chicago; his circle of mixologist friends spanned the globe.

I decided after he had dropped me off that it wasn't too late to call Marlise at her hotel. "Marlise, it's Jessica. Hope I'm not waking you."

"Fat chance. Sleep doesn't come easily these days."

"I don't wonder. Marlise, I'm going to be leaving Chicago, probably late tomorrow."

"Had enough of the insanity, huh?"

"It's not that. I have to be in Italy to provide an ID for the Italian police."

Her silence reminded me that I hadn't told her my tale of having been at the scene of an art theft and murder in Italy a few months earlier. I explained what had occurred, and that the Italian police had apprehended the man they believed to be the murderer and needed me to make an identification.

"You never cease to amaze me," she said.

"It's not something I aspired to," I said. "As it happens, Tony Curso will be there as well."

Another silence, this one not only indicating surprise but also hinting at a sense of displeasure.

I hastened to explain how we both were required to be in Rome at the same time. When I'd finished—and I wasn't sure why I felt compelled to explain anything—she asked, "Has Tony finished his appraisal of Jonathon's collection?"

I almost corrected her and added Edgar Peters to the ownership list but didn't. "I don't know," I said. "He didn't say anything to me, but it's something you might ask him."

"I thought you had all the answers, Jessica," she said coldly.

"Marlise, are you unhappy that I am spending time with these people?"

She forced a laugh. "Oh, no, Jessica. You'll have to excuse me if I sound a little testy. This nightmare is taking its toll. I have no idea what the future has in store for me. I wish I were as free to go about as you are."

I responded with my own reassuring laugh. "I'd be testy, too," I said, "if I were in your shoes. I'd like to see you before I leave. Can we get together tomorrow?"

"I'm not sure. Joe Jankowski is coming to the house again in the morning, and so is Willard Corman. Seems I can't stay away from the place, even if I want to."

"Why do they need to come to the house?"

"Willard wants Wayne to take a lie detector test."

"That makes sense."

"It's about time. Willard also wants me to take one. He's bringing in an expert tomorrow. He thought it would be more convenient to have us all in one location."

"Has Wayne agreed?"

"He'd better."

"Sounds like tomorrow is an especially busy day."

"I just want to end it, Jessica. You said you wanted to come by. Please do. We'll find time to talk during breaks in the madness."

"I'll be there, Marlise. Get some sleep. You sound as though you could use some."

I should have given myself the same advice. I was wide awake when we ended the conversation, and I paced the living room of my suite, thoughts and images coming and going, questions suddenly appearing out of the blue and disappearing just as quickly.

I sat at the room's desk and started making notes before those thoughts and questions could vanish completely. It was hard focusing on Jonathon Simsbury's murder, and the dynamics surrounding it, with my unexpected trip to Italy interfering. I made a list of things I had to accomplish before leaving, starting with calling my travel agent in Cabot Cove, Susan Shevlin, first thing in the morning to book a flight to Rome. I'd also have to call Jed Richardson to arrange for transportation to Boston.

I was still busy making notes when the phone rang.

"Mrs. Fletcher, it's Diane Albanese at the *Trib*. Hope it's not too late to call."

I was tempted to say that I preferred not to receive calls from the press at any hour, but stifled the urge.

"We're going with a feature in tomorrow's edition, Mrs. Fletcher, about the Simsbury murder, and I need to clarify something you said to me earlier."

As far as I could recall, I'd said nothing to her.

"When I mentioned that I'd been led to believe that you doubted Wayne Simsbury's accusation that his stepmother had shot his father, you said—just a minute, I wrote it down—you said that you 'hadn't come to any such conclusion.' Does that mean that you might suspect that your friend Marlise Simsbury had something to do with the murder?"

I tried to summon a recollection of having said that but wasn't successful. "Ms. Albanese," I said, "if I did say that, it was only because I didn't want to indicate having come to any conclusions whatsoever about the case. I'm here in Chicago as Marlise Simsbury's friend, to lend moral support. It's not my role to make judgments about who's responsible for Mr. Simsbury's death. That's the responsibility of the police."

"Fair enough," she said. "May I ask a favor?"

"You can ask."

"I've been trying to nail down an interview with Mrs. Simsbury ever since the murder took place, and especially after Wayne Simsbury leveled his charge at her. I was wondering, since you are friends, if you might, say, run interference for me and help arrange an interview."

"I couldn't possibly do that," I said.

"The feature in tomorrow's paper doesn't paint a particularly flattering portrait of her, Mrs. Fletcher, and it would be in her best interest to give her side of the story for a follow-up piece."

"That would be entirely up to her," I said, masking my annoyance. "I really don't wish to discuss this further, but I don't want to be rude and hang up on you."

"What about when Wayne Simsbury came to your home in Maine?" she asked. "What did he tell you that—?"

"Please, don't cause me to be rude," I said. "I have nothing further to say."

"I find it interesting that he chose to come to your home and—"

I grimaced as I held the phone away from my ear, as though I was about to do something terribly painful. I heard her fading voice as I gritted my teeth and slowly lowered the handpiece into its cradle. "I'm sorry," I said to the dead phone.

Chapter Fifteen

Marlise answered the door the following morning. "Come in," she said. "Have you seen today's paper?"

I hadn't.

"According to the *Trib*, I'm no better than the Wicked Witch of the West," she said, chuckling. "I know who that reporter's been talking to. Nice to have your enemies so close at hand, isn't it?" She glanced down the hall, then said, "Follow me. Joe is already here, bugging Consuela for a snack, and Willard will be arriving shortly with the lie detector examiner."

"Wayne has agreed to take the test?"

She guffawed. "No, he hasn't, the twerp. He's holed up with his precious grandmother, who treats him like he's twelve years old. Talk about spoiled. Maybe you can convince him, and her. He's listened to you before."

"I'm not sure I agree with that, but I'll be happy to talk with him."

"Oh, good." She led me to the parlor, which by now had become familiar territory. Seated in her wheelchair and covered with a heavy tartan blanket was the elder Mrs. Simsbury. Next to her on a hassock he'd drawn up at her feet was Wayne, who wore jeans, a maroon sweatshirt with the Chicago Cubs logo on it, and flip-flops.

"Here's your chance," Marlise said under her breath.

Grandmother and grandson looked at me, but said nothing as Marlise quickly left.

"Good morning," I said in as upbeat a voice as I could muster.

They offered nothing in response.

I entered the room and stood at a respectful distance from them. The old woman glared at me, her expression lethal.

"Do you mind if I sit down?" I asked, taking a wing chair without waiting for their answer. "I realize that I'm an outsider," I said, "but I can't help being concerned, Wayne, that you refuse to take a lie detector test. After all, what you've accused your stepmother of doing is deadly serious. Surely you'd want to prove that you've been truthful."

Mrs. Simsbury answered for him. "No one," she said in a voice far stronger than her frail physical condition promised, "is going to accuse my grandson of lying."

"I didn't say he was," I hastily added. "All the more reason for him to take the test willingly. One person is already dead, and the life of another person hangs in the balance." I switched my gaze to Wayne. "This isn't a game, Wayne," I said. "Please reconsider your decision."

He started to respond, but his grandmother cut him

short. "You say nothing to her, son. You say nothing to anyone. You've already done what's right and that's that!"

It was evident that as long as his grandmother was present, my chances of changing the young man's mind were nil. We were sitting quietly, occupied with our own individual thoughts, when Mrs. Tetley bustled down the hallway and opened the door to admit Corman and an older man wearing a heavy brown tweed suit and carrying an oversized briefcase.

"Good morning, ladies, Wayne," Corman said as they joined us. "This is Mr. Lowden. He's a former FBI lie detector expert who now administers the test on a freelance basis."

Mrs. Simsbury pushed Wayne's shoulder, and the young man responded by getting to his feet and heading for the door.

"You're making a mistake, Wayne," Corman said.

Wayne stopped and snarled at the attorney, "I'm not taking any damn lie detector test and nobody can make me."

"That's right, Wayne," said Corman, "nobody can make you. But by refusing to take one—and I believe the prosecutors will feel the same—you cast doubt upon the veracity of your statement regarding your stepmother's involvement in your father's murder. Think about that."

For a moment I thought that Wayne might change his mind. His expression was one of utter confusion. He looked back at his grandmother as though she held the answer to his dilemma, and in a way she did. She propelled her wheelchair to the center of the room, stopping only a few feet from Corman. "You leave my grandson alone," she demanded. "You hear me? You leave him be. You want to defend that harlot, that's your dirty business. But my grandson told the truth." She said to Wayne, "Go on, son, leave now. Go to your room. They won't bother you again."

She followed him, wheeling around in the doorway to look back with a satisfied smile.

Corman sank down in a chair, slowly shook his head, and blew an imaginary lock of errant hair from his forehead. "The kid's lying," he said, "but proving it's another matter. Oh, Mrs. Fletcher, say hello to Jim Lowden."

I shook the lie detector technician's hand. "I wish he'd let you administer the test," I said.

Lowden, who looked like a man who'd seen every aspect of the human condition, good and bad, simply shrugged. It wasn't his role to decide who took the test. His responsibility was to give it to anyone who'd agreed to take it and who would pay his fee.

"Marlise is taking the test this morning," Corman said.

"I hope it will help her case," I offered.

"We feel that way," Corman said, "but it won't be admissible in court, should it ever come to that."

I'd participated in a one-day Mystery Writers of America seminar on the use of lie detectors and took from it an understanding that the test has a certain degree of fallibility, especially where false positives are involved. Still, should Marlise's result indicate that she was telling the truth, it would go a long way toward salving her hurt, to say nothing of bolstering her case and possibly forcing the issue where Wayne was concerned.

Lowden made a point of looking at his watch, a sign to

Corman that his fee meter was running. Corman rose and asked, "Will you be here when we're through, Jessica?"

"I'm not sure," I replied. "Probably."

They'd no sooner walked out when the other attorney, Joe Jankowski, and Jonathon Simsbury's administrative assistant, Susan Hurley, replaced them.

"How's it going?" Jankowski asked me in his familiar loud, gruff voice. He looked down and brushed some crumbs off the front of his jacket.

"Just fine," I answered. "Hello, Ms. Hurley."

"Hello, Mrs. Fletcher. I see that you're still here." Her tone made it clear that she would have preferred that I not be. Dressed in a form-fitting beige suit, a tailored white blouse, and cinnamon-colored snakeskin heels, she gave every appearance of having arrived for a routine day at the office. She crossed to a desk in the corner and began pulling files from a drawer.

"I'll be leaving shortly," I said.

"Marlise is taking the lie detector test," Jankowski said as he lowered himself into the room's largest chair.

"I know," I said. "Will anyone else be tested?"

"The kid refuses," said Jankowski. "Makes you wonder, huh?"

Hurley shoved the file drawer closed. "Why is everybody on Wayne's case?" she said angrily to Jankowski. "He said what he saw, pure and simple."

"But Marlise has denied what he's said," I offered. "Surely her version of things should be considered."

A self-satisfied smirk crossed Hurley's face. "I don't see why. I learned right after coming to work for Jonathon that nothing Marlise says can be believed. Your friend is an inveterate liar, Mrs. Fletcher. Sorry to break that to you, but it happens to be the truth."

"Perhaps your version of the truth is not without a bias," I said as she stacked the files on the desk.

Her head came up. "What's that supposed to mean?"

"Simply that your admiration for Jonathon may have colored your opinion of his wife."

"See? Marlise has been filling your ears with lies, hasn't she?" She gathered the files and exited the room.

"She's a piece of work, isn't she?" Jankowski said.

"She's certainly not fond of Marlise," I said. "It seems that no one in this household is."

"Hurley has her reasons. As you've apparently learned, she did more for Jonathon than open his mail."

"I've heard that they were romantically involved. Marlise was well aware of it."

"Not a bad reason to shoot the guy, is it? Jealousy. A staple motive in the homicide business."

"Whose reason would that be? Marlise's or Ms. Hurley's?" I asked.

He raised a finger and aimed it at me. "Good point." He shifted in the chair and grimaced as he did. "Bad back," he said. "How's your back?"

"My back?" I said, laughing. "It's just fine."

"You must be the exception. Figured that everybody on the wrong side of fifty has a bad back."

I got off the subject of bad backs and said, "Not only does it seem everyone is lined up against Marlise, but they're also protective of Wayne. He told me when he was at my house that his father had been disappointed in him, his leaving college to join a rock band, his lack of ambition."

"Yeah, Jonathon had high expectations for his kid, maybe too high. The problem with Jonathon Simsbury was that he never faced reality. Running the business was more like a hobby, nothing like his old man. Jonathon's father was one tough dude, Mrs. Fletcher. I drew up his will before he died, and leaving the business to Jonathon wasn't easy for him. He knew that his only son was a playboy, infatuated with gadgets and toys and all the things the old man had no use for. I suggested that he structure his will so that Jonathon would share in owning the company, have some people around him who cared about running a business, but the old man said he'd feel guilty if he did that. Guilty about what? Making a sound decision? Jonathon ran the business into the ground." His laugh was rueful. "But I suppose he had a good time doing it, enjoying his plane and yacht and—and Ms. Hurley."

I was surprised Jonathon's lawyer would speak so freely about his client, but perhaps he reasoned that death cancels any requirement for confidentiality. While I was a bit uncomfortable hearing such intimate details about Marlise's husband's life, I was also eager to learn more. Somewhere, somehow, the answer to Jonathon's murder rested with those who knew him best.

I wanted to ask Jankowski follow-up questions, but he stood, arched his back against his pain, and said, "I have to get back to my office. You said you were leaving soon. Back to Maine?"

"Only for a short stopover to repack. I'm going to Italy to help in that case I told you about."

"Oh, yeah. They find the perp?"

"It seems that way. They want me to provide identification."

"You lead an interesting life, Mrs. Fletcher."

"I'd prefer a simpler one," I said. "I'll be meeting Anthony Curso in Rome."

"No kidding. What's he say about his appraisal of the art collection?"

"Nothing, at least not to me."

"I understand Peters intends to sell the collection as soon as all the legalities are ironed out. Too bad."

"As the surviving owner, doesn't he have that right?"

"So their agreement stipulates. The estate will get its share of the profits. Jonathon never should have sold him a half stake in the collection. He was desperate for money, I suppose, but Peters isn't—well, let me just say that he's not the sort of partner I'd look for. He paid a pittance for his half interest. That's how hard up for money Jonathon was. I advised against it, but he wouldn't listen." He twisted his torso again, groaned, and said, "Travel safe, Mrs. Fletcher."

"Thank you. I hope your back improves."

"It won't," he said glumly. "Comes with age. You get old and everything is patch, patch, patch. See ya."

I debated leaving with him but decided to stay. I knew it was silly to think that my presence in the house would somehow make the answer to Jonathon's murder become apparent, would cause it to make itself known like some aura, a vision floating down the stairs. But each time I'd been there, another little piece of the puzzle had dropped into place. And selfishly, I wanted to wait until Marlise had completed her test. From what I'd learned about lie detectors, the examiner would come to an immediate conclusion. If Marlise passed, I wanted to be present to share in her victory, as legally meaningless as it might be.

Twenty minutes later she entered the room with Corman and Lowden. The broad smile on her face testified to the result.

"I passed," she said.

"Wonderful," I replied. "I knew you would." Frankly, I was as relieved as she was. I hadn't been completely comfortable standing by her when the possibility existed that Wayne had told the truth. Of course, Marlise's passing the test wasn't a foolproof indication of her innocence, just as she hadn't been exonerated by the negative finding in the gunshot residue test the police had conducted the night of the murder. But the two results went a long way toward satisfying me, as they obviously did her.

Marlise escorted Lowden to the door, came back, and collapsed on a love seat. She extended her long legs and kicked them in the air. "I passed," she proclaimed, then giggled. "That should end this nightmare."

Corman smiled, but I could tell that he was refraining from saying anything that would dash her enthusiasm.

"I feel like celebrating," she said as she got to her feet and pumped a fist into the air. "How about it, Jessica? A celebratory lunch or maybe dinner? You, too, Willard."

"Afraid not," he said. "I want to get hold of someone from the prosecutor's office to let them know of the test result. I'm hoping it will help them rethink taking legal action against you."

"He seems like a good attorney," I commented after he was gone.

"I hope so. Jessica, dear, a favor?"

"If I can."

"Now that I've passed the lie detector test, I want Wayne to know about it."

"That makes sense. Mr. Corman thought your passing it might spur Wayne to change his story."

"That's what I'm hoping, too. Would you tell him?"

"Me? Why not you?"

"I can't. He sees me and runs the other way, usually behind his grandmother's wheelchair. But if you were to tell him the news, he might reconsider."

"I already spoke with him this morning, Marlise, and he didn't listen. Mr. Corman and I tried to reason with him, but he angrily declined to take the test, with his grandmother's staunch support."

"That miserable old witch."

There was a knock at the door, and Mrs. Tetley poked her head in to curtly inform Marlise that she had a phone call.

"Marlise, I'd better be going. I'm flying home this afternoon and then off to Italy."

"Oh, that's right, your little tryst with Tony Curso."

"Hardly that," I said, giving her a quick hug. "I'm glad you passed your test. I'll be back in touch when I return."

She left to take her call, having forgotten her suggestion that we celebrate. I was relieved. I had a five o'clock flight to Boston, where Jed Richardson was scheduled to pick me up for the trip to Cabot Cove.

When I walked out the front door, hoping to hail a taxi,

I heard loud voices coming from the rear of the house. Curious, I took a path that circled around to the driveway until
I reached a point where I could see the participants. The
elder Mrs. Simsbury was in her wheelchair next to a garage
where the chauffeur, Carl, was waxing one of the cars. The
loud voice belonged to her. She was berating him about
something, and although I couldn't make out her words, her
angry tone was evident. I was about to turn around and go
back to the front gate when she spotted me and pointed a
finger as though it were a weapon. Then, to my surprise, she
spun the wheelchair around and headed down the driveway
at me, her arms spinning the large wheels on either side of
the chair like a physically fit contestant in a race for the
handicapped. When it became apparent that she intended
to run into me, I jumped out of the way. The chair passed
where I'd been standing and came to an abrupt stop. In a
voice dripping with menace she barked, "What are you
looking at? Why are you even here? You're not wanted here.
So go! Go on! Go away!" With that, she used one of the
wheels to turn the chair and headed back toward the garage.

This aggressive confrontation shocked me and I found
myself breathing hard, my hands trembling at my sides. I
considered pursuing and challenging her, but discretion
won out over valor. What had I done to incur such wrath on
her part? This was someone who despite her age, and whatever physical problem confined her to a wheelchair, had
some very healthy anger genes.

I retraced my steps back down the driveway and in minutes had waved down a cab and was on my way to my hotel,
where I was happy to be in the quiet, comfortable surround-

ings of my suite. Up until that moment I hadn't been especially happy about making the trip to Italy. But it now had a new and urgent appeal—a chance to get away, if even for a few days, from the family madness within the Simsbury household.

Chapter Sixteen

I t felt good walking into my house after the flight to Boston and being ferried to Cabot Cove by Jed Richardson. It was after eleven, too late to call anyone to announce my arrival, or to return the half dozen calls on my answering machine. Susan Shevlin had booked me on an Alitalia flight from Boston the following evening, which didn't give me much time to accomplish everything on my list.

I unpacked and started a load of laundry. While the washing machine performed its sudsy task, I started packing for the next leg of my trip. I should have been tired, but my adrenaline had kicked in during the flight with Jed and I was wide awake. Flying with him in his single-engine Cessna was always a treat, especially since this trip afforded me some nighttime hours at the controls. I'd flown at night only a few times during my training with him and I enjoyed gaining the additional experience. Everything looks so different at night from five thousand feet, so serene and peaceful. Of course, having someone with all Jed's hours as a commercial pilot in the next seat relieved any tension I might have felt as an amateur.

Eventually I turned off the light at two and slept until seven, reveling in the familiar feel of my own bed. Fortified with an English muffin and a cup of hot Earl Grey tea, I sat in my office and started making calls. The first was to Seth Hazlitt, who I knew was an early riser.

"Good morning, Jessica," he said. "This is an unexpected surprise. Calling from Chicago?"

"No, Seth, I'm calling from here in Cabot Cove. I got home last night at about eleven."

"Welcome back. Staying for a while?"

"No. I'm off to Italy tonight to identify the young man the authorities there have in custody."

"Ayuh, you did mention that was a possibility. How did things turn out in Chicago?"

"Still up in the air. My friend, Marlise, passed a lie detector test before I left, which takes some pressure off her. But they still haven't determined who shot her husband. It's a strange household."

"I'm sure you're happy to be away from it."

"Yes," I said, although the feeling of having left unfinished business behind bothered me.

Everything that had happened since my arrival in Chicago continued to prey on my mind—the assortment of characters in the Simsbury house, the overt animosity and petty jealousies among them, the underlying scenario of adultery. What kept coming to the forefront of my thoughts was the new will that Jonathon had never gotten around to signing. His son, Wayne, would have lost forty percent of what he was to gain from the previous will, which certainly gave him a strong motive to prevent his father from signing the new one. It also undermined Marlise's motive to kill Jonathon. She was to benefit from receiving the forty percent Wayne was to lose, coupled with the fifty percent she'd already been promised. She knew about the new will and had pressured her husband to execute it as penance for his affair with Susan Hurley. I didn't admire her for doing that, but I was hesitant to pass judgment. How they lived their lives, as alien as it might be to me, was none of my business—except for the fact that someone in that dysfunctional family, or perhaps someone else altogether, had committed murder.

Who had killed Jonathon Simsbury? I knew that I wouldn't be able to rest until I had the answer.

But that would have to wait until I'd taken care of the business at hand, flying to Italy to identify the man who'd killed Detective Fanello and stolen the Bellini. Memories of that fateful day were never far from my consciousness, and the notion of seeing the gunman again wasn't pleasant. But it had to be done, and I was committed.

"Free for lunch?" Seth asked. "I'd suggest Peppino's, but you'll be having your fill of Italian food in Italy."

"Oh, thanks, Seth. I'd love it, but I can't. Jed Richardson is flying me to Boston at two."

"Looks like you're keeping our local flyboy in business."

"And thank goodness he's here. I'll only be away a few days and—" I almost mentioned that I'd be going back to Chicago once I returned home from Italy, but I didn't want to hear any of my friend's objections. "We'll have that lunch when I get back," I said.

"Travel safe, Jessica," he said.

"Thank you, my friend."

I managed to take care of everything on my list by the time the taxi picked me up at one forty-five to take me to the airport, where Jed had just finished filling the plane with fuel and doing his usual walk-around to be sure that everything was in order. It was a beautiful, calm day to fly, and we arrived at Boston's Logan Airport without incident.

The flight to Rome was smooth and I used some of the time to make notes for what would happen in the next chapters of the novel I had abandoned when I'd taken Wayne home to Chicago. But my mind kept straying, alternating between the mystery of who shot Jonathon and my apprehension at having to identify the killer of Mr. Fanello.

Rome's Leonardo da Vinci Airport was bustling as I headed for the area where taxis waited, girding myself for the cab ride into town. To my surprise, a uniformed man stood at the door holding a sign that read JESSICA FLETCHER.

"*Buon giorno,*" I said. "I'm Jessica Fletcher."

"*Perfetto!*" he replied loudly and with a broad smile. "Signore Curso has arranged for me to meet you and drive you to the d'Inghilterra."

"I didn't expect that," I said, "but I'm pleased that you're here."

A slender young man with a mop of blond hair, who'd been standing behind the driver, suddenly took a few steps to the side, raised his camera, and pressed off a rapid series of photographs. I didn't have a chance to ask who he was or why he was taking my picture before he turned and ran toward the exit.

"Do you know what that was about?" I asked the driver.

His shrug was accompanied by, "The paparazzo. *Testa vuota!*"

"Pardon?"

"The paparazzo. No brains. *Somaro!* A moron."

The driver, whose name was Luigi and who spoke excellent English, led me to his black Mercedes parked at the curb and we chatted all the way to the hotel on Via Bocca di Leone. It was located in the Piazza di Spagna, on a charming, flower-laden street of older buildings, some of which had been converted into luxury hotels like the d'Inghilterra. The outdoor sidewalk café was busy as Luigi carried my suitcase into the lobby and wished me a pleasant visit. I learned at the desk that I'd been preregistered by Curso, and I was handed a key and told that my luggage would be delivered to the room within minutes. As I walked to the elevators, Curso appeared from nowhere and intercepted me. "You're here, safe and sound," he observed. "Good flight?"

"Fine, although it was a rush to make it." I gestured toward the lobby. "It's lovely," I said.

"I knew you'd like it. I've reserved you a deluxe room, all the amenities, splendid view, fresh fruit and champagne ready for you to enjoy. Go freshen up. I'll meet you in the bar in half an hour."

The room was everything he'd said it would be. The large, beautifully made-up bed beckoned—a nap would have been heaven—but I didn't want to disappoint him. Besides, I had to contact Detective Maresca and arrange a time to go to police headquarters, a call I decided to put off until after meeting with Curso.

When I walked into the wood-paneled bar off the lobby—it had all the trappings of a British gentlemen's club—I immediately spotted Curso in a corner booth with another man. It wasn't until I got closer that I recognized Detective Lippi of the Carabinieri's art squad, who'd treated me to lunch the last time I was in Rome. Both men stood as I approached. Lippi shook my hand and Curso kissed it.

"What a pleasant surprise," I said to Lippi.

"Anthony called and suggested that I be on hand to greet you, Mrs. Fletcher. After all, you've come here at great personal sacrifice to help us."

"Oh," I said, "having an excuse to come to Rome again could never be considered a personal sacrifice."

Curso, dressed in a double-breasted tan suit, a blazing red tie, and a pale blue shirt, was working on a martini despite the early hour. The detective sipped an espresso. I ordered sparkling water with a slice of lime.

"Well," I said, "I suppose I should know what's in store for me over the next few days. Do you use a lineup in Italy the way we do back in the States?"

"Yes, it is very much the same," Lippi said.

"The young man won't be able to see me behind a one-way glass?"

"Exactly. He will never know that you are there, except that—"

Curso and Lippi looked at each other before the detective continued. "This case has become—how shall I say it? It has become the source of interest for members of the press."

I immediately thought of the man who'd taken my picture at the airport and mentioned it.

Lippi sighed. "Damn media vultures," he growled. "They care nothing about privacy or how their intrusions affect ordinary people."

"But why would he single me out at the airport?" I asked. "He obviously positioned himself by the driver who held up a sign with my name on it. Why would I be of interest to him, or to anyone else in the media, for that matter? I'm not giving any talks and I'm not here to promote my books."

Lippi gave another furtive glance at Curso before answering. "Unfortunately, there has been a disclosure from our department, a leak, as you say. Someone—if I knew who he was he would be fired immediately—someone told a reporter that you would be coming to provide an identification in the case. Because you are such a popular writer, Mrs. Fletcher, they naturally grabbed on to that bit of news." He leaned over, withdrew a copy of a newspaper from his briefcase, and handed it to me. It was in Italian, of course, and I couldn't read it. But the picture of me spoke louder than any words could. It was a photo that appeared on the back of some of my novels, many of which had been translated into Italian.

"This is terrible," I said.

"It couldn't be helped," said Lippi. "These reporters, they have contacts in every government department, including the police."

"But how did that photographer know that I'd be arriving on that flight?"

"They have their associates in the airlines, too, I am afraid. They are like mice, able to squeeze through even the smallest of openings, always finding a way to get what they want."

I wasn't sure that I would have used that analogy to describe the paparazzi, but it was as good as any at the moment. What was of considerably greater concern to me was what it would mean having my photograph in the newspaper. If the young man under arrest read the papers, he would know who I was, and, more important, he would know that his fate might rest in my hands. Of course, he wasn't in any position to harm me—but what of his accomplices? What of others of his ilk?

"Have you arrested the second man involved in the murder?" I asked.

"No, we have not. I hope that with your positive identification, the man we have in custody will provide us with information about others in the ring."

I hadn't examined the newspaper article beyond my photograph, so I picked up the paper again and scanned the page. Mine wasn't the only photo accompanying the piece. Staring out at me was the young man who'd shot Mr. Fanello, the one I was there to pick out of a police lineup.

"That's him!" I blurted.

"*Si*," said Lippi.

"What does the caption say?" I asked, referring to the words in Italian beneath the photo.

"That he has been accused of murder and art theft. The entire story is about how the theft of art in Italy has become big business, a lucrative source of income for the Mafia. That other photo is of Enzo Felice."

I focused on the photo Lippi pointed to. Enzo Felice, a corpulent man wearing a three-piece suit and sporting a wide smile, was being taken into custody by uniformed police.

"He's in jail?" I asked.

"No, he is very much a free man. We arrest him, his lawyers get him off. Men like Felice create many layers between themselves and their crimes. Felice is a very big man here in the Mafia," Lippi further explained. "He controls numerous gangs, including those whose job it is to steal valuable paintings. The young man in custody worked for him."

I felt a knot develop in my stomach. It hadn't occurred to me that the Mafia would be involved, although its connection to art theft had been mentioned in earlier conversations.

"What does the article say about me?" I asked.

"Only that you are a famous writer of murder mysteries and are an eyewitness to the crime for which *l'idiota* Lombardi has been accused."

"That's his name?" I asked. "Lombardi?"

"*Si.* Danilo Lombardi."

Curso, who'd remained silent during the conversation, finally spoke. "Nothing to worry about, Jessica," he said, his words accompanied by a laugh. "The only person you have to worry about is this young punk Lombardi, and he's already behind bars and will remain there for the rest of his wretched life once you have identified him. Besides, the police will be with you every step of the way, and so will I."

I smiled at my new friend but didn't say what I was thinking. As charming as he was, Anthony Curso didn't represent a source of physical security for me.

"So," Lippi said in an attempt to lighten the mood, "I propose a toast to our lovely guest, Jessica Fletcher."

"Thank you," I said, raising my glass to touch his espresso cup.

Our toast was interrupted by a light going off in my face. I looked up to see the same young man from the airport standing a few feet from us, his lens raised, the camera's motor whirring as it captured shot after shot. Lippi jumped to his feet as members of the restaurant staff ran across the room in our direction. Lippi grabbed the photographer by the front of his jumpsuit and propelled him across the handsome room and out the door.

"*Mi dispiace*, so sorry, so sorry," the bar's maître d' said to Curso, wringing his hands and rolling his eyes. "How dare he intrude on you like this?"

"It is nothing, signore," Curso said. "Forget about it."

Lippi returned. "Scum!" he muttered angrily. "I am sorry, Mrs. Fletcher."

"It isn't your fault," I said. "I do wish there wasn't all this notoriety associated with my arrival. I assumed I'd show up quietly, take part in your lineup, feel good about having done it, and return home."

"Ah," Curso said as he motioned for another drink, "life is never as simple as we would like it to be."

Lippi checked his watch and said, "I'm afraid I must go now. We are grateful to you, Mrs. Fletcher, for being here, and I apologize for any hardships it might entail."

"I must admit that I'll be glad when it's over, Detective. When will the lineup take place?"

"We have scheduled it for late tomorrow afternoon. I have a suggestion."

"Yes?"

"It will not help our cause if the lawyers for Lombardi know that you have seen this newspaper article with their client's picture in it. They will claim that your having seen it has tainted your objectivity."

"I understand," I said, "but I won't lie if I'm asked."

"No, of course not. I only suggest that you not offer the information without being prompted."

I agreed.

"One final bit of advice," said Lippi. "If you decide to venture from the hotel alone, please take care with your personal possessions. Street crime is on the rise here in Rome, with young thieves snatching purses from the unsuspecting. Be aware of your surroundings at all times."

"Thank you for the warning," I said. "I'll certainly heed it."

When Curso and I were alone in the booth, he said, "Now, my friend, maybe we can find time to discuss the book I have proposed."

I heard what he said, but the words seemed far away. As I stared down at the newspaper that Lippi had left on the table, the knot in my stomach grew and I felt a wave of fatigue wash over me.

"Are you all right, Jessica?" Curso asked.

"What? Oh, yes, I'm fine. It must be jet lag, my circadian rhythms out of kilter."

"I was asking about the collaboration between us, but it seems that now is not the time. This lovely lady needs a rest."

I smiled. "Yes, that's exactly what I need. Would you excuse me?"

"But of course. I want to see you rested and relaxed when we go to dinner."

"Dinner?" Food was the last thing on my mind at that moment.

"I have a surprise for you this evening," he said.

"I'm not sure that I'm up for any surprises, Tony."

"Nonsense. Come, you must go to your room and nap. I promised the bartender, a very good friend, to show him a variation on the Hurricane, a popular cocktail in New Orleans. The last time I was there I stopped in to see the bartender at Pat O'Brien's, who showed me this new approach to making the drink. It's all in the mix and—"

I placed my hand on his and said, "If I don't get to that nap, you'll be carrying me."

"Of course, of course."

He escorted me to the elevators. "Sleep tight," he said, squeezing my hand. "I'll call you at, say, five. We'll have an early dinner, yes?"

"Yes, fine, Tony. That will be fine."

I didn't realize how upsetting seeing my photograph in the newspaper had been until I'd gotten out of my clothes, stretched out on the bed, and pulled the comforter over me. I hadn't bargained on this sort of intrigue. It was to have been a simple matter of showing up, peering through a piece of one-way glass, identifying the culprit (assuming that he was in the lineup), and going home (or, more accurately, back to Chicago). Instead, I'd ended up the subject of media scrutiny—the sort no one seeks or is comfortable with.

I dozed off in the midst of these thoughts and awoke two hours later, groggy but rested. It was only noon, which gave me some time before Curso called for me at five. I decided to shower, slip on comfortable clothing and walking shoes, have lunch sent up, and take a leisurely stroll.

An hour later I stepped out onto Via Bocca di Leone, ready to do a little exploring. I knew that the hotel was only a short walk from Rome's fabled Piazza di Spagna, the Spanish Steps, 137 of them built by the French to create easier access to their church of Trinità dei Monti from the plaza below. I rounded a corner and headed for the plaza along Via Condotti, Rome's fashionable shopping street, stopping at window after window to admire the endless array of high-priced clothing and fashion accessories offered by shops with famous names. The pleasant, sunny weather had brought Romans and tourists to the streets, and walking was sometimes slow going because of the crowds clogging the sidewalks. I reached the Spanish Steps ten minutes later and stopped at the base to get my bearings. Should I make the trek up? I put off that decision, opting instead to follow the charming Via Margutta off to the left, lined with art galleries and stalls erected on the sidewalk by artists. As I perused the works for sale, I thought about how tragic it was that such beautiful works of art had become fodder for organized crime like drugs and extortion and prostitution. I spent a few minutes admiring a landscape by a young female artist, envisioning it on that blank wall space in my home, but decided this was not the time to be making a major purchase.

Instead I retraced my path back to the plaza at the base of the steps and stopped in at the Keats-Shelley Memorial, the final home of the poet John Keats. I bought two small volumes of the poets' works before going to the rococo fountain, Fontana della Barcaccia, from which tourists and locals alike who were about to climb the steps satisfied their thirst before making the ascent. I, too, drank from the fountain, which is in the shape of the boats that plied the waters of the nearby Tiber River, then drew a few preliminary breaths and started up. I made sure to check that the money belt I always traveled with was secure around my waist, Detective Lippi's admonition firmly in mind.

The steps were as crowded as the sidewalks had been. Along with tourists and locals out for a day in the sun were what seemed to be hundreds of men and women of all ages heavily made up and wearing a variety of costumes. I stopped to observe a group of them who were posing for tourist cameras, and asked a man taking pictures who they were.

"Models," he said in a British accent. "They pose here hoping to catch the eye of an artist from the fine arts academies that seem to be everywhere. Appears they'd be better off getting a real job."

I smiled, thanked him for the information, and continued my climb.

I reached the first of three landings on which dozens of artisans hawked their products and enjoyed a few minutes' rest before continuing. I'd gotten halfway to the second landing when I found my path blocked by two young men playfully jostling each other. I stopped, then tried to skirt them. As I passed behind one of the men, the other pushed him against me, sending me toppling backward into a family of tourists. The husband tried to break my fall but was unsuccessful. I knocked down the family's teenage daughter and, as I did, I continued falling over her, headfirst, until my forehead came to rest against the edge of one of the steps. I felt a searing pain where contact had been made and my hand automatically went to my head. Blood—my blood— ran through my fingers. Everything went black, replaced by shooting stars and jagged lightning. I heard voices—"Are you all right, lady?"—and someone knelt next to me and placed fingertips on my cheek.

I looked up into blurred faces. My vision cleared somewhat and I used my left arm to attempt to right myself. The moment I put pressure on it, pain radiated from the shoulder down to my hand.

"Take it easy," someone said.

"Get an ambulance."

"No," I said, now able to at least sit up.

Someone handed me a rag, which I pressed to the bleeding wound on my forehead.

"I don't need an ambulance," I protested as I struggled to regain my equilibrium. It was at that moment, while sitting on the Spanish Steps surrounded by strangers, my head pounding and my shoulder and arm aching, that I peered up into the eyes of the young man who'd crashed into me and sent me sprawling. He and his friend smiled, actually smiled, before they stepped out of my sight and were gone.

"No," I muttered.

A woman leaned close. "No what, signora?"

I didn't answer her because she wouldn't have understood. I wasn't certain myself. All I knew from my fleeting glance at my assailant—it was an assault, wasn't it?—was that he looked like the second young man who'd barged into the church, stolen the Bellini, and escaped with his accomplice, who'd slain Mr. Fanello.

Chapter Seventeen

Despite my protests, two members of the local Polizia, the civilian arm of Italian law enforcement, aided by two medical emergency technicians, carried this embarrassed woman down the Spanish Steps to a waiting ambulance that whisked me to a nearby hospital, the Ospedale San Giacomo, where I was taken to the emergency room and examined by the doctor on duty. He insisted upon a CAT scan of my head, which was negative, and an X-ray of my shoulder, which also didn't show any serious damage—"a strained muscle" was the diagnosis. As I waited in one of the examining rooms after I'd been told I'd been discharged, I glanced at a clock on the wall. It was almost four; Curso would be calling my hotel room soon.

"Could I make a phone call?" I asked one of the nurses who spoke fluent English.

"Of course," she said.

I didn't know the number for the hotel, but she got it from Information and placed the call, asking to be connected to Mr. Curso's room. When he came on the line, she handed me the phone.

"Tony, it's Jessica. There's been a slight change in plans. I'm in the hospital."

He gasped.

"I'm all right, Tony. I had an accident, that's all. I'm fine."

He asked which hospital I was calling from and I gave him the name.

"I'll be there in fifteen, twenty minutes, Jessica, depending on the traffic. Stay right where you are."

The doctor, a sweet-natured middle-aged man, told me, "I suggest that you rest for a day and do not hesitate to take the pain medicine you have been given whenever you need it. You will require transportation to your hotel?"

"No, thank you. Someone is picking me up."

"Good. You are fortunate that your injuries aren't more serious."

"I'm grateful for that, and for your care. *Grazie!*"

Despite my protests that I felt perfectly capable of walking under my own steam, they insisted that I be wheeled from the ER to the lobby. As we moved through the hallway I thought of the elder Mrs. Simsbury and wondered what it was like to be permanently consigned to a wheelchair. Not a pleasant thought. Was her nasty disposition the result of her condition? Probably not. I suspected that she was one of those people born with a difficult personality, something in the genes, possibly enhanced by her upbringing.

The orderly who took me to the lobby wished me a "better" day and left me to await Curso's arrival. Fifteen minutes later, he came to a screeching halt directly in front of the

hospital—the car he drove was sporty and fire-engine red—
and burst through the doors, threw up his hands at seeing
me, and exclaimed, "What have they done to you?"

"They've been very nice to me and—"

"You look as though you have been beaten up," he said as
he came to where I sat, went down on one knee, and took
my free hand. My other arm was in a sling.

"I guess I have been," I said. "I'm ready to leave."

"Of course." He stood and pulled me up out of the chair.

While my injuries were restricted to my forehead and
shoulder, I expected my entire body to ache as I walked with
careful steps toward the door. It was when I was almost
there that I caught a glimpse of my reflection in the glass. A
large compression bandage dominated my forehead, and the
white sling covered one side of me. "I do look a mess," I said,
more to myself than to him.

His red sports car was difficult to enter, but I managed.
He closed my door, ran around to the driver's side, got in,
and started the engine, which came to life with a roar.

"Where did you get this car?" I asked as he navigated
traffic.

"A rental. I always use a rental agency that specializes in
sports cars when I'm in Rome. It's a Ferrari Scuderia 430,
top of the line." He was looking at me as he spoke and had
to jam on the brakes to avoid piling into a double-parked
delivery truck. The pain in my shoulder elicited a moan.

"Mi dispiace," he said. "Sorry. I'll drive more slowly."

The doorman at the hotel took one look at me and
winced. "What happened, signora?" he asked as Curso
helped me out of his car.

"An accident," I said. "I fell."

"Or was pushed," Curso said angrily as he guided me into the lobby and to the elevators.

I'd told him during the trip that two young Italian men had been horsing around and had bumped into me, causing me to tumble backward. I also mentioned that one of them resembled the second armed thief in the church in L'Aquila, and added that they'd looked down at me and smiled as though pleased that I'd fallen. My tale elicited a string of Italian curses, or at least what sounded like profanity. I didn't ask for a translation.

A mirror in the entranceway to my room drew my attention and I moved closer to examine the damage. "I look like who-did-it-and-ran," I said.

"A dreadful experience," Curso said. "Did the police make a report?"

"I suppose so, although it appeared to them to be nothing more than an unfortunate accident."

"But from what you've told me, it doesn't sound as though it was."

"No, I think it was deliberate," I said as I settled in a chair by the window.

"Then we must take every step possible to protect you while in Rome," he said. "I will call the police and demand that they provide twenty-four-hour guards."

"Oh, no, Tony. I really don't think that's necessary. Maybe it *was* an accident."

"Still, better to be safe. They owe you protection, considering the reason you are here. I'll call Maresca and Lippi."

He used his cell phone to place the call, reached Lippi at

police headquarters, and told him what had happened, speaking mostly in Italian. After he'd hung up, he said, "They will assign security for the duration of your stay, Jessica."

I was in no mood to argue and simply said, "Thank you."

"You must rest," Curso said.

I nodded. I was having trouble keeping my eyes open.

"I will cancel dinner plans," he said.

"That's not necessary," I said. "I'll be fine after a nap. You said you had a surprise for me."

"I do. I did. Perhaps you are not up to it."

"No, I'll be fine. Just let me rest. Give me half an hour?"

"I'll call you in an hour. Rest now. I will see you later."

I heard him close the door and breathed a sigh of relief. As much as I enjoyed his company, I needed time alone to sort out what had occurred that day. I couldn't be sure, of course, that the young man who knocked me down was one of the two men at the church. I'd caught only a fleeting, blurred glimpse of him. What stayed with me was the cruel smile on both men's faces. While others scrambled to help me, they'd exhibited smug pleasure at what had happened. Why would anyone do that—unless my plight was the result of a deliberate act on their part?

Aside from a slight stinging sensation where my head wound had been stitched, I was surprisingly pain free, despite not having taken any of the medicine given me at the emergency room. All in all, I felt pretty good considering what I'd just gone through, which fortified my decision to go through with dinner that night.

After dozing off in the chair for a little while, I got up, took my arm out of the sling, and gingerly moved my shoulder. Not bad, not bad at all. Maybe New England's fabled stoicism was at work.

I wondered where and when the uniformed security Curso said would be provided was going to show up. I didn't relish the idea of having armed guards, no matter how discreet they might be. Would they be in uniform, or would plainclothes officers be assigned? I abandoned that question to focus on my appearance. Another trip to the mirror wasn't comforting. I decided to carefully remove the compression bandage and see if I could fashion something less conspicuous. It took a few minutes to peel it away, and the resulting image wasn't nearly as bad as I had imagined it would be. The surgeon had done a skillful job with the stitches, and aside from some mild swelling and a bluish green hue, the wound wasn't grotesque. Hopefully we'd have dinner in a dimly lit restaurant.

I watched a portion of a John Wayne western with Italian subtitles, then got in the shower, careful to avoid disturbing the wound, and dressed for the evening. I elected to go out sans the sling but tucked it in my large purse in case my shoulder started aching later.

Curso came to my room and escorted me downstairs to where his rented red Ferrari waited at the curb.

"How are you feeling?" he asked as he settled into the driver's seat and turned the ignition key.

"Surprisingly well," I said.

"That's wonderful to hear, Jessica. I would hate to think of you going through the evening in pain."

"I have some pills if I start to hurt, but I don't expect I'll need them. Now, where are we going, and what is this surprise you mentioned?"

"To answer your first question, we are going for an early dinner in the town of Calcata, thirty miles north of the city."

"Calcutta? I know I blacked out this afternoon, but I didn't think I'd gone to India."

His laugh was gentle as he skirted a traffic tie-up by turning off the main road and racing down a narrow side street. "Not Calcutta, Jessica. Calcata. It's a most interesting town, perhaps the grooviest village in all of Italy."

"'Grooviest'? You make it sound like some sort of hippy commune."

"Exactly what it is. Hundreds of unusual characters, including many fine artists and performers who live and work there. The village was condemned by the government back in the thirties because officials were convinced that the cliffs on which it sits were ready to crumble. Inhabitants were forced to build a new town about a half mile to the north, and the old town was abandoned for years until artists and other bohemians decided to ignore the government's warning and started moving in. These new Calcatesi have rejuvenated the village."

"Evidently the government's fears were unfounded," I said.

"So far. As of today, the old village is still standing, inhabited by an eclectic mix of people. I thought you might enjoy seeing a part of Italy that most tourists miss."

"I'm always open to seeing new things," I said as he took a corner at a speed that caused the car to tip a little. "Would you please slow down, Tony?"

"Yes, I'm sorry. I forgot I have a patient with me."

I contented myself with taking in the passing countryside as we traveled on a highway—the sign said it was the Cassia Bis—and finally came to a stop at an open gate that was too narrow for a vehicle to pass through. Curso turned off the engine, looked at me, and smiled. "We're here," he announced.

"We can't drive any farther?"

"Afraid not. We leave the car here and walk into the village."

My silence reminded him that I might not be up to taking a walk, especially considering that the cobblestone lane was uphill.

"If you are not able to walk, Jessica, I certainly understand. I should have taken that into consideration."

"I'll be fine," I said, hoping that I would be.

"We'll walk slowly, take our time. We have the whole night ahead of us, huh?"

I hoped not, but I didn't argue. I'd been looking for signs of the security detail but saw no one who fit that bill. I asked Curso about it and he said, "They will be discreet, Jessica. Good security officers fade into the background."

I looked back in the direction from which we'd come in search of someone who might qualify as a security officer, but we were alone.

"Did you tell the police that we were coming to this town?" I asked.

"No."

"So how would they follow us?" I asked, thinking of the speed at which Curso had driven.

"They have their ways," he replied. "Not to worry, Jessica. You're in very good hands."

"If you say so," I said, not brimming with confidence.

We set off up the path at a slow gait, stopping now and then for me to rest, although I really didn't need to. I was feeling fine, so we picked up the pace until we reached a small plaza amid a jumble of ancient stone buildings that appeared to be built one atop the other. Curso said the town dated back to at least the thirteenth century, and from the looks of it, it might have been even older. At the center of the plaza was a small provincial church, which we stopped to admire.

The plaza was lively. Outdoor cafés were crowded with an assortment of men, women, and children. Some of the men wore saris and sported long ponytails. The attire of their female companions ran the gamut from jeans and T-shirts to floor-length flowered dresses from another era. I noticed one couple in pajamas enjoying a drink in a café. A man put on a puppet show, and two guitarists competed at cafés opposite each other. Everywhere were signs advertising art galleries, many tucked away down tiny streets off the plaza, others on the square itself with outdoor displays of the artists' latest works.

"Hungry?" Curso asked.

"As a matter of fact, I am," I reported.

"Good. I've made reservations at a charming restaurant, Grotta dei Germogli, owned by a friend, Pancho Garrison. He's an American. His partner, Paul Steffen, was a dancer and choreographer in Hollywood during its heyday. His stories about the great stars he knew are always amusing. Don't let the surroundings throw you off, Jessica. It's in a cave lined with mosaic tiles. But the food is good—nouvelle Italian, I suppose you could call it."

"And of course you know the bartender there," I said playfully.

"The owner mixes the drinks. He's quite good at it, although I suggest we stick to wine. Come, it's only a short walk."

The restaurant certainly was built inside a cave. You had to duck to enter through the cave's mouth, and the space between tables was just enough to slide by sideways. Curso was greeted by his friend, the owner, and we were seated in the deep recesses of the space. A few other tables were occupied by tourists who spoke Italian. "Calcata is a favorite getaway for Romans," Curso explained. "For them it's like traveling to a different world only thirty miles away."

Our dinner was excellent. The owner insisted that he choose the menu for the evening—I'm not sure what all the ingredients were, but the result was tasty and not heavy, for which I was grateful. The only problem was that sitting for more than an hour in a cramped space caused my shoulder to begin to throb, not to the point that I pulled out the sling, but enough to cause me to shift position frequently.

We eschewed dessert and stepped out of the cave into a pristine evening. Guitar music led us back to the plaza, where even more people crowded into the cafés or sat on many benches ringing the area.

"Up for another walk?" Curso asked.

"The surprise you mentioned?"

"Yes." He took my hand. "Come. It isn't far. It's called Giancolo Hill, near the church of Santa Maria di Loreto and the American Academy. There's someone there that I want you to meet."

"I'll do my best," I said, and we left the plaza and went down a street that gradually became steep.

"You're all right?" Curso asked frequently.

"Yes, although my shoulder is beginning to protest. I think I'll put on my sling."

We stopped as I placed my arm in the sling. It worked, taking the pressure off and alleviating any pain I'd been feeling.

Ten minutes later, we came to the entrance to another cave that had been turned into a living area. Curso stuck his head through the entrance and yelled, "Hey, Vittorio. It's me, Tony Curso."

I looked past Curso into the cave, which was illuminated by oil lamps and candles. Curso repeated his call. Soon, an imposing figure filled the interior of the cave and emerged. He was a mountain of a man, easily three hundred pounds, who towered over me and the shorter Curso. Vittorio had a salt-and-pepper beard that reached his chest, and hair of the same color flowed down over his shoulders. His brown eyes were watery and puffy, with fleshy bags hanging beneath them. He wore a badly stained pair of brown farmer's coveralls over a T-shirt that had been white many years ago. His large feet were encased in sandals.

He squinted at Curso, then at me, before grasping Curso in an embrace that threatened to smother my friend. "Hey, Curso. What are you doing here?" he asked, his voice eroded by too many cigarettes, cigars, and, I presumed, alcohol.

"What, you aren't glad to see me?" Curso asked.

"Oh, yeah, sure, I am always glad to see my rich American fan." He looked at me. "You have a new girlfriend, huh? You beat her up?"

"She's not my girlfriend, Vittorio. She's Jessica Fletcher. She writes books, murder mysteries, good ones, big sellers."

Vittorio extended a hand the size of a ham and enveloped mine. "He tells the truth?" he asked. "No girlfriend?"

"No, I'm not his girlfriend," I said.

"*I* need a girlfriend," Vittorio said through a loud rumble of a laugh. "Maybe you stay around, huh, be my girlfriend."

Curso saved me from responding. "So, Vittorio," he said, "I've come, like I promised I would, and brought this lovely lady with me."

I was confused about what was going on. Was Vittorio the "surprise" Curso had promised? If so, I couldn't imagine why he would have thought that my meeting his friend was worth the trek to Calcata.

"*Benvenuti*, come in," Vittorio said, stepping aside to allow us to enter his cave. I had a momentary fear as I entered that I would find a colony of bats hanging upside down above me, or would hit my head on one of the stalactites suspended from the ceiling. Both fears were unfounded, of course, simply the result of my too vivid imagination at play.

We followed Vittorio from the small outer room into a vastly larger space, off which two other smaller areas were visible.

"Welcome to my home," Vittorio said. He noticed me attempting to peer into the other rooms and said, "Just my bedroom. The other is for storage. You want to see?"

"No, thank you."

Because of what Curso had told me about the town of Calcata and its attraction for artists, I'd entered assuming that our host was an artist. Once I was inside the main part of the cave, my assumption was verified. It was the quintessential painter's studio, replete with multiple easels, shelves lined with tubes of oil paint, dozens of brushes, and an array of canvases piled against one another along the walls. Unlike the lighting in the entryway, here the illumination was electric, a succession of bare bulbs strung from the ceiling and across two of the stone walls.

"Here, sit down," Vittorio said as he unfolded three battered director's chairs and positioned them around a small table. "Drink?"

"A martini, cold, dry, and shaken," Curso said.

Vittorio laughed heartily. "You still drink those fancy drinks, huh, Tony? None of that here. Grappa or Genepi, take your pick." He held up a bottle of what he said was grappa, its contents clear as water.

I looked at Curso, who said, "An acquired taste, Jessica. Fermented peels, grape stems and seeds, potent stuff."

"Nothing for me, thank you," I said.

Vittorio held another bottle in front of me. "Maybe some Genepi, huh? It's from the Alps, the Aosta Valley. Good stuff. Puts hair on your chest."

I grimaced. Vittorio laughed. Curso said, "You have water, Vittorio?"

To my relief he produced an unsealed bottle of spring water, uncapped it, and poured it into three glasses that appeared to be relatively clean.

"To the beautiful lady," Vittorio said, raising his glass in my direction. Curso matched his gesture.

"So, Tony, you got my message," Vittorio said, downing

his water in one swallow and refilling his glass from the grappa bottle.

"Yes, I did," Curso responded. "That's why I'm here. You're serious?"

Vittorio's expression changed. Until that moment he'd had a sparkle in his eyes and an almost perpetual hint of a smile on his lips, at least the portion of them that I could see behind the beard. Now he turned solemn and lowered his head, deep in thought.

"It's a big decision," Curso said.

Vittorio slowly shook his head. When he raised it, he said, "I've had enough, you know? These *sanguisughe* are too greedy, Tony. They would steal from their own mothers."

Curso noticed my puzzled expression and said, "He calls them bloodsucking leeches, Jessica."

"Who?"

"The Mafia."

I looked at Vittorio. "He's—?"

"No, no, Jessica. Vittorio is not one of them. But he has worked for them."

If he worked for them, wasn't that the same as being one of them? I silently questioned.

Vittorio started to say something but stopped, looking at me as though it was the first time he was aware of my presence.

"It is okay that she is here," Curso said. "We are working together, writing a book."

"Actually," I said, "we've only discussed that possibility."

"A book, huh?" said Vittorio. "You better not put me in it."

"Not by name," Curso reassured him. "Never by name. But your story will make the book a bestseller."

I'd become impatient at the vague references being bandied about and now asked, "Just what *is* your story, Vittorio?"

The big man looked at Curso, who'd struck a cavalier pose in his chair, one leg crossed over the other, a small smile on his face. "Tell her, Vittorio," he said.

Vittorio's response was to haul himself up out of the director's chair, which had sagged beneath his weight, and motion for me to follow him. He went to a far wall of the cave where dozens of framed oil paintings were stacked vertically against one another. He picked up one and held it for me to examine. It looked like the work of some old master, but I couldn't identify the artist. I must admit that while I appreciate fine art, I'm not well versed in it. The subject was a pretty young woman draped in a gossamer robe that allowed a veiled view of her naked body. Cherubs seemingly floating in the air above looked down on her.

"What do you think, huh?" Vittorio asked in his deep, gravelly voice.

"It's very nice," I said. "Did you paint this?"

"*Si*, I painted this."

"You're very talented," I said.

"So was Gozzoli," Vittorio said.

"I don't know that name," I said.

"Benozzo Gozzoli, an artist from the mid-fifteenth century," Curzo said from where he sat. "He was pupil and assistant to Fra Angelico. Very prolific, best known for his series of murals in the Palazzo Medici."

"This particular work is very different from his usual settings and subjects," Vittorio said. "Like most Italian Renaissance painters, he focused on religious subjects, but he had his lecherous side, too," he added, winking at me. "This painting represents that side of him. It was probably hidden in a closet or beneath his bed." The large man laughed. "She is pretty, huh, the young woman in the painting?"

"Very pretty, but I don't understand. You say this is by an artist named Gozzoli, but yet you claim that you painted it."

Vittorio looked back at Curso, who nodded.

"I *did* paint it," Vittorio said. "This version."

"You mean you've copied it," I said.

"*Si.*"

"Why would you do that?" I asked, hoping I didn't sound too naïve.

Vittorio erupted in a laugh that started somewhere deep in his gut. "*Why?* What other reason is there? For the money, lovely lady, for the money."

"Who pays you to make a copy?" I asked.

The minute I asked, I knew the answer—and the expression on Curso's face confirmed it.

Chapter Eighteen

Curso and I stayed in Vittorio's cave for another hour, one of the more fascinating hours I've ever spent. The artist showed me painting after painting that he had copied for wealthy art collectors.

"Let me explain," Curso said after we'd resumed our chairs and Vittorio had finished what was left in his bottle of grappa. "There are few artists in the world with Vittorio's skills, Jessica. You've already heard of one in Los Angeles."

"He's an amateur compared to me," Vittorio mumbled.

"That's right, he is," Curso said, "but he's still good enough to attract plenty of business. The point is, Jessica, that Vittorio's copies are not made for the collectors who've purchased great works of art. He copies them on behalf of unscrupulous dealers, as well as thieves here in Italy. A wealthy art collector, say, in the United States, is offered a painting by a dealer. The original painting may have been stolen from a church like the one in L'Aquila. It happens every day. More than six hundred thousand works of art have been stolen over the past thirty years, with more than forty percent taken from churches and private collections. These thieves steal not only the art; they even steal the pews."

"Why would they do that?" I asked.

"They recycle the benches, which are then used to stretch the canvases of fake paintings. The wood from these pews can be several centuries old, and the counterfeiters use it as proof that the paintings are also ancient. But the salient point is that Vittorio's commissions come not from the collectors but from those who *steal* the art."

"Wait a minute," I said, as what was being explained began to sink in. "If Vittorio here is making copies for the thieves, does that mean that the originals aren't being delivered to those collectors who've paid for them?"

"Exactly," Curso said. "A collector pays a large sum to an unscrupulous dealer here in Italy for a work painted by a master. But instead of receiving the original, he or she receives a superb copy painted by none other than Vittorio. The dealer then has the original to sell again to a more astute and discerning collector."

I drew a breath before saying, "Jonathon Simsbury?"

Curso replied solemnly, "He was among the naïve and easily duped. Jonathon was too trusting. He believed that every work of art he bought was an original. More worldly collectors hire people like me to examine their intended purchases before going through with a deal. Jonathon put his faith in those he was dealing with in Italy and elsewhere. Art theft isn't unique to Italy. It takes place all over the world, thousands of pieces each year from every corner of the globe."

I sat back in the chair and sighed. Our talented host
was seemingly content with his role in duping naïve co
tors, was an accessory to multiple crimes. It was not so
thing I dared comment on in his presence, but I would
Curso later, after we left. It was no surprise to me that w
of art were stolen, of course, but I hadn't thought bey
that. I had no idea how vast the network was or the ex
to which those behind the thefts went to squeeze even m
money out of unsuspecting buyers like Simsbury.

I tried to put it into a clear perspective and to draw n
understandable lines between the players.

A dealer contacts Jonathon and says he has a work of
for sale. They agree on a price. The piece of art has be
stolen and the dealer knows it. The thieves bring the origin
to someone like Vittorio—how many Vittorios are there?
and he makes an excellent forgery, which is delivered to t
unsuspecting collector. In Jonathon's case, he himself has
forger in Los Angeles make a copy of the copy to hang o
the wall of his home, and then he sleeps well at night, think
ing that the original is safe and sound in his warehouse. Bu
the dealer still has the original to sell for a second time to
more knowledgeable collector who will have the work'
provenance verified by an expert like Anthony Curso.

Amazing!

Was it possible that Jonathon Simsbury and his new partner, Edgar Peters, owned a warehouse filled with phony art?

I sneaked a few glances at my watch and saw that the
hour matched my growing fatigue. Curso's explanation, enhanced by Vittorio's personal experiences, had given me a
clear understanding of how things worked in the big-time

world of art theft and forgery. But what I didn't understand was why Curso had brought me here. He'd mentioned to Vittorio that we intended to collaborate on a book together, presumably based upon Vittorio's story. But there had to be more to it than that. I'd never actually committed to work on the book with Curso, after all. I decided that I would wait until the drive back to Rome to seek an answer. We had much to talk about. But our departure wasn't to happen until another hour had passed, during which Curso's real reason for visiting that night was revealed.

"Let's get down to brass tacks, as we Americans say," Curso said to Vittorio, who'd opened a fresh bottle of grappa. "You're sure you want to go through with it?"

"You bet I do," was the artist's response. "No more dealing with those *avvoltoi*. They treat me like dirt, huh, like some worthless *idiota*, always telling me to hurry up and trying to pay less money. Faster! Faster! Too much money! Pigs! I detest them."

I looked to Curso, who said, "He's talking about the Mafia, Jessica. He calls them vultures. The Mafia is behind much of the art theft. He is fed up with having to deal with them and wants out."

"Can't he just say that he's closing up shop, retiring?"

"It's never that easy with the Mafia," Curso said with a stern shake of his head. "You don't just walk away. Besides, what Vittorio knows can be detrimental to the Mob's operations." He looked at Vittorio, who appeared to be on the verge of falling asleep in his chair. "It is all right, my friend, that I tell the lady what we plan to do?"

Vittorio shrugged his massive shoulders and his glass fell

from his hand, the sound as it smashed on the cave's floor snapping him to attention. He kicked the shards of glass under his chair with his sandal.

I wasn't sure I wanted to hear what sounded like a scheme between them, but I sat stoically as Curso continued, having gained his friend's tacit approval.

"You see, Jessica, Vittorio and I have been discussing his desire to leave this life. When I spoke to you about collaborating on a book, it is Vittorio's story that is the basis of it."

"I gathered that."

"And there's the TV documentary."

I sat up straighter. "What TV documentary?"

"The one that exposes the Mafia's role in international art theft based upon Vittorio's experiences. I have already secured funding for it. An Italian film crew was here for two days recently, filming Vittorio in his natural habitat." He said to Vittorio, "I must say, I was impressed with how you managed to lay off the grappa during the filming."

He turned to me. "Our book would be a natural extension of the film, Jessica. Besides, it would be a wonderful opportunity for you to provide your own on-camera experience with this sordid business of art theft that finances the Mafia's drug trafficking."

I held up a hand. "Wait a minute, Tony. I'm afraid that you're speaking with the wrong person. I write books, novels, works of fiction. Being involved in an exposé like this isn't something I'd be interested in."

"Then the book will be a work of fiction based upon this true story."

A sharp pain suddenly radiated down my arm, making

me grimace and adjust the sling. "This has been fascinating," I said, "but I'm afraid the events of today are catching up with me. Could we please leave?"

"Yes, of course. I understand that this is all so new to you, so sudden, that it is impossible for you to fully understand the importance of it. We can discuss it tomorrow after you've had a good night's rest. Come, we'll go now."

Vittorio, now fully awake, walked us out of the cave. A full moon bathed the area in soft natural light, and the fresh air was welcome. Curso turned to Vittorio and said, "So it is set. Tomorrow, in Rome. I will have everything you need."

"Good," Vittorio said, then laughed. "Those *avvoltoi* will be plenty surprised, huh?"

"They certainly will," Curso agreed as he took my arm, and we turned to begin our walk back to the car. I'd taken only a few steps when a pebble that had gotten into my shoe caused me to stop, remove the shoe, and shake it out. As I did, I noticed two men standing in the shadows approximately thirty feet from the cave's entrance. Curso, too, saw them and sensed my concern. "The police," he whispered. "Undoubtedly your security."

He drove at a sensible speed back to the city. Despite my intention to press him to answer my many questions, we said little to each other. My head was full of what had transpired since I'd arrived in Italy, and I was so tired I could barely organize my thoughts. But one question nagged at me: I asked Curso why Vittorio was coming to Rome the next day.

"To pick up his airline ticket and cash from me for his trip to the States. It's not safe for him to have them at his home, since someone might decide to search the place."

"That sounds like his life could be in danger," I said. "The Mafia isn't restricted only to Italy, you know. And what about the Italian police? I'm sure the officers in the art squad would love to hear Vittorio recount his story in front of a judge."

"All in good time, Jessica. I've arranged a place for him to stay in Chicago while the filming continues there. I just need to get him out of Italy first. Then I can see that he's safe. I've thought of everything."

Curso offered to walk me into the hotel, but I declined.

"You're deep in thought," he said as I prepared to get out of the car.

"I'm just wondering whether Jonathon Simsbury's murder is in any way connected with what I've learned tonight about his art collection."

"It wouldn't be the first time someone was killed over a piece of art, Jessica. Go now; climb into bed and rest. You have your police lineup tomorrow afternoon. I have appointments in the morning, but I will pick you up after lunch, say at three, and drive you to police headquarters."

I exited the car and looked down the street, where I saw a young man dressed all in black leaning against a light pole smoking a cigarette. A member of my security detail? If so, his presence was welcome.

I entered the hotel, paused in the lobby, and went back outside. The young man in black had come to the front of the hotel and was peering through the doors. My sudden appearance seemed to startle him. He stared at me, a hard expression on his youthful face, before quickly turning away and walking down the street. Somehow, he didn't look like a policeman, and I felt a chill run up my spine. It was at that moment that I realized the situation I'd ended up in was far more threatening than I'd ever dreamed it would be. I returned to the lobby, rode the elevator to my floor, entered my room, and bolted myself in.

Chapter Nineteen

I couldn't remember a time in recent memory when be-ing alone was so appealing. So much had happened since I'd arrived in Italy that had sent my mind swirling, my imagination soaring.

I found myself almost resenting Anthony Curso. While he was a delightful gentleman with a wide range of interests, he was also someone who obviously enjoyed intrigue. I'd been drawn into his mysterious life without the benefit of being forewarned. I could only assume that he'd kept from me the "surprise" he'd promised until it was too late for me to decline to be involved. The documentary about big-time art theft and forgery must have been in the works for a long time; filming in Vittorio's cave had already taken place, and now the artist was being flown to Chicago for more, and presumably to get him away from any people in Italy who didn't want him to expose their business. It was also clear to me from what Curso had said about arranging financing for the project that he was the force behind it.

I had to remind myself not to feel used by him. My arrival on the scene in Chicago came late in the game, which meant that including me in the documentary had to be a last-minute thought. Why he felt that I would add anything to the project was beyond me, unless he was hoping my relative fame as a writer of mysteries would help enhance the documentary's appeal. Of course, the fact that I'd witnessed firsthand the theft of a piece of art, and the cold-blooded murder that accompanied it, may have given me the sort of credentials that he felt warranted my inclusion in the tale. But I knew one thing: I would not be roped into participating in the making of any documentary.

I was deep in these thoughts when the phone rang. I looked at the clock. It was close to midnight. Someone from home? It was late for anyone to be calling from Rome. Carefully, I lifted the receiver. "Yes?"

"Go home, signora," a male voice said. "It is safer there."

"Hello? Hello."

The line had gone dead.

As I pondered what to do, it rang again.

The same voice said, "Mind your own business, signora. You are too lovely a lady to end up in a Dumpster."

"Who is this?" I said into the lifeless line.

I called the front desk and asked that no calls be put through to my room.

Where was my alleged security?

I placed a call to police headquarters, but of course Detectives Maresca and Lippi had been long gone for the evening. I tried to explain to the officer who took the call that I'd been receiving threatening messages and that I was scheduled to view a lineup the following afternoon. He sounded interested, although my limited Italian and his limited English got in the way of what I was attempting to get across. We finally reached an agreement—I hoped. He would try to reach Maresca or Lippi at home and ask one of them to call me at the hotel.

"*Grazie,*" I said. "Thank you very much."

It was after I'd hung up that I remembered having banned calls from being forwarded to my room. I dialed the desk again and explained that I wanted that prohibition to stay in place, but that if a detective named Maresca or Lippi called, he was to be put through. I wasn't sure the clerk understood my intention, but he agreed nonetheless.

The anonymous threats had set my nerves on edge. Every sound from the hallway caused me to flinch. I turned on the television, but a war movie, with its explosions, whistling bullets, and cries from the wounded, was hardly the sort of background I needed.

I paced the room, stopping repeatedly to open the drapes to see whether the young man with the cigarette was anywhere in sight. *Calm down, Jessica,* I told myself a number of times. *Nothing is going to happen to you. You're safe here in this room.*

The problem was that I wasn't convinced.

Detective Maresca called a little before one a.m. I told him about the threatening messages and asked what I should do. "Inform the desk that no calls are to be put through," was his suggestion. I told him that I'd already done that. "There is nothing else that can be done, certainly not tonight," he said. "If the calls persist tomorrow, I can arrange for a trace to be put on your hotel phone. In the meantime, try to get some rest. Oh, Mrs. Fletcher, there will be a plainclothes detective assigned to you tomorrow. I look forward to seeing you at the lineup. *Buona sera.*"

Over the next hour, I fluctuated between edginess and anger, concern and relief. This roller coaster of emotions took its toll, and by two o'clock I felt as though I'd been awake for two days. I collapsed on the bed in what I was wearing and awoke at seven the following morning.

I was groggy from so little sleep, but a long session beneath the shower did wonders to revive me. My shoulder was mildly sore and my head wound looked less angry. I dressed for the day in clothes I hoped wouldn't stand out in a crowd. While I did want my police escort to see me, I didn't want to give any criminal elements an easy target.

My growling stomach dictated the need for a hearty start to the morning. Downstairs, as I crossed the lobby to the dining room where breakfast was being served, I noticed a man dressed in a gray suit who sat reading a newspaper. I don't know why he attracted my attention, but he did, and I took a moment to observe him. He seemed engrossed in the paper, and I decided I was being paranoid. But after I passed him I stopped suddenly and turned. He'd placed the paper on his lap and was looking intently at me. I glanced past him to where two other men sat talking. *They* looked like policemen; were they the ones assigned to keep an eye on me? Just their presence relaxed me.

The maître d' seated me at a table for two next to a spectacular vase of tall, colorful flowers and handed me a menu. I looked around the pretty, sunny room. Most of the tables

were occupied and waiters moved quickly to serve everyone. Moments later, with coffee and juice in front of me, and
my order given for two eggs over easy, bacon, and wheat
toast, I settled back and drew a deep breath. My adventure
was almost at an end, and that realization swept a wave of
relief over me. I was eager to participate in the lineup, put it
behind me, and board a plane home. The contemplation
brought a smile to my face as I sipped the steaming-hot coffee. I'd allowed my imagination to run rampant last night,
something I'm usually able to keep reined in.

Breakfast was delicious, the eggs perfectly cooked, the
bacon crisp and flavorful. As I pondered how to spend the
morning—was there time for a little shopping before Curso
picked me up?—a man who'd been sitting with three others
at another table approached. He smiled and said, "Please
excuse me, signora, for intruding on your breakfast, but I
have been told that you are Jessica Fletcher, the famous
American writer."

I returned his smile. "I don't know about famous, but I
am American and I do write books."

He was a large man with a craggy face accented by a
large, broad nose, high cheekbones, and pink cheeks. Something about him was familiar. An actor perhaps? Or a politician? But he had all the trappings of a wealthy Italian
businessman: three-piece suit, silk tie, large gold cuff links
protruding from his jacket sleeves. What was also noticeable
about him was the heavy aroma of aftershave.

"You are much too modest," he said. "May I?" He indicated the vacant chair.

"Actually, I was about to leave and—"

He sat. "I just want to tell you how much my wife and my daughters enjoy your books, signora. They are all translated into Italian and I believe that my wife has read every one. She anxiously awaits publication of the next."

"That's kind of you to say," I said, smiling. "Please tell them I write as fast as I can."

"I am sure you do," he said. "I was wondering how you come up with your stories. You must be a very creative person."

Since he certainly didn't fit the profile of most of my fans, I assumed he wanted more details to take home to his wife and daughters. I could have explained how I worked, but I didn't want to prolong the conversation, as pleasant as he might have been. "I'm sorry to cut this short, but I really must go," I said, motioning to the waiter for my check, folding my napkin and placing it next to my plate.

"A woman like you must lead a very busy life," he said.

I nodded but didn't reply as the waiter placed a small silver tray next to me on which was a pen and the check showing my breakfast charge.

I started to sign my name and indicate my room number when my uninvited visitor leaned closer. The man's voice changed dramatically and he said in a low, menacing tone, "Go home, signora. Go home now and write your books. Don't be a fool. If you stay and cooperate with the police, you will never get to write another book."

I looked up sharply and noticed that his three breakfast companions had risen and taken a few steps in our direction. I pushed back in my chair to put space between us, ready to make a commotion if necessary.

The man stood and his smile returned. It was at that moment that I recognized him. His photograph had appeared in the newspaper Detective Lippi had shown me. What was his name? It came to me. Felice. Enzo Felice. The Mafia boss.

"Buon giorno, signora," he said. "It has been a pleasure talking with you."

"I wish I could say the same," I muttered as Felice and his three colleagues walked from the room, stopping to say hello at a table of people who seemed to grovel in his presence.

"Everything was satisfactory?" the maître d' asked as I headed for the exit.

"What? Oh, yes, everything was fine, thank you."

When I emerged from the dining room, Felice was still in the lobby, greeting people like a popular politician, shaking hands and slapping backs, his cohorts surrounding him, one on either side, the third bringing up the rear. The two men who'd been in the lobby when I'd arrived, and who I'd assumed were police officers, had gotten up and followed Felice and his entourage outside, where a long black limousine waited. Felice and his bodyguards got in; the men I'd assumed were police climbed into an unmarked car also parked at the curb and fell in behind as the limo joined the traffic. *Well, they weren't here on my behalf,* I thought, disappointed.

But someone else was. As I stood watching, a young man tapped my elbow. I jumped.

"Scusi, Mrs. Fletcher," he said. "I did not mean to alarm you. I am Detective Amato. I have been assigned to be with you for the day."

"Did you see that man who just left?"

"Enzo Felice? Of course. He's everywhere. We have tails on him twenty-four hours a day."

"He came to my table and threatened me," I said, not realizing that my voice was louder than I'd intended. Several people in the lobby turned to see what was happening.

Detective Amato led me to a pair of chairs and indicated I should take one while he sat in the other; he removed a notebook and pen from his pocket. "Tell me, please, signora. What did he say?"

I related the scene at breakfast as best as I could remember, my anger rising as I relived the conversation.

"I am so sorry this has happened to you," the detective said. "I assure you that he will not bother you again. I will stay out of your way, but please be confident that I will always be close."

"I appreciate that," I said, meaning it. But the threatening words Felice had used haunted me as I went through the rest of the day.

Despite the unpleasantness in the restaurant, I was determined not to let it send me scurrying back to my room to cower behind a bolted door. I purposely went shopping, defying those who tried to bully me, and bought small gifts to take home. I chose an outdoor café at which to have a leisurely light lunch while I watched the colorful parade of Romans and tourists enjoying the city. From time to time, I noticed Detective Amato trailing me, staying at a discreet distance, and I was grateful the police had kept their promise.

At two thirty I returned to the hotel and waited in the lobby for Curso's arrival. I recognized the red Ferrari when it pulled up to the entrance. Detective Amato escorted me to the car and opened the door, checking to make sure no one other than Curso was inside. Curso motioned for the detective to come closer. "I am driving Mrs. Fletcher to police headquarters," he said. "I suggest you meet us there." I half expected Curso to invite him to ride with us, but I couldn't see how another person would be able to fit in the sports car. Even if he could have squeezed in, the detective undoubtedly would have declined the offer.

I recounted for Curso the calls I'd gotten the night before and my confrontation with the Mob boss.

"Yet here you are," he said. "Others might have run away, gotten on the first plane out of Italy."

"I considered it," I admitted, "but I feel even more strongly now about helping convict this young punk."

He laughed.

"What's funny?"

"Calling him a 'young punk.' It doesn't strike me as a term you would use."

"I'm sure you'd be surprised at some other terms I use when I'm angry. Have you seen Vittorio today?"

"No. Typical of him to be late. We were supposed to meet at your hotel for lunch, but he never showed up. He's probably at the bar now, drinking his beloved grappa. We'll look for him after you take care of your business with the police."

Detectives Maresca and Lippi were waiting for us when we arrived along with Detective Amato. They led us to a conference room where coffee and biscotti were served by a female officer. When we were seated, I described for them my encounter with Enzo Felice.

"Unusual for him to deliver such a message personally," Lippi said to Maresca.

"It says to me that he's especially concerned about what happens to Lombardi." Maresca turned to me. "Generally, he'd have sent one of his goons to try to scare you off."

"Well," I said, "I think he may have tried yesterday, but he didn't succeed."

"What do you mean, Signora Fletcher?"

I gave the detectives a brief account of the incident at the Spanish Steps, then waved away their apologies for not ensuring my protection. "It's not important anymore," I said. "I'm here. Are we ready for the lineup?"

Maresca checked his watch. "They'll be bringing in Lombardi and the stand-ins in twenty minutes."

"I wish I didn't know his name," I said.

"Why?" asked Lippi.

"It makes it, well, somehow personal."

"This young punk is *personal*?" Curso said. To the detectives: "Mrs. Fletcher called him a young punk."

"Please," said Maresca, "don't say such a thing in front of his defense attorney."

"He'll be here?" I asked.

"Of course. Offer him nothing in the way of comment, Mrs. Fletcher. Simply view the lineup, pick out the man who murdered Fanello, and leave."

"Whatever you say," I said, keen to get the whole matter over with.

A uniformed officer entered the room and announced that the participants in the lineup were ready. Curso stayed behind as we followed the officer to a small room with a floor-to-ceiling window that spanned the wall. A heavy green drape was drawn across it. I was introduced to the prosecutor, a handsome young man with a pleasant demeanor. There was another man in the room, considerably older than the prosecutor and dressed more elaborately. His dark blue suit looked expensive, as did the multiple thin gold chains on his wrist and a gold tie tack that glistened in the room's lights. Introduced to me as the alleged shooter's defense attorney, he had a perpetual sneer on his deeply tanned face; I wondered whether it was for my benefit.

Up until now I'd been relatively calm, but as the moment of truth arrived, I felt a slight quivering in my legs.

"Ready, Mrs. Fletcher?" Maresca asked.

"Yes."

"The curtain will be opened and the men will file in. There are six of them. Take your time and look closely at them. What is most important is that you be absolutely sure of your identification."

"If there is one," the defense attorney said.

"That's right, Counselor, if there is one," Maresca agreed with a sigh.

"Where do you get the men to take part in the lineup?" I asked.

"Mostly police officers who look somewhat like the accused, although we sometimes go out to the street to enlist a look-alike. Here we go." He said into a microphone, "Open the curtain and bring them in."

I watched with fascination as the six men entered the brightly lit room on the other side of the glass. The room was devoid of any furniture. Behind the men was a marked chart on the wall against which their height could be judged. They were dressed similarly, in jeans, dark T-shirts, and sneakers. None wore a hat or glasses.

"All right," Maresca said into the microphone, "stand up straight and face the window."

He said to me, "Okay, Mrs. Fletcher, step up to the window and take a long, hard look. There's no rush. Take your time."

Although the six young men looked alike, I immediately recognized the one from L'Aquila. But I withheld announcing it because I didn't want to appear to have rushed to judgment. I methodically took in each man's face, going from left to right, from subject number one to subject number six. I could sense the tension in the room. My declaration had significant ramifications for the accused.

"Mrs. Fletcher?" Maresca said.

"Number two," I said.

"Are you certain?"

"Yes. I'd recognize him anywhere."

"If you'd recognize him anywhere," the defense attorney said, "why did it take you so long to make the ID?"

"I didn't want to appear to be too hasty."

"I suppose you saw his picture in the paper along with yours."

Maresca interrupted the defense attorney's challenge by speaking into the microphone. "Number two, please step forward."

The young man, whose name I now knew was Lombardi, took a few steps toward the glass. His expression was one of sheer defiance and anger, the same expression as when we had locked eyes in L'Aquila. Although I knew that he couldn't see me, I had the feeling that he was challenging me.

"You're sure, Mrs. Fletcher?" Maresca said.

"Yes, I am positive," I said.

"Thank you," Maresca said to the men through the speaker system. "Please leave now."

The curtain closed.

The defense attorney laughed. "This is a joke," he said. "The event happened more than two months ago. It was a chaotic scene, people breaking into a church, guns being fired, a man shot to death right in front of you. Don't tell me that you have a clear vision of him. It's nonsense." With that he stormed out of the room.

Before I left, I gave an official deposition indicating that I had identified the suspect.

"All I can say is thank you, Mrs. Fletcher," Detective Lippi said.

"I'm happy I was able to help," I said. "Now, if you gentlemen don't mind, I'd like to leave."

"Of course."

Detectives Lippi and Maresca accompanied Curso and me as we walked out of the building. Before we parted, Maresca asked how long I would remain in Italy.

"I intend to book a flight for tomorrow," I replied.

"I ask because now that you've made your identification, I'm sure Felice and his men won't be bothering you. Their intention was to intimidate you, to scare you off, which didn't work. There's nothing to be gained by threatening you again."

"I hope you're right," I said.

"*Buona fortuna*, Signora Fletcher."

Curso and I drove to the hotel, where he looked for Vittorio. The big man wasn't there; he hadn't left a message for Curso, nor had anyone seen him.

"Something is wrong," Curso said.

"You said he wasn't especially punctual, Tony. Maybe he had too much to drink and fell asleep, or perhaps he simply forgot."

"Possibly, Jessica, but I'll be uneasy unless I find out what happened. I'm going to drive up to Calcata."

"I hope everything is all right," I said.

"Will you be returning to Chicago?"

"I'm not sure," I said.

"Well, I hope I'll see you again."

He kissed my cheek and started across the lobby.

"Wait, Tony," I called after him.

He stopped and turned.

"I'll come with you."

"You're sure?"

"Yes. If I don't, I'll just spend the time worrying and wondering where he went. After all, you've drawn me into Vittorio's life and your plans for him. I feel like—well, like part of the team."

"Good," he said. "I would be grateful for the company."

He drove fast and skillfully, maneuvering the powerful sports car through Rome's impossible traffic and really speeding up once on the highway. We parked where we had left the car the night before and walked into the village. The plaza wasn't as busy as it had been during our previous visit, and I wondered why. We approached Vittorio's cave, and I paused outside.

"Something the matter?" Curso asked.

"I had a chill, that's all," I said, looking around.

"Stay here," he told me as he entered the cave. "I will call for you if everything is all right."

I shivered, shook it off, then followed him into the gloomy interior.

At the entrance to Vittorio's studio, I saw the outline of Curso's figure standing in the center of the room and turning in a slow circle. It was eerily dark in there; the lights were off and the only illumination was a shaft of light coming from the outside entryway, which I was partially blocking. It took a few seconds for my eyes to adjust to the dim surroundings. The first thing I noticed was that the paintings that had been stacked against the wall were gone. Then I saw the brown form crumpled against the opposite wall.

"Tony?"

"Yes?"

I pointed.

Curso muttered a string of profanity in both Italian and English and knelt beside the large man.

"Is he—?"

"Yes," Curso said. "He is dead."

Chapter Twenty

Vittorio had been killed execution style, with a single gunshot to the back of the head. Whoever had done it—and there was no doubt in my mind that the Mafia was behind it—had added a cruel afterthought. Grappa had been poured over Vittorio's face and the half-empty bottle left propped against his cheek.

I sat down heavily in one of the director's chairs. "How horrible," I murmured, more to myself than to Curso, who stood over the body, fists clenched, an anguished expression on his face.

With a pained sigh, he pulled out his cell phone and called Detective Maresca at police headquarters, informing him of the murder in Calcata.

"They're sending a squad," he said as he sank into another chair.

"I assume they want us to wait," I said.

"Yes," Curso replied, "but not in here."

We left the cave and walked to the plaza, where activity

had picked up. If any of the villagers were aware of the murder that had taken place in their midst, it wasn't evident by their demeanor. There was a festive atmosphere. Musicians performed, artists set up their works in front of the small shops, and children ran around with abandon while their parents sat in cafés drinking wine or coffee in the late-afternoon warmth.

Curso approached one of the artists, a matronly woman dressed in a flowing yellow caftan, and asked if she knew Vittorio.

She laughed. "Sure, I know him, the big fool."

"Did you see him today?" Curso asked.

"No."

"Did you see anyone leave his studio carrying many paintings?"

"No."

I was curious about the same thing. There had to have been at least two dozen works in the cave when we'd first visited Vittorio. The only exit from the cave faced the plaza, and ferrying those works to a vehicle would have required someone to move directly through the center of town and across the square. Surely someone had to have seen the paintings being taken.

Curso questioned a few other people, all of whom gave the same response. No one had seen anything. I decided to do some questioning of my own and approached a group of men seated at an outdoor café. There were four of them, three in their twenties or early thirties and the fourth an elderly gentleman in a wheelchair. Although the temperature was warm, the older man was wrapped up in what looked like a gray horse blanket, its color matching his unruly hair and shaggy beard. A thin half-smoked cigarette hung from his lips.

"*Scusi,*" I said. "*Lei parla inglese?*"

The old man stared at me through cold, dark eyes while two of his younger companions giggled, maybe because of my faulty pronunciation.

"Does anyone speak English?" I asked.

"Me," a young man said. "I speak the English, a little."

"You know the artist Vittorio?"

He looked at the old man before answering. "*Si.* Yes."

"Did you see him today?"

Again a glance at the old man. "No. I don't see him."

"His paintings. Many of them." What was the Italian word for ten? "*Dieci, si?* Maybe two times *dieci.* They are missing. Vittorio is—he is, ah, dead. *Morto.*" I remembered the Italian word for "dead," having used it in a book. "Did you see any men take his paintings away?"

The old man in the wheelchair had observed our exchange without reacting or responding, with just that cold, hard stare. Now he waved a gnarled hand to end the conversation.

I ignored him and said, "Surely you saw what was going on. Vittorio is dead, shot to death. Didn't you hear anything? Any of—"

The old man's action cut off my words and caused me to gasp. He'd withdrawn his other hand from beneath the blanket. It held a handgun, which he pointed directly at me. "*Se ne vada!*" he rasped, waving the weapon at me. "Go! Go!"

Curso, who had witnessed the conversation, grabbed my

arm and pulled me away. "Come, Jessica," he said. "Leave them alone."

"But why would he—?"

"He's Mafia," Curso said. "They are everywhere, even in a town like Calcata. We have to get out of here. Now."

"But the police will be coming."

"They know where to look. We'll talk to them back in Rome. Please, let's leave. It's dangerous to stay here with them."

We drove back to Rome and went directly to police headquarters, where Detective Lippi was in his office. He'd been informed of the murder in Calcata and wanted a statement from us. Curso provided most of it, although it wasn't necessary to go into detail about the documentary and Vittorio's part in it. Curso had been working closely with the police from the first day, and I learned that Lippi had already been interviewed on camera.

Back at my hotel, Curso ushered me into the d'Italia bar, where he was warmly welcomed by the bartender. We settled at a table and he ordered his usual martini while I chose club soda with lemon.

"I'm so sorry, Jessica," Curso said.

"About Vittorio? I'm sorry, too."

"That, and about how your trip has turned out. Too many bad things have happened."

"I certainly never expected to have another gun pointed at me, or to have the Mafia boss personally deliver a threat on my life, but it isn't your fault, Tony."

"You'll leave tomorrow?"

"Yes. If I can."

"To your home in Maine?"

"To Boston. I'll have to arrange for transportation home. What about you? Are you staying extra days in Rome?"

"No. I think I'd better get back to Chicago and figure out how to proceed with the documentary now that Vittorio is dead." He took a sip of his drink and looked at me with sad eyes. "Thank you for not being angry with me."

"Why should I be angry with you?"

He shrugged. "Bringing you to Vittorio. Trying to push you into my documentary. And then it ends up like this. I thought if I could get him out of Italy, I could make sure he was safe, but instead they got to him first, and I put you in danger at the same time. You're a brave lady, Jessica Fletcher, a real trouper."

"I appreciate the compliment, Tony, but I don't deserve it. However, if you'll excuse me, I think I'll go upstairs and make arrangements for my flight."

"May we have a last dinner together tonight?"

"If we make it early and light."

"Then that's what it will be. Six? That's early for dinner here in Italy."

"Six will be fine."

We ate in an intimate brasserie a block from the hotel. Naturally, the conversation revolved around the events since I'd arrived in Rome and our reactions to them. It was after Curso had paid the check that he asked, "Did you succeed in getting a flight tomorrow to Boston?"

"No."

"The flights are full?"

"No, there was available space, but I've changed my mind. I'm flying directly to Chicago."

Chapter Twenty-one

"Marlise?"

"Jessica, dear, where are you calling from?"

"O'Hare. I just got back from Italy." I'd called her house the minute I got off the plane and was pleased that she'd personally answered.

"Good trip?"

"Well, I accomplished what I went there for. Marlise, I'd like to see you."

"I'm here."

"Has anything new developed?"

"Plenty. My wayward stepson has disappeared again."

"When did that happen?"

"Yesterday. I haven't bothered to try to locate him, although Willard is making calls. Frankly, I don't care if they never find him."

How peculiar, I thought. By running again, Wayne had focused the spotlight on himself as a suspect in his father's murder. Was he regretting his accusation against Marlise?

"Where are you staying?" she asked.

"I haven't made a hotel reservation. I'm about to make some calls."

"Stay here. We have oodles of guest rooms, and I could use the company."

"Sure it won't be an inconvenience?"

"Not at all. Grab a cab. See you soon."

It was raining hard by the time my taxi driver navigated city traffic and arrived at Marlise's house. Jet lag had caught up with me and I'd dozed during the last half of the trip, until I was awakened by the driver's "Hey, lady, we're here."

Marlise answered the door. "Mrs. Tetley has taken off for parts unknown," she said as she led me to the parlor. "It's good to see you," she said. "I want to hear all about your trip. How's Tony Curso? Flamboyant fellow, isn't he?"

"He certainly has extravagant taste in cars," I replied. "He's fine. Flying in later today, I believe."

Marlise looked older and more haggard than the last time I'd seen her, even though it had been only a few days. Serious lines had developed beneath her eyes and at the corners of her mouth. Before I'd left for Italy, she'd taken pains to look her best, makeup deftly applied, hair shiny and carefully coiffed, clothes out of the pages of a fashion magazine. Now her hair had been haphazardly pulled back into an untidy ponytail. Her face was bare of paint, and her tan slacks were in need of pressing. I couldn't help but notice that her usually pristine nail polish was chipped in two places. Stress will do that to you, especially the sort of pressure she'd been under lately. But I wasn't looking my best either. She noticed the bruise and the stitch line on my forehead and asked about them.

"An accident in Rome. A couple of young men were horsing around on the Spanish Steps and knocked me down. I'm fine. But you said on the phone that Wayne had taken off again. What happened?"

"Just vanished."

"Was there an incident that prompted him to leave?"

"Yes, I suppose there was. We've been avoiding each other since Jonathon was killed—the advantage of a large house. And I've been spending time at the corporate suite at the hotel. Being in this house is like taking steady doses of poison. But Wayne and I had a run-in just before he left. He'd been drinking or was on drugs. I couldn't tell which. He didn't smell of alcohol, but he certainly behaved as if he was inebriated. He swore at me and kept calling me a murderer, used every four-letter word in the book. It was horrible."

"It must have been."

"I challenged him about taking a lie detector test, told him I had passed, suggested he might not. Maybe that's what sent him running."

"You say that the housekeeper left. Now that Wayne is gone, who's still here?"

"I've persuaded Consuela to stay, or we'd all starve. I haven't been near a kitchen in more years than I care to count. Carl, the chauffeur, is here, but he's talking about leaving, too. I actually wish he would. The financial situation is looking worse than I was led to believe. And, of course, the charming Ms. Hurley shows up, although I have no idea who's paying her. She probably knows where the money is stashed, if there was any left to stash. Who else? Oh, I almost forgot—there's Jonathon's mother, that old witch. How could I possibly forget her?"

I stifled a yawn. It wasn't that I wasn't interested in the conversation, but the long flight had taken its toll and I was desperate for a nap. Even twenty minutes with my eyes closed would be a boon. Marlise sensed my fatigue, or perhaps my stifled yawn was not as subtle as I hoped. She suggested that I get settled, and I readily agreed.

"You have a choice of rooms," she said. "You can stay in Mrs. Tetley's suite on this floor. She demanded that she have quarters in the house; she was always demanding something, that one." Marlise snorted. "Or you can stay in one of the guest rooms upstairs, but I give you fair warning, my mother-in-law is up there." She gave a mock shiver. "What's your pleasure?"

"Whatever is closest," I said with a weary smile.

"Mrs. Tetley's it is, then." She led me to the room, which was at the rear of the house. "Actually, it's quite a nice suite," she said as she opened the door to what would be my room during my stay, as long or as short as it might be. "I changed the sheets and did some dusting after she left," Marlise added. "Judging from what Joe Jankowski tells me, I'd better get used to making my own bed." She plopped down in a small rocking chair by the room's only window, shook her head, and sniffled into a balled-up tissue.

"It's that bad?" I asked.

"It sure is. Every time I talk to him, it gets worse."

The front doorbell chimed.

"Expecting someone?" I asked, as I lifted my travel bag onto a suitcase rack.

"No. And I look a mess." She dabbed at her eyes, checked herself in a mirror, and walked out of the room, leaving the door open. I had started to survey my new surroundings when I heard Marlise say, "Hello, Edgar. I wasn't expecting you."

Peters sounded agitated. "What the hell is going on with Curso?" he demanded.

"What do you mean?" Marlise asked.

"Curso. He's making a documentary about art forgery."

"A documentary? I know nothing about that."

"Yeah, well, Marlise, the guy is obviously a loose cannon. He's supposed to be appraising my art collection and—"

"*Your* art collection?" Marlise snapped. "You mean the one you cheated Jonathon out of."

"A contract's a contract. He needed money and I ponied up. Now Jonathon's dead, which makes it my collection. I paid plenty to become Jonathon's partner."

"He was desperate and you—"

Peters's voice became even louder. "So I made a good deal for myself. That's just business, Marlise. Now you listen to me. If Curso is double dealing, claiming that the works aren't originals because it helps his damned documentary, I'm out big money."

"Edgar, calm down," Marlise said. "I assure you I know nothing about Tony Curso's intentions with this documentary, but maybe Jessica Fletcher does."

"Her? Why would she know anything about it?"

"Because she just came back from Italy. She was there with Tony."

"She was? Yeah, maybe I ought to be talking to her."

"Maybe you should." Marlise raised her voice. "Jessica,

dear," she called out. "Sorry to interrupt your nap. Would you please join us?"

When I entered the parlor, Edgar Peters stood in the center of the room, his face red, his posture combative.

"I didn't know you were here," he said.

"I just arrived."

"You went to Italy with Tony Curso? How come?"

"I didn't go *with* him. We both had business there."

"What was his business?"

"You probably should discuss that with him. I went at the behest of the Italian police to identify a murderer who shot a man the last time I was there. I told you about that incident."

"Yeah, you did. So, what was Curso doing there?"

"Again, Mr. Peters, I think you should ask him. He's due to arrive back in Chicago later tonight."

"What's going on?" he asked.

"Concerning what?" I asked.

"You and Curso."

"I haven't the slightest idea what you're talking about, Mr. Peters."

"What the hell is this documentary all about? I just found out about it. What's Curso doing, using my collection as proof of some kind of nonsense about art forgery?"

I thought for a moment before saying, "He told me about the documentary, but he never mentioned using the collection as proof of anything. I'm sure that whatever appraisal he comes up with will be an honest one. How did *you* hear of the documentary?"

"I know people, including one of Curso's backers. He

tells me that Curso has been filming in my warehouse—without my permission, I might add. If that scoundrel claims that a lot of the art in the collection is forged, I'll sue his socks off. I should have known better than to have him appraise it. As far as I'm concerned, he's a fraud." He guffawed. "*He's* the forgery."

"What do you know about this, Jessica?" Marlise asked.

I'd been going through a mental debate with myself about whether to recount the events in Italy, particularly in Calcata, and decided that it wasn't my place to reveal anything more than people already knew. Marlise probably wouldn't benefit from the art collection. It now belonged to Edgar Peters by virtue of the contract he'd put together with Jonathon, having bought in as a partner. But no matter who ultimately benefited, if Curso was convinced that most of the collection consisted of forgeries, it wouldn't be worth much of anything—to anyone.

Peters had gotten his anger under control and now spoke in a calmer voice. "Look, Mrs. Fletcher—Jessica—I don't have a quarrel with you. But it seems that since you arrived, you've gotten yourself involved with everybody. What do you know about Tony Curso?"

"You introduced us," I said, "and told me what a wonderful person he was. We had dinner together, remember?"

"Sure, and I meant what I said. As far as I knew, he was a straight arrow, with all sorts of credentials as an art expert. But I'm beginning to think he's more of an operator than an impartial appraiser. A documentary? That's a conflict of interest as far as I'm concerned. From what I hear, Curso has to find examples of art fraud if the documentary is to work.

He'd better not use my collection to make his point. I'll take him to court so fast his head will spin."

I didn't see the validity of his claim of a conflict of interest but didn't argue. His disenchantment with Curso was something to bring up with the appraiser himself, not with me. It also occurred to me during our exchange that this man who'd bought into Jonathon Simsbury's art collection had a solid motive for wanting his partner dead. As far as he'd known, the collection contained only legitimate paintings by great artists that would be worth millions at auction.

But what if he'd come to learn that the warehouse might contain forgeries, worthless works? That, too, might have angered him to the point that he would have killed Jonathon for having sold him a half interest in bogus art, albeit skillfully executed by an oversized drunken Italian artist named Vittorio, who'd sold out his talent for money. I thought of the big man lying there in his cave, a bullet hole in the back of his head, his beloved grappa bottle nestled against his cheek. It was a dark, upsetting vision that I knew would haunt me for a very long time.

I changed the topic. "How did you and Jonathon get along?" I asked.

My question seemed to jar him. He looked at me quizzically before answering, "Why would you ask that?"

"Just curious," I said. "While all this talk of Anthony Curso and forged art is taking place, there's still the matter of Jonathon's murder. That should be more important to you."

"Oh, I get it," he said. "I forgot that you write murder mysteries for a living. What are you suggesting, Mrs. Fletcher? That I shot Jonathon?"

"I'm not suggesting anything, Mr. Peters, only that his murder is still to be solved."

"I'm not ignoring Jonathon's murder. What can I do about it, anyway? I just want to know that he was straight with me. I paid a fortune for that collection. It had better be legit."

I sighed and stretched my neck. The notion of catching a nap became appealing again, so I said, "I suggest that you bring all this up with Tony Curso once he's back in Chicago. If you'll excuse me, I've just come off a long flight and I need to rest."

He said nothing as I walked away and returned to my room at the rear of the house. I heard the front door close, and then Marlise joined me.

"What a fool," she muttered, perching on the edge of the bed.

"I'm not sure I'd say that about him," I said as I began unpacking.

"I'm talking about Jonathon. He sold a half interest in the art collection for a pittance."

I was tempted to tell her what Curso had hinted at in Italy, that most of the pieces in the collection were forgeries, but I held back. It was Curso's responsibility to break that news to her and to Peters, not mine.

It isn't easy keeping such things from a friend. The temptation is to share what you know. But discretion was certainly the better part of valor in this case.

"I know you're tired, Jessica, dear, so I'll leave you alone. Before I go, though, I have to ask about this documentary Peters is talking about. Curso must have told you all about it."

"He gave me a brief description," I said.

"And it's about art fraud?"

I nodded and continued my task of hanging clothes in the small closet.

"Does it involve Jonathon's collection?"

Here's where it becomes difficult to withhold what you know from a friend. Once a direct question is asked, you're faced with lying, fudging, or telling what you know despite your promise not to. I dislike the two former options, so I answered truthfully. "I don't know to what extent Jonathon's collection is involved in Tony Curso's documentary, Marlise. I do know that Tony was involved with an Italian painter who made his living painting forgeries of works by the masters. His name was Vittorio."

"*Was* involved?" she said. "He isn't any longer?"

"No. The artist died recently."

"How recently?"

"A day or two ago. He was murdered."

"Oh, Jessica Fletcher, why do I suspect that there's a lot you're not telling me?"

"Because you're right," I said. "But at the moment, I desperately need to climb into this bed before I fall on my nose. Please understand, Marlise. You can ask anything you wish about the art collection when Tony Curso is back. He knows a lot more than I, and I don't want to give you incorrect information."

"The art collection means nothing to me, Jessica. My lawyer says it now belongs to Peters. I won't see a cent from it. It's just that maybe the collection had something to do with Jonathon's murder. I wouldn't put it past Peters. He's smarmy."

"We'll talk later," I said. "I promise." This time I didn't try to stifle my yawn.

She left and quietly closed the door behind her.

I took off my shoes, fluffed up the pillows, and stretched out. It felt heavenly to be in a prone position after spending the long trip strapped into an airline seat and the backseats of cabs. As I hovered between wakefulness and sleep, I questioned my decision to return to Chicago. I could be home in my own bed in Cabot Cove. And I could leave the resolution of this case to the Chicago police, who were undoubtedly capable of seeing through Wayne's lies, as I was convinced they were.

The situation surrounding Jonathon Simsbury's death was tangled at best, and had the potential of ending up among the one-third of murders that are never solved. Would my presence make a difference? It appeared that it wouldn't, and I second-guessed my entire involvement with the Simsbury family and its muddled relationships.

Finally I dozed off, but slept for no more than an hour. I was awakened by a commotion somewhere in the house, loud voices from a male and a female. One belonged to Marlise; the man's voice could have belonged to Wayne Simsbury, although I couldn't be sure. I slipped into my shoes, went into the small bathroom adjacent to the bedroom, splashed some water on my face, and headed for the parlor. My assumption had been correct. The prodigal son had returned.

Wayne was sprawled in a chair in front of Marlise. From where I stood in the doorway, he looked bedraggled, unkempt. His eyes were red and watery and his speech was slightly slurred.

"You're drunk," Marlise said. "You reek of alcohol."

"So what?" he responded, as his head fell back against the cushion of the chair.

"Were you drunk when you shot your father?" she pressed, standing over him.

"Shut up, Marlise."

"Don't tell me to shut up, you sniveling excuse for a man. Where have you been?"

"Away from here—and you."

They seemed not to realize that I was witnessing the confrontation. Marlise turned suddenly, saw me, and said, "Look what the cat dragged in, Jessica, dear."

I stepped into the room and greeted Wayne.

He looked up, startled that I was there.

"Any chance of getting some hot tea, and maybe some sweets?" I asked Marlise. "Is there any coconut custard pie? I know that's a favorite of Wayne's."

Marlise looked at me quizzically—actually it was more of a bewildered expression. "Why should I wait on him?"

"I'm thinking we need to sober him up, and food is the first step."

"All right. I'll see what Consuela has."

"Hi, Mrs. Fletcher," Wayne said, as the sound of Marlise's heels on the floor echoed down the hall.

"Hello, Wayne." I pulled up a hassock in front of him and sat. "I'm glad to see that you're home."

"I just couldn't stand it here," he said, avoiding my eyes.

"The way you felt when you came to my house. I understand."

I thought for a moment that he might cry, but he inhaled and ran a fist over his eyes.

"Where did you go this time?" I asked.

He shrugged. "Just a girl's house. I didn't really drink that much. I just spilled a beer on my shirt, and came home to change."

"And who is this 'just a girl'?"

"She used to be my girlfriend. We were in a band together."

"I remember you telling me about her and the band. Are you still playing music?"

He guffawed. "Nah. I jam with myself sometimes, you know, play along with CDs. I'm not that good."

"But you were good enough to go on the road with the band before. Maybe you need to practice, become more serious about your music."

"I don't care about it. I don't care about anything anymore."

"But other people care about you, Wayne. I do, and your grandmother does. I'm sure that Marlise does, too, when she isn't furious with you for accusing her of murder."

He twisted in the chair and locked eyes with me. "Give me a break," he said. "The only person she cares about is herself."

"Don't be so quick to judge," I said. I didn't know how far to take my soft approach with him. He seemed to have reacted positively to it when he was at my house, and I hoped that discussing things in a calmer atmosphere would be productive. His disappearances weren't of particular concern to me. What I was hoping was that I could lead him into a conversation about his claim that he'd seen Marlise shoot his father. I didn't expect my effort to be successful, but it seemed worth a try. I still didn't believe him, although I had nothing tangible upon which to base that feeling.

Consuela interrupted as she delivered a tray with tea and two slices of coconut custard pie.

"See what you miss by running away?" I said to Wayne.

He managed a smile, and reached for a piece of pie.

"Wayne," I said, as I poured a cup of tea for myself, "I know this is something that you don't want to hear, but I'm going to say it anyway. You accused Marlise of shooting your father. But there's no other evidence to support that claim."

"Isn't my word good enough?"

"Probably not, especially since you recanted your first story. Any good lawyer will use that to cast doubt on your new statement. It might be enough to sway the jury if the case ever got that far."

He started to say something, but I held up my hand. "Please, just hear me out," I said. "Without any additional evidence, it's highly unlikely that the case will even get to court in the first place. I doubt Marlise will be charged with the murder. But that's all right. I'm convinced that someone else killed your dad. My point is that since accusing Marlise won't result in anything happening to her—and *if* you were mistaken—then now is the time to retract what you said and put an end to what is obviously a painful situation for both you and Marlise."

Taking another slice of pie was his response.

I continued. "You and Marlise both have lives to get on with, Wayne. I don't know how much will be left in your father's estate for either of you."

He stopped eating and stared at me.

I forged ahead. "Which means that she'll have to put together a new life, maybe going back to working as a journalist, and you have—well, you have your music if that's what you wish to do. Think of how wonderful it would be if the two of you could recapture a pleasant relationship and support each other as you move into the future. But that can never happen if your accusation continues to hover over both of you."

He stood up abruptly, almost knocking the tray over.

"I don't want to talk about it," he snapped.

"That's your prerogative," I said. "All I ask is that you *think* about what I've said. Life is really just a matter of making decisions. You make good ones and things go pretty well, barring acts of nature or other unforeseeable calamities. You make bad ones and things don't go so well. You can have a bright future, Wayne, but only if you make the right decisions."

For a moment, I thought I'd gotten through to him. His bloodshot eyes pleaded for understanding. He looked down at me and extended his open palms as though to say, "I'm scared."

That prompted me to add, "Nothing bad will happen if you tell Mr. Corman and Marlise that you misspoke about seeing her kill your father. Because if you don't tell the truth about that, you'll have to carry that burden for the rest of your life." I deliberately chose the term "misspoke" as a gentler substitute for "lying." Wayne had seen enough talking political heads on television to recognize the euphemism.

He cast a final glance at what was left of the pie on his plate before leaving the room.

Marlise returned a few minutes later.

"What was the tea and pie routine all about?" she asked.

"I wanted to have a calm, rational conversation with him," I explained.

"And?"

I shrugged. "We'll see," I said. "We'll see. Have the detectives been back?"

"Not recently."

"I'd like to speak with them again," I said.

"Why?"

"I have some ideas about the investigation I'd like to share with them. Do you know if they questioned Edgar Peters?"

"I don't."

"The household staff was questioned."

"Sure—anybody who was here the night of the murder."

"Was there any indication that Jonathon might have had a visitor the night he was killed, someone whom he let in, perhaps met with privately in his office, without anyone else being aware of it?"

"Are you referring to Peters?"

"Or others."

She shook her head.

"Is it possible that his mother might have heard someone with Jonathon?"

Marlise's laugh was dismissive. "God, no, Jess. She's half deaf and plays her TV at maximum volume."

"Where is her room?"

"Upstairs, at the head of the stairs."

"I'd like to see it."

"Go on up. I'm sure she's there."

"I'd rather see it when she *isn't* there."

"She'll be down for dinner. She always eats alone, before anyone else, then heads back upstairs."

"Would you take me there while she's having dinner this evening?"

"Sure, although I don't know what you hope to see in the dragon's lair. By the way, did you get your nap in?"

"A short but refreshing one. Marlise, I need to make some calls back home."

"Use the phone in this room," she said, pointing to a cordless telephone on the small desk. "I'll leave you alone."

She closed the door behind her and I finished my cup of tea. The pie was appealing, but I fought the urge. The trip to Italy had been a high-calorie indulgence, thanks to Tony Curso, and I wasn't pleased with the few extra pounds I'd put on.

I crossed to the desk and picked up the sleek black phone but then put it back down and took my cell phone out of my purse. The atmosphere in the Simsbury house served to heighten my paranoia. There were undoubtedly extensions throughout the house, and I didn't want to chance anyone listening in on my conversations.

Chapter Twenty-two

Marlise led me to the elder Mrs. Simsbury's room while her mother-in-law was dining alone downstairs. The room was surprisingly messy, although I couldn't expect a wheelchair-bound elderly woman to spend much time tidying up. Hadn't the housekeeper taken on that chore? It didn't look as though she had. Perhaps the old woman had barred her from the room.

"When they were looking for the murder weapon, did the police search this room, too?" I asked Marlise.

"Without question," she replied with a wry smile. "They left no pillow unturned. Mrs. Tetley was in a snit for days. They even searched the elevator. Jonathon had it installed when his mother was no longer ambulatory. She's the only one who ever uses it."

"Where is the elevator?"

"Just down the hall. I'll show it to you when you're finished here."

Even though Marlise had brought me to see the room, I

felt a bit guilty inspecting it without the owner's permission and didn't stay long. I'm not sure what I was looking for, perhaps just a sense of how other people in the household lived. We took a quick look at the elevator—only large enough to hold a wheelchair and perhaps an attendant pushing it—and returned to the parlor. We waited until Mrs. Simsbury had finished her meal and gone back to her room before taking seats at the dining room table, at which point Consuela served our own dinner.

"I hope you don't mind my saying so, Jessica, dear, but you look exhausted."

"I think the jet lag is catching up to me," I said.

"Well, I'll let you go in a minute," she said. "Tell me your plans for tomorrow?"

"I'd like to meet with the detectives on your case, if they'll talk to me. Marlise, just how dire is the financial picture for you?"

She blew a stream of air at a lock of hair that had fallen over her forehead before answering. "According to Joe Jankowski, Jonathon was flat broke. He'd borrowed a gazillion dollars to keep the company afloat, and all those loans are long past due. Apparently, each time Jonathon needed money, he ceded a little more of the art collection to Ed Peters. The whole thing now belongs to Peters, so I won't see anything out of it. The house belongs to his mother and—"

"It does?"

"Yes. How's that for a slap in my face? Jonathon put it in her name for tax reasons, or so he said, and he never changed it after we were married. It seems I've been a tenant here for years with the old lady my landlord. Joe says she can't kick me out until the will is probated, and he's holding off on that to see what happens with the murder investigation."

Marlise shook her head and sighed. "I used to think that I was pretty savvy—you know, worldly. I thought I had street smarts and could avoid the pitfalls that so many people end up falling victim to. But I was blinded by Jonathon's charm and optimism, always ready to have my curiosity about our finances bought off by a trip to Europe or a cruise on the company yacht, a new piece of jewelry or a shopping spree at an upscale store, all of it bought on the come, as they say, borrowed money, leveraged money. I can't believe how stupid I was."

"You're not the first person to have been taken in by charm, Marlise. Look at all the victims of deceitful Wall Street investors who promised great returns and then used the money of those who trusted them to keep their Ponzi schemes afloat."

"Those investors must have been so naïve."

"Or greedy," I said, fighting a yawn.

"You're suggesting I was greedy?" She gave me a sardonic smile. "I guess I was."

I admired her honesty when it came to admitting her own fallibility under the circumstances, but I certainly wasn't brimming over with sympathy. As I'd told her stepson, life involves making decisions. Blinded by her rich lifestyle, Marlise had obviously made some bad ones, but at least she recognized her mistakes.

"Did Susan Hurley know what was going on? You once said she knew more about Jonathon's affairs than you did."

"If she did, she wasn't about to share that knowledge with

me," Marlise said, her mouth a tight line. "If Jonathon's murder holds one consolation for me, it's that Susan didn't get to complete her campaign to steal my husband. Unless, of course, she was the one who killed him."

"Do you think she did?" I asked.

Marlise shrugged. "I only know it wasn't me, despite what Wayne claims." A sly grin crossed her face. "Wouldn't it be ironic if Jonathon promised to take care of her, and then she learned he had run out of money? Is breach of promise a legal excuse for murder? I like that idea."

Marlise was being flippant, and I was too tired to respond in kind, but a thought occurred to me. "Joe Jankowski seems like an intelligent man, Marlise. He's been Jonathon's adviser, as I understand it. Didn't he ever step in and stop the financial bleeding?"

"Joe is someone who collects his fees and doesn't lose a minute's sleep over whether his clients go under. I suppose he advised Jonathon of how grim things were, but that doesn't mean that Jonathon would listen. He didn't listen to anyone. For Jonathon, everything would miraculously get better. He personified the term 'cockeyed optimist.'"

"What about Jankowski?" I asked, rubbing an eye. "I assume that he's owed money, too."

"Plenty. He told me that he hadn't been paid for months."

"Then why would he keep working for Jonathon?"

"He must have his reasons, Jessica. Frankly, I don't really care whether Joe hasn't been paid or not. I have myself to worry about. Now go to bed before you nod off in front of me. I tend to be offended when people fall asleep while I'm talking."

I thanked Marlise for her hospitality and her understanding, and went to my room. Just walking down the hall revived me a bit. I sank into an easy chair and tried to sort things out. It took me less than ten minutes to decide that if I couldn't make headway in solving Jonathon Simsbury's murder over the next two days, I'd pack up and go home. *Home*. Cabot Cove, Maine, never sounded so good.

The house was quiet that night. I climbed into bed intending to finish the last chapter of a novel I'd started reading on the flight from Italy, but my eyes refused to stay open. The next thing I knew it was six the following morning. I showered and dressed, and read the last four pages of my book before going downstairs. Marlise was in the kitchen with Consuela.

"Good morning, Jessica, dear. Sleep well?"

"As a matter of fact, I did. Good morning, Consuela."

The cook nodded and busied herself at the sink.

A harsh voice from the dining room said, "I want more tea!"

"Jonathon's charming mother," Marlise said. "She's always shouting at somebody for something."

Seconds later Mrs. Simsbury wheeled herself into the kitchen. She stopped just inside the door and looked at me. "You planning on taking up residence here?" she growled.

"Good morning," I said pleasantly.

Wayne Simsbury appeared behind her. He was sober and looked considerably more put together than he had the previous afternoon.

Marlise excused herself and swiftly exited the room by another door.

"Where's my tea?" Mrs. Simsbury demanded of the cook.

"The water is boiling, ma'am," Consuela replied.

"You can't even boil water properly," the old woman snarled.

"Yes, ma'am," Consuela said, checking the kettle. "It will be ready soon."

"I hear you've been lobbying my grandson," Mrs. Simsbury said to me.

"We did have a nice talk yesterday."

"You leave him alone," she said. "You pack up your things and leave. This is my house. We don't need the likes of you snooping around."

"I'm Marlise's guest," I said. "She invited me to stay."

"I'll be glad when she's gone, too. A bunch of leeches and interlopers." She muttered something else under her breath, pivoted her wheelchair, and pushed past Wayne, who stood transfixed. The door closed behind him and he stepped into the kitchen.

It was evident to me that he wanted to say something. I waited.

The whistle of the kettle on the stove startled us both. Consuela poured the boiling water into the teapot and carried it past Wayne to his impatient grandmother in the dining room.

"Have you thought over what we discussed yesterday?" I asked him.

"I don't know what to do," he said, almost in a whisper.

"It's simple," I said. "Do the *right* thing. Tell the truth."

He started to speak, but his grandmother's reappearance in the doorway stopped him.

"Don't talk to that woman," she said.

When he didn't move, she added loudly, "Come with me, Wayne, and do it now! My tea is getting cold."

He left with her. It was now clear that if I were ever to be successful in persuading Wayne to change his testimony about Marlise, it would happen only outside the presence of his overbearing grandmother.

After Mrs. Simsbury departed, Marlise rejoined me in the kitchen and we shared breakfast before I called for a taxi to take me to police headquarters. I had made up my mind to simply show up rather than phone ahead. It was a ploy I'd used before, knowing that it would be more difficult for the officers to put me off in person than over the phone.

When I reached headquarters, I was informed that Detective Witmer wasn't there but Detective Munsch would be able to accommodate my request for a few minutes of his time. He came to the main reception area shortly and greeted me, although he gave off a vibe that said he wasn't sure why I was there. I quickly explained.

"I've just returned from Italy," I said, "and I'm staying with Marlise Simsbury at her home. I've been doing a great deal of thinking about Jonathon Simsbury's murder and would appreciate the opportunity to speak with you about it."

"The department is doing everything we can, Mrs. Fletcher. Pressuring us won't make a bit of difference."

"Of course. I wouldn't presume to pressure you, Detective Munsch. I'm not here to criticize either. I promise I won't take up much of your time. Surely you can spare me fifteen minutes."

He said through a sigh, "Sure. Come on back."

His office was cramped and littered with file folders. He wore a red-and-white striped shirt, red suspenders, and a burgundy tie. A handgun was nestled securely in a holster beneath his arm. "Have a seat," he said, "if you can find one."

I moved a pile of papers that had been on a chair to the floor and took a seat.

"Okay, Mrs. Fletcher, what's on your mind about the Simsbury murder?"

"May I first ask what progress you've made in the case?"

"Sure. If we'd made any progress, I'd cut you off right now. But the truth is, we don't have any leads aside from what the Simsbury kid claims, that he saw his stepmother shoot his father. As far as I'm concerned, that should be enough to bring her in, but the DA has a different view of it. He wants corroboration. We don't have any at the moment, but we're working to change that."

"Let me be frank with you, Detective. I don't believe Wayne Simsbury's allegation."

"Neither does Mrs. Simsbury's attorney. But unless the kid recants, his accusation is still hanging out there."

"The last time we talked, you or your colleague Detective Witmer indicated that the murder weapon was never found. I assume that your search for it was extensive."

He looked at me as though I'd accused him of corruption. "You bet it was," he said. "What makes you think otherwise?"

"Please don't misunderstand," I said. "It just seems strange to me that whoever killed Jonathon Simsbury was able to get rid of the weapon—unless the killer was someone from outside the household and took it with him or her. Did you interview his business associates?"

"Like who?"

"His partner in his art collection, Edgar Peters."

"Peters? Yeah, we talked to him."

"Can he account for his whereabouts that night?"

"As a matter of fact, he did; it's not an airtight alibi, but enough to satisfy us. We weren't looking at him as a suspect anyway, but he did give us a rundown of his activities during the time of the murder."

"With someone to confirm it?"

"Look, Mrs. Fletcher, I've got a busy day ahead of me. What else is on your mind?"

"The weapon," I said. "If the shooter was someone from the Simsbury household, getting rid of the weapon wouldn't be easy unless—"

"Unless that 'someone' took it with him when he left the house, like the son. He flew the coop right after we questioned him."

"Correct. Or unless the weapon is still somewhere in the house."

"Unlikely."

"But possible."

"Forget it. If the weapon *was* in the house the night of the murder, and somehow my guys missed it—and I doubt that very much—it'd be long gone by now."

"Would you consider conducting another search?"

He shrugged. "I wouldn't, but I'll run it past Detective Witmer. He's the lead investigator."

"I can't ask for more than that," I said. "You're aware that the housekeeper, Mrs. Tetley, has left."

"Uh-huh. We ruled her out as a suspect."

"I'm sure you were right in doing so. The victim was having an affair with his administrative assistant, Susan Hurley.
How closely did you question her?"

His bored demeanor changed. He leaned forward in his
chair and said, "Are you a PI in your spare time, Mrs.
Fletcher?"

"I'm not a private investigator, but I do notice things and
remember what I hear."

"Well, suppose you tell me what you've heard about Mr.
Simsbury's adultery."

I explained how Marlise Simsbury had confided in me
about the affair, ending with, "A jealous or betrayed woman
has been known to kill before."

He took his first note since we'd started talking.

"That could be applied to Marlise Simsbury, you know."

"But also to Ms. Hurley."

He grunted and jotted another note on his pad.

"And surely you know about the new will that Jonathon
never got to sign, leaving ninety percent of everything to his
wife."

He made another note without commenting.

"That gives Wayne Simsbury a strong motive to kill his
father before Jonathon was able to execute it."

He looked up from his notepad. "And gets the wife off
the hook. Did she know about the new will?"

"She did. She was eager for her husband to sign the new
one, which would have cut Wayne's share down to ten percent. There's simply no motive for her to have killed him in
advance of the new will being signed."

He held up his hand. "Wait a minute," he said. "You were

talking about jealous women killing people. Maybe she was upset about the affair and shot her husband to get even."

"Good point," I agreed, "but knowing Marlise Simsbury the way I do, I'm certain that money would have trumped jealousy."

"Maybe he changed his mind about the will, and she got furious and popped him off."

"If Jonathon had had second thoughts, Marlise would have been far more likely to redouble her efforts to convince him to sign—in a loving manner."

He conspicuously looked at his watch.

"I know," I said, "my time is almost up. Give me a few more minutes to tell you about an experience I just had in Italy." I gave him a shorthand account of what had happened to me while in Rome, along with the story about the artist Vittorio and Tony Curso's involvement with him.

"So you see, the art collection may not hold the value people expect it to, and if it's made up primarily of forgeries, that might have played a role in Jonathon Simsbury's murder. That's why I was interested in Edgar Peters's whereabouts the night of the shooting. He was Jonathon's partner in ownership of the collection."

"Interesting story, Mrs. Fletcher, but we interviewed Peters and he is not a suspect at this time."

"Fair enough. I just wanted to be certain you had all the facts to consider. Jonathon led a complicated life and had dealings with many people who may have had reason to kill him."

I thanked Detective Munsch for his time and left. When I returned to the house, I spotted Tony Curso's blue Austin

Healey parked in front. It brought a smile to my lips. Despite the harrowing experiences he'd led me into, it would be good to see him again.

Curso was in the parlor with Marlise when I came in. He jumped to his feet, crossed the room, and gave me a hug, followed by a peck on the cheek. "Lovely seeing you again," he said. He was dressed in a black-and-white checked sports coat over a crimson button-down shirt open at the collar, jeans, and loafers sans socks.

"Tony was just telling me about your adventures in Rome," Marlise said. "You held out on me. God, you ended up in the hospital after being pushed down some steps, and you and Tony were together when you discovered the body of this Italian artist. What was his name?"

"Vittorio," Curso provided. He said to me, "You're just in time, Jessica. I was about to reveal to Marlise the true value of her late husband's art collection."

I took a chair and listened. Marlise took the news calmly, which didn't surprise me. After all, she didn't have a stake in the collection. When Curso paused, she laughed. "You'll have to excuse me for finding this funny," she said, "but it's just another example of Jonathon's blindness. He laid out millions of dollars for art that he was sure would appreciate, but it turns out to be worthless, like everything else he was involved with." She laughed even louder and longer. "And Peters. I want to be a fly on the wall when you tell him what the collection is worth, Tony. I wouldn't want to miss seeing his face when he gets the news." She slapped her thigh. "What a hoot."

I couldn't share Marlise's mirth at learning that her

husband's paintings were forgeries. Her reaction seemed inappropriate, even given the fact that the diminished assessment of the collection would have no impact on her. I didn't say anything, but silently I pitied Jonathon, a man who'd been handed a lucrative family business and who'd run it into the ground through impetuous, ill-informed choices, including buying expensive European art based upon the false assurances of others. I also felt a modicum of sympathy for Edgar Peters, although that feeling was tempered by the man's greedy self-interest in his transactions with his partner.

Marlise's laughing jag passed and she asked Curso, "When will you tell Peters?"

"The next time I see him. I promised to have a final appraisal of the art in the warehouse by tomorrow. There are some originals in the mix, but none of those are of high value."

A question struck me at that moment. Had Jonathon been as naïve as Marlise made him out to be? Had he become aware that most of his art collection consisted of forgeries, and had he knowingly suckered Peters into buying a half share? In some regards, that possibility was more satisfying than Jonathon's reputation as a hopeless romantic and bungler.

We were interrupted by the arrival of Joe Jankowski. He lumbered into the room, muttered a hello to everyone, and took the largest chair.

"What brings you here, Joe?" Marlise asked.

"I need to talk to you, Marlise."

"Here I am, Joe."

Jankowski glanced at Curso and me.

"We'll leave you two alone," I said, motioning for Curso to follow me. We walked down the hall toward the kitchen, and Curso stopped to peruse the art on the walls. "These are probably worth more than the whole damn warehouse," he said, "provided they aren't forgeries, too."

"Funny," I said, "but I hadn't even looked at them. You're back in Chicago to work on the documentary?"

"Right. I also have a few classes to teach at the university. Look, Jessica, we've been through a lot together the past week."

"No argument from me."

"I really want you to work with me on the documentary *and* a book."

"Tony," I said, "this is not the time to discuss it. I will say that the documentary is out of the question. As for a book, I can't even consider the possibility at the moment."

"Okay, but having you on the documentary would add immediacy to the story. You've lived it, first when you were in that church when the theft and murder took place, and now where Vittorio's involved. Horrible what happened to him. I met with Maresca and Lippi after you left. No question that it was a Mafia hit."

"Will they ever find who shot him?"

"Doubtful, but maybe they'll be able to track down the paintings the thieves took from his cave. Come to dinner with me tonight and I'll tell you what I've learned."

"Thank you, no," I answered, but something prompted me to reconsider. "On second thought, dinner would be fine, but we must include Marlise in the invitation."

"Of course. I'd be delighted."

"I wouldn't have looked forward to having dinner here, and it's even more uncomfortable for Marlise. Have you met the senior Mrs. Simsbury?"

"No, haven't had the pleasure."

"She's not happy that I'm here. She's accused me of 'snooping.' I don't know, Tony, maybe she's right. Originally, I came here to get Wayne Simsbury to return to Chicago, thinking that he wanted to help Marlise. It turned out to be quite the opposite. I shouldn't have come back to Chicago after the last episode in Rome. I've been thinking a great deal about it. I belong at home in Cabot Cove with my friends, sitting at my computer writing my next novel. My dear friend Seth Hazlitt—he's a physician and a very good one—is always critical of me when I end up involved in real-life murder, which has happened with too much regularity."

"Sounds like you lead a dangerous life," he said.

"I never considered it dangerous. The problem is that it's brought me into contact—too close contact—with too many bad people, people whose greed and outsized ambition and arrogance have led them to do terrible things. Back in Cabot Cove, we treasure peace and the respect we have for each other. At least most of us do."

"Sounds like an idyllic community. Is there a man in your life there?"

"Many."

"Oh," he said with a chuckle.

"But not in the sense you're talking about. I had a wonderful marriage to a man named Frank, a gentle, bright, caring person. He died. Since then, I've busied myself writing and nurturing the many friendships I'm blessed with. There is one man who looms large. He's a Scotland Yard senior inspector, lives in London. His name is George Sutherland. He would like to carry our relationship to another level, and I have to admit that it is an appealing idea. But I'm not ready for a serious commitment, and not sure I ever will be."

"You never know what life will bring."

"That's true. What about you, Tony? Have you ever been married?"

He chuckled. "No. I've come close but never found the perfect woman."

"Is there such a thing?"

"I suppose not. I have to admit that I'm selfish. I kind of enjoy being footloose and fancy-free, able to pick up and go someplace on a whim, indulge myself without having to be concerned about someone else."

"It's good that you recognize that about yourself, Tony. It'll save grief for you and that 'perfect' woman, should she ever materialize."

I walked him to the front door.

"Pick you up at seven?" he asked.

"That'll be fine. I look forward to it."

Marlise was still closeted with Joe Jankowski after Tony Curso left, so I decided to walk off some of the extra pounds I'd accumulated while in Italy. I headed in the direction of Lake Michigan, which wasn't far away. Once there, I strolled along the lakeside, enjoying the brisk breeze off the water and the sun on my face. The change in my mood here on the lake was dramatic. I felt closed in back at the house, almost suffocated by the ill will that existed there. I was witnessing the deterioration of a family that from the outside appeared to have been blessed with riches and the good life that money can buy. But inside that impressive house were bitterness, jealousies, greed, and accusations that had torn the family apart.

I could have stayed at the lake for the rest of the day but thought I'd better get back to the house to tender our dinner invitation to Marlise. The door was open, but she wasn't in the parlor. Rather than hunt through the house for her, I went directly to my room. At five thirty, Marlise knocked on my door. "Up for dinner out?" she asked.

"I was going to ask you the same thing," I said. "I've made arrangements to go out with Tony Curso."

Her eyebrows went up. "You two are becoming quite an item."

"Don't be silly, Marlise. He asked me to dinner and I accepted, but I was hoping you would join us. Will you? It'll be fun being together."

"How will Tony feel about that?"

"He said he'd be delighted. May I call him and tell him you said yes?"

Curso reaffirmed his pleasure in having Marlise join us for dinner, and I passed along that message to her. He also said that he'd bring his other car, which had more room than his two-seater Austin Healey.

Curso's larger vehicle was a long, shiny black Cadillac with a red leather interior and a dashboard replete with electronics that looked like the inside of a space capsule.

"How can a man get so lucky to be going to dinner with a lovely lady on each arm?" he said as we drove to the restaurant, which was on Milwaukee Avenue, away from down-town. "We're going to Bob Chinn's Crab House, the best seafood in Chicago. Absolutely the best, fresh from the cold, deep waters of the ocean and cooked to perfection."

Tony Curso at his superlative best.

The Crab House was big and bustling—Curso told us that it served more than three thousand dinners every night and at one time had been the highest-grossing restaurant in the country. He knew, of course, not only one of the bar-tenders but the manager as well, and we were given a prime table on the outskirts of the busy scene. Curso and Marlise ordered drinks, his usual martini made to order by his friend behind the bar, and a double scotch on the rocks for her.

"It feels so good to be out," she said as we scanned the sizable menu.

"You've been through the wringer," Curso said, patting her hand. "But I may have something to pick up your spirits."

"Oh? What's that?"

"Well, as you know, I'm producing a documentary about art theft and forgery. I've invited Jessica to participate, but she's declined." He cocked his head at me. "Still your deci-sion, Jessica?"

"Yes," I said.

"Which I graciously accept. But you, Marlise, would be a perfect fit. You've had on-camera experience when you worked as a TV journalist, and you're very familiar with the impact of art theft and forgery. In other words, I'm offering you the job of hosting my documentary, accompanied by a substantial fee, of course."

I had to smile. Anthony Curso was, among many things, the consummate operator, ready to pounce at every opportunity. I didn't view him negatively; he was an honest man with multiple interests. Nothing wrong with that. I looked at Marlise, and from the expression on her face I could tell she was weighing the offer.

"What do you say?" Curso asked as the waiter came for our food order.

She checked me before exclaiming, "I say let's do it!"

Chapter Twenty-three

The dinner ended on a decidedly upbeat note. Marlise was thrilled at having work on the documentary to look forward to, and Curso spent the rest of the meal waxing poetic about the project and giving Marlise, and me, a scene-by-scene account of how it would be put together and distributed. He was working closely with the Italian art detectives, and the direct link between Vittorio's brutal murder and the Italian Mafia's role in international art theft and forgery would add an undeniable and unexpected dramatic dimension to the documentary.

He dropped us off at Marlise's house and bid us good night with, "You two lovely ladies make my heart sing. *Buona sera. Siete belle.* You both are beautiful."

Marlise was in high spirits when we entered the house. She kicked off her shoes and flopped on a love seat in the parlor. "Maybe there is a God after all," she said. "Isn't he charming?"

"Yes, he is, and I'm so pleased for you, Marlise."

"The cavalry has arrived in the nick of time. Joe told me today that I'm on my own. There's nothing to inherit, and the estate owes him a small fortune. I wasn't sure what I'd do once this nightmare was over. If the documentary is a success, it could open doors for me to get back in the business."

"I'm sure that will happen," I said, stifling a yawn. I looked at my watch. "It's after eleven," I said, this time through the yawn that insisted on coming. "I'm heading to bed."

"And you sleep tight, my friend. If you hadn't invited me to join you and Tony at dinner, this might not have happened. I owe you, Jessica."

"What you owe me is to get on with your life. Good night. See you in the morning."

I undressed for bed and used the adjoining bathroom for my nightly ablutions. I climbed under the covers and sighed. Although nothing had been resolved where Jonathon's murder was concerned, my friend seemed poised to start a new life on a positive note. Without corroborating evidence, Wayne's allegation against her likely wouldn't hold up. More important, I'd finally dismissed even the possibility that Wayne had been truthful and that my friend was a murderess.

I considered starting another book I'd brought with me, but my drooping eyelids dictated otherwise. A series of images flashed across my mind like a slide show as I hovered between sleep and wakefulness.

The first was of Vittorio's cave, a pleasant vision that had him very much alive, a glass of grappa in his hand, while he entertained me and Curso. But the slide that replaced it was distinctly more ominous. Vittorio was slumped in a corner, the back of his head blown away, his grappa bottle propped against his face as though the killer had created a piece of performance art.

I squeezed my eyes shut against that picture until the next visual appeared on my mental screen. It was of the young man who'd knocked me down the Spanish Steps, a crooked, satisfied smile on his face. That image morphed into the face of the art thief and killer Danilo Lombardi. He, too, smiled as he held a gun to my face. I had to both shut my eyes and shake my head to make him disappear.

Visions of my home and the streets of Cabot Cove came next, happy, smile-inducing snapshots of the town and people that I love. I sighed and smiled during that portion of my personal visual journey, the perfect note on which to turn off the projector and go to sleep.

But the projector wouldn't shut off. I was back in Calcata, in the plaza, and that scene snapped me awake and had me sitting straight up in bed. I got up, found my slippers, put on my robe, and stepped into the hall. It was dark except for one small lamp high on a wall. I went to the room occupied by the elder Mrs. Simsbury and put my ear to it. The TV was on—a sitcom, judging from the canned laugh track. I knocked. When there was no response, I tried again, louder this time. Still nothing. I turned the doorknob, and the door opened. All lights were off in the room; the only illumination came from the TV set. Mrs. Simsbury wasn't there.

I closed the door and went to the head of the stairs. I heard voices from somewhere downstairs, muffled voices, the words indistinguishable. I carefully descended the stairs in the dim light, holding the banister tightly until I reached the ground floor. I knew now that the voices came from the parlor, and that one of them belonged to Mrs. Simsbury. The parlor door was closed and I stood outside until I recognized that the second voice was Wayne Simsbury. I drew a deep breath, opened the door, and stepped through.

Mrs. Simsbury was in her wheelchair, covered with her usual red-and-black plaid caftan that shrouded her from the waist down. Wayne was in a robe and slippers, and stood a few feet in front of her. My unannounced arrival startled them. Wayne looked at me and turned away. His grandmother jutted her chin out and said, "What are you doing here?"

"I couldn't sleep," I said, "and heard you here. But—"

"Get out!"

My response was to close the door.

"I told you to get out," she repeated.

"Not before I ask a few questions," I said defiantly.

Wayne turned to face me. "Maybe it's better if you leave, Mrs. Fletcher."

I stared Mrs. Simsbury down. As I did, the sight of her was replaced by a different one, one I'd seen while in bed, the aging Mafioso in a wheelchair in the Calcata plaza, covered with what appeared to be a heavy gray horse blanket, his eyes as dark and cold as pieces of anthracite, the handgun he pulled beneath the blanket menacing.

Mrs. Simsbury replaced that picture.

I said to Wayne, "I know that you lied about Marlise, and that your grandmother won't let you tell the truth." I directed my next comment to her. "Why, Mrs. Simsbury, don't you want your grandson to be honest?"

Wayne started to answer, but she stopped him with, "Keep your mouth shut. Say nothing to this prying trouble-maker. She wants to hurt you the way they did."

"'They'?" I said. "Who? Marlise? His father?"

"I told you to leave," she said.

"Not until I prove something to myself," I said in a strong voice to match hers. I addressed Wayne. "There was a time when I thought you might have shot your father and were blaming Marlise to get yourself off the hook. Now I believe you when you say you didn't do it. But I don't believe you when you say Marlise did. She didn't kill your father. But you know who did."

"You're wrong! He saw that witch of a stepmother do it," the old lady said, rolling her wheelchair a few feet in my direction. "My grandson wouldn't lie."

"I don't think lying comes naturally to him," I said, "but he might lie to please someone else."

When she didn't respond, I added, "Someone like you, Mrs. Simsbury."

"Don't listen to her," she growled at Wayne. "She and that witch are in cahoots. They're working together to get you jailed. She's evil, like Marlise and, and—"

"And like the man who was your son?" I interjected.

"That weakling! He was no man. His father, my husband, was what a man ought to be, strong and willful, sure of himself, with no patience for the flunkies who tried to take him down. He crushed them all and left what he'd fought so hard for all his life, a thriving business. But none of that skill, that shrewdness, that power was passed on to his sniveling son." Her expression was pure disgust. "Jonathon was weak. He fell victim to everyone and anyone who wanted something from him, the men he surrounded himself with, every one of them a bloodsucking leech. And then that woman batted her eyes and shook her bottom at him, and he fell for it." Her voice was now a shout. "He married her! I told him that she was poison, was after his money, the money my husband worked so hard to make. I've cursed her every day since she sashayed into my home. May she rot in hell for the way she twisted my son around her little polished finger, getting him to change his will to—" Her voice rose until it was a shout. "Change his will to cut my grandson out and give it to *her*!"

Wayne stood silently by the window during her tirade, hands clenched at his sides, his face a mask of confusion, torment, and pain.

"And you shot him to prevent that from happening," I said.

She fell silent.

"You took Jonathon's gun from his bedside table, didn't you?" I said. "You've had it hidden in the wheelchair under that caftan ever since the night you killed him. The police looked everywhere, but they would never violate an old lady's dignity and privacy. Do you have it with you now? Give it to me and put an end to this madness."

She slumped in her wheelchair as though someone had pulled a plug and let all the energy out. She turned to Wayne and said in a sweet voice, "I did it for you, darling. You know that, don't you?"

Wayne looked at me with pleading eyes.

"Tell her to go away, darling," she said in that same cloying, saccharine voice. "Tell her that this is our house and we don't want her kind in it."

"Did your grandmother tell you to blame Marlise?" I asked him. "Was that the way she decided to cover things up?"

"I—"

Her voice regained its strength. "Don't be a coward like your father was," she snapped. "Your grandfather wouldn't stand for it."

She reached beneath the caftan, pulled out the gun, and pointed it at me. "I told you to get out and leave us alone," she said. "Now you'll wish you had."

I flinched, as I expected to hear the discharge and feel the bullet enter me. But Wayne sprang at her and grabbed the weapon. It went off, boring a hole in the ceiling. He wrestled the gun from her, dropped it to the floor, and collapsed on top of it, his sobs filling the room.

Chapter Twenty-four

Marlise heard the gunshot and ran to the parlor. "Oh, my God! I was afraid it was happening again."

The sight of her sent Mrs. Simsbury into a frenzy of cursing her daughter-in-law and accusing her of everything that had gone wrong in the family, crying and raging at the same time. It was a pathetic display; I admired Marlise for not responding. She stood in wonderment as the woman with whom she'd had such a toxic relationship melted before our eyes.

When the police responded to my call and came to arrest Mrs. Simsbury, she met them with a sweet smile and asked if they wanted something to eat. She had either succumbed to dementia or was putting on a convincing act that would support a temporary insanity defense. She explained she was a woman who'd adored and admired her late husband and expected everyone else to emulate him. When no one responded, she turned venomous, spewing a stream of profanity directed at Marlise. She shifted between lucidity and fantasy, one minute talking like a little girl, then without missing a beat becoming tyrannical.

As the house filled with police officials questioning everyone in attendance, the one I felt particular sadness for was Wayne.

"My father told me he was cutting me out of his will, leaving me a minimal amount. He said it would force me to grow up and learn how to take care of myself," he told the police. "I was pissed. I admit it. I could have killed him myself. I would have if I'd had a gun in my hand. I yelled at him, accusing him of choosing Marlise over his own flesh and blood. I told him that his father didn't cut *him* off. You know what he said? He said, 'Maybe he should have.' My grandmother came in in the middle of the conversation and things got really hot."

"I expected things would blow up when Jonathon talked to Wayne about the new will, but I didn't want to get involved," Marlise whispered to me. "It was Jonathon's decision. He felt he had Wayne's best interests at heart. I supported him, but I knew how it would look. If I'd known Jonathon was talking to Wayne that night and that his mother would be there as well, I would have gone in to even the odds."

"If you had, you might have been killed, too," I reminded her.

"My grandmother said no one was going to cut me off, and when my father told her to keep out of it, it wasn't her business, she pulled out a gun and shot him. I didn't know what to do. I had no idea she meant to kill him. I didn't even know she had his gun. I started to cry. She said to me, 'You needn't worry any longer, dear. Nana has taken care of everything.'" He broke down now, the tears coursing down his cheeks as he recalled the terrible scene.

Mrs. Simsbury had instructed Wayne to tell the police he'd seen Marlise pull the trigger. That's when he ran, and came to my house in Cabot Cove. "I didn't want to lie to all of you," he said to Detective Witmer, "but I had to protect her, didn't I? She killed him to protect me."

Mrs. Simsbury sat straight in her wheelchair, a small smile on her lips. While she didn't admit to having shot Jonathon, she didn't deny it either. Her final words as they escorted her to a special police van were: "My husband would be so proud of me."

Marlise, of course, was relieved that she was no longer considered a suspect. I was pleased when she expressed concern for Wayne, what would happen to him for providing false sworn testimony, and more important, what the rest of his life would be.

"I'm sorry," he told her.

"I know you are," she said. "I'd like to try to give our relationship another chance. I know I can never replace your real family, but you'll always be welcome wherever I am."

His response was noncommittal, but I had a hunch that they might reconnect one day after the dust had settled and clear thinking had emerged.

I caught a flight to Boston the following day, and Jed Richardson delivered me home to Cabot Cove, where I quickly settled in at my house and got back to work on my novel. Naturally, Seth, Mort Metzger, Susan Shevlin, and many others were eager to hear of my experiences in Italy and Chicago, and I filled them in over a succession of dinners. Seth, bless him, refrained from saying, "I told you so," and even hosted a welcome home party for me. While I've run across quite a number of bad people over the years, I'm fortunate to have my loyal, loving friends in Cabot Cove to renew my faith in humankind.

Months later, we gathered to watch the premiere of Anthony Curso's documentary on our public television channel. Marlise was a charming and professional on-camera narrator, and I was surprised when my name appeared in the list of those to thank at the end of the show. The documentary was a wonderful, thoughtful insight into art fraud and forgery and brought back a flood of memories for me, not all of them negative.

The week after the show aired, FedEx delivered a large package to my house. It consisted of a rigid wooden framework covered with multiple layers of foam and brown paper. I carefully opened it, peeling through the layers until I came to what was encased. It was a magnificent oil painting. A note from Tony Curso was included:

Dear Jessica,

Please accept this as a sincere expression of my respect for and gratitude to you. You'd mentioned that you had a large space on a wall in your home that needed a piece of art, and I hope this will fill that need. I should tell you that this work is Alessandro Botticelli's *Portrait of a Youth*. It's a copy, of course, provided to me by the Italian police as a thank-you for including them in the documentary. They found it among the paintings that had been taken from Vittorio's cave, most of which they recovered. The original hangs in the National Gallery of Art in Washington, D.C. I wish it were an original, but that's a little out of my league. However, it's a wonderful example of Vittorio's skill, a testimony to his sensitivity, talent, and artistry. I hope you'll proudly display it. He would have liked that.

Tony

The painting wasn't the only item in the package. Shrouded in many layers of bubble wrap was a pint bottle of grappa with another note from Curso. He suggested I drink it as a shot after dinner, or add it to espresso. *Or freeze it and drink it straight from the freezer. It loses a little when frozen, but what the devil, huh?*

My forged Botticelli now occupies a proud spot on my wall, and if I ever forget about my Italian adventure, I need only to look at it to remind me of all the young men—good and bad—I encountered.

On the basis of her appearance in Tony Curso's documentary, Marlise was hired by a Chicago TV station to produce and narrate documentaries. The last I heard, Wayne had sold his grandmother's house and was living with Marlise, although he wasn't home very much. He'd gotten serious about music and had joined a rock band that toured frequently. Luckily for him—and I'm sure it involved a substantial fee for Willard Corman—his lawyer was able to persuade the police not to charge him with false testimony, and he was given a clean slate.

Tony Curso keeps in touch. He's busy teaching courses in art history and consulting with the Italian police on matters of art theft and forgery. I treasure knowing him and look forward to catching up again in person one day.

According to Marlise, Susan Hurley went to work for Joe Jankowski. "He needed a good accountant. I'm sure they're trying to figure out if there's anything left in the estate to pay his fee."

Marlise also passed along the information that Edgar Peters took the pieces in the art collection, sold the originals for not much money, and put the others up for sale on eBay, advertising them as coming from the hand of history's greatest art forger, the Italian painter Vittorio.

As for me, I finished my novel and took a one-month hiatus to relax and catch up with friends. My travel agent, Susan Shevlin, called me a few months after I'd gotten home to say she had a wonderful Italian tour package that she knew I would love.

"*Grazie*," I told her. "Maybe another time. The only 'Italian' I want to hear for a while are the items on the menu at Peppino's restaurant."